Killian Farm

Copyright © Lisa M. Meehan 2025

All Rights Reserved.

Edited By Lauren Lepkowski

Cover Art By Lisa M. Meehan

Published in the United States by Whisper Woods Productions LLC

Paperback ISBN 979-8-218-59310-0
Ebook ISBN 979-8-218-60689-3

Dedication

For my Nana, who taught me to love reading and, more specifically, reading horror. I cut my teeth on her hand-me-down Stephen King, and Dean Koontz paper-backs. The occasional chocolate thumb print marked the pages where she needed a little snack to keep reading deep into the night. I still sometimes glance at the margins of a freshly turned page, hoping to find that telltale smudge.

And for my friend Mike DeLuca, who taught me how to tell stories with enthusiasm and how to bait the hook, sometimes years in advance. His dedication to amusing himself—and us—at our expense is legendary among those lucky enough to have called him a friend.
Who knows how many dangling hooks are still out there?

To quote Guardians of the Galaxy II, "I'll see in you in the stars."

The Devil's Hour

The woods surrounding Killian Farm grew quiet as the devil's hour closed in. Flashlight beams flickering through the trees in the distance stilled like pale fireflies stalled in flight. The scattered calls of the missing boy's name that, just minutes ago, filled the night like a chorus of frogs dwindled until there were none. Even the forest itself seemed to sense the time and grew silent in anticipation.

Pete ran a calloused hand through his dark hair, then checked his watch for no good reason. He knew the time. The coming hour sparked across the raw edges of his frayed nerves. He leaned up against a tree, not trusting his legs.

"No. No. No." Across the clearing, Kent Buckner, a thin and fidgety man, shook his head from side-to-side, painting streaks of light across the ground with his headlamp.

Pete watched Kent's light pace at the edge of the clearing. When he left his house six hours ago, running on an hour's sleep and the fumes of the coffee churning like acid in his stomach, he wanted nothing more than to find the boy before it came to this again. Find him and be done with it.

For better or worse.

Pete swallowed hard against the lump in his throat. Somewhere out there, the boy's parents desperately searched for their son, needing to find him alive and well, as surely as they needed to breathe.

Kent poked at the leafy ferns carpeting the forest floor with his walking stick as he paced. His headlamp jerked from shadow to shadow with a dizzying tempo. The tragic conductor of an orchestra only he could hear.

Pete hissed, sucking in a breath, as he watched the light veer too close to the drop off, waiting for it to disappear down the ravine. Kent needed to calm down. One wrong step and the man would be a pile of broken bones amongst the boulders that covered the valley floor.

At least his body will be easy to find.

To Pete's left, Henry Clevenger sighed. He walked over to a felled tree, gave it a kick to check its soundness, then sat his burly frame down with a creak. He clicked off his flashlight, sat it on the log, and pulled out a pack of Marlboros from the breast pocket of his grease stained t-shirt. The plastic wrapper around the pack crackled and Kent spun as if he'd heard a gunshot. He pinned Henry in a beam of light and held it there until the big man looked up with an unlit cigarette dangling between sneering lips and stared Kent down.

Kent turned away and continued painting the woods in chaotic light.

Henry flicked his lighter a couple of times, his face ghosting out of the darkness with each spark, until the flame caught. The tip of his cigarette flared, and he closed the lighter, becoming a floating ember in the dark.

Pete switched off his flashlight. The night closed in and clung to his skin like sweat. His thumb twitched, wanting to turn the light back on, but the quivering beam gave away the shake of his hand and he couldn't have that. Not in front of Kent and Henry, especially Henry. It had been beaten into him from the day he was born, until the day he left this very farm at the age of sixteen, that weakness was a cardinal sin. And though Killian's were often sinners, they were never weak.

He felt Henry's stare through the gloom. The man couldn't see him in the dark, but the tip of the Henry's cigarette pointed right at him. Every time the big man took a drag, the tip would flare, but the smoldering light never pointed away. The man was suspicious of him, like the rest of the town. Pete got it. You leave a small town for fifteen years—you come back a stranger. It didn't matter that he had returned a family man, fresh from the Army. He was still a Killian, and that name carried a certain reputation.

And the boy had gone missing on his land, under his watch. He'd be suspicious, too.

Pete glanced in the direction of the farmhouse, whose lights he couldn't see through the thick trees, thankful his family was too far away to hear what was coming.

The boy had been missing for three days and it came every night since. He checked his watch again, though he still didn't need to. He could feel it in the air, a resonance on the wind, faint like the decaying twang of a guitar string.

Kent sensed it, too. He slowed his pace around the clearing, gave the underbrush one more half hearted poke, and leaned against his walking stick facing the woods.

Henry took a final drag, ground the cigarette butt into the dirt with the toe of his boot, and disappeared into the darkness.

Across the woods, someone cried out, just a few syllables of anguish that kind of sounded like the boy's name. Pete wondered if it was Victor's father.

After that, no one made a sound. They all strained to listen for the thing that they had dreaded hearing all night. For the sound that would come to haunt them in their darkest moments. They listened for it, in the same way they might search the dark shadows of a room for the cause of a floorboard creak. They listened, hoping to find nothing.

But it found them.

Somewhere in the woods of Killian Farm, Victor Pennridge screamed.

He screamed with all the might a skinny ten-year-old boy could muster. It was the scream of a throat torn raw. A scream of terror, of pain. Grating, guttural and devastating in its frailty.

Pete shook, every muscle in his body clenched. His fists curled tighter and tighter until he felt like his knuckles would pop through his flesh. His fingernails dug deep into the meat of his palms, finding the grooves from yesterday, drawing fresh blood.

The scream came from everywhere and nowhere. Lasting uncounted seconds that seemed to go on forever. Then it fell abruptly silent, cut off.

Just like last night and the night before.

In its wake, muffled sounds of crying drifted through the forest.

Pete wiped the tears from his eyes with the back of his shaking hand and sniffed back fresh ones while listening to the strangled sobs nearby. It surprised him to realize the sounds came from Henry's direction.

"You okay?" Pete winced at the crackling of a voice that didn't sound like his.

"Leave me the fuck alo-"

Crack.

A heavy crumble followed, then the rolling, muffled impacts of a body hitting the ground. Henry's panicked scream faded fast into the distance.

Pete fumbled for the switch on his flashlight and swung the beam to where Henry had been. The trunk of the tree where the man had been sitting lay in scattered pieces of rotten pulp and disintegrated crumbs of wood. Henry's flashlight sat unmoved on a still solid section of trunk just a foot away from the destruction. Beyond the fallen tree, darkness at the edge of the ravine swallowed the beam of light.

Pete rushed to the edge, Kent right behind him, and pointed his light down. He let out a whoosh of breath when he saw Henry sitting at the bottom at least fifty feet down. The man was conscious, pissed, and cradling his left arm to his chest. Even from that distance, Pete could tell Henry had dislocated his shoulder. The big man was lucky. He landed in a patch of tall, scruffy grass. Inches in either direction, and he'd be coming up on a stretcher, or worse, in a body bag.

Leaving Kent at the top, Pete made his way down the embankment. He followed the torn underbrush and used the gouged earth and jutting rocks in the path of Henry's fall as footholds as far as he could. When it got too steep, he sat and slid, wincing at the small rocks that poked through the denim of his jeans. He picked up speed near the end, and his stomach lurched when the hill went vertical, sending him free falling the last five feet. He hit the ground feet first, driving a rush of pain up his ankles. Momentum sent him staggering forward, and he threw his hands out in front of him. Stopped himself before his face smashed against a boulder the size of a small car. The flashlight in his hand took the hit and flickered, but kept shining.

"That," Henry said, an edge of pain in his voice, "was well thought out."

Pete, panting with adrenaline, swung his light to Henry. "Nah. If I stopped to think about it, I would've sent Kent."

Henry's mouth contorted into a painful grin, stretching a bloody cheek scraped raw against the side of the hill during the fall. He hugged his left arm tight against his chest through the shaking laughter.

"How's your shoulder?" Pete asked. He could see the bump of the joint poking up through Henry's t-shirt where it shouldn't. It was going to be tricky getting him out of there.

"How's it look?" Henry's brow scrunched like he wasn't sure he wanted to know.

"Better than your face."

The big man nodded. "That's not saying much on a good day."

Pete held out a hand. Henry reached up with his uninjured arm, grabbed it, and pulled himself up. Halfway to standing, the big man's eyes went wide and he let go. He fell back hard, hit a chunk of granite with a meaty thud, and screamed.

Pete shined the flashlight at Henry, who lay sprawled against the boulder. He stared past Pete, his face pale, quivering. Pete turned and saw it for himself, illuminated by the dim light of Kent's headlamp stretching from the top of the ravine. Knowing he shouldn't, he aimed his flashlight at the boy.

Victor was caught up against a sapling jutting out of the underbrush growing on the side of the hill. It was as if the tree cradled him in its embrace. One branch supported the boy's back. His arm, tucked around it, hung limp, but kept the body from sliding off. The thin limb bent with the weight of Victor, but held. The boy's legs rested on a lower branch tucked in the angle of his knees, letting his feet dangle. One shoe was untied, and the laces drifted lazily in a breeze too faint for Pete to feel.

But it was the boy's face that held Pete. Milky eyes stared up at the night sky from a face untouched by insects and scavengers, preserving its rigid mask of terror. A ghost of the scream that had torn through the woods minutes ago, now ripped through Pete's head, made more visceral by the sight of Victor's face. The boy's gaping mouth hung open, locked in the endless scream of a terrified child. His lower jaw lay unhinged, and flopped against a throat that would never carry sound again, yet would never be silenced.

1

Twenty Five Years Later

Thud.

The pen in Vernon Hinkley's hand hit the stack of papers on the desk with a deafening thud.

No, not a thud, not much more than a loud tap. But Laney felt the tremble of its impact, heard the rattling clink of secondhand dishes against the wooden table. Her son's cries, the scratchy infant wails of her daughter resonated, fading into the high-pitched hum of the many dinner conversations blending together in the crowded restaurant beyond the office door behind her.

"You need to work more night shifts," Vern said. "Hustle more."

Tap.

"You're an assistant manager. You set the tone."

Tap.

He punctuated every point with that damn pen. Laney fixated on its point of impact, watching the table assignments that she stayed late to finish the night before shudder with each hit.

"You need to make sure they're only taking the breaks they're supposed to be taking. I'm not paying them to smoke. And I don't know what I'm paying you for half the time."

Tap.

"Why do you make me have to tell you this every time?"

Tap.

"Why do you always try to piss me the fuck off when I'm sitting down to eat?" The voice was deep and gravelly.

Vern's nasal drone faded away, taking the office with it, leaving Laney back in the apartment on Hickory Street. Back there with Troy. She sat at that wobbly legged kitchen table across from the boogeyman of her memories. A dark and brooding shape vibrating with intensity. The shape's fist slammed down on the scarred table with a deafening thud, sending a tremor across its surface.

"Why?" The word a growl, tearing through her head, bounced against the sides of her skull.

A pounding on the thin apartment wall signaled the neighbor had enough of Troy's nightly routine. But Troy hadn't, and the pounding on the wall only made him want more.

She looked down at her hands clenched in her lap and watched a drop of blood fall on her knuckle. She tried to wipe it off, but there was nothing there.

"Well?" Vern asked.

Laney looked up at her boss, a man who by all basic standards was a loser. A cheap suit wearing, insecure, potbellied man who for the past twenty years spent most of his days bullying employees in the same old bargain chain restaurant, and most of his nights watching TV with his mother. A loser that Laney couldn't afford to piss off if she wanted to keep feeding her kids and paying her rent. So what did that make her?

She cleared her throat, thought back to that TED Talk about projecting confidence that she watched a dozen times, straightened her shoulders, and stammered, "well...well, Vern, I've closed three times this week. And...and last week four times because of your bowling tournament-"

"I'm sorry." He cut her off. "Is my personal life inconveniencing you?"

"No. No." Laney tried to recover. She shifted in her seat, took a deep breath and started again. "I'm just saying that I, um, I do work nights. I've been taking extra shifts, and the new ordering process I set up has been working and really saving us time-"

"Okay. Okay." He waved his hand in the air, trying to cut her off.

But Laney was on a roll and feeling more confident with every second. "I really feel like I've been an asset to this place. The wait staff have been happy with the restructured schedule I put together and-"

Her phone chirped where it laid on the desk in front of her. She glanced at the message on the screen, and the name on the text hit her like a punch in the face.

VINE.

"Wow." Vern sat up straight, a gleam in his eyes, his face a contortion of something between mock disappointment and glee. "How many times have I had to talk to you about the phone?"

Tap.

"You can't even ignore a text message in the middle of your workday? Hell, in the middle of your performance review?"

Tap.

"Do you need to take a break to answer it? Have to call someone?"

Laney's hand went to the scar on the side of her head, unseen beneath her blond hair pulled taut into a ponytail. The three inch long, raised line of flesh where hair no longer grew marked where the plate in her skull was from the last time she shared the same room with Troy.

"I...I..." Laney looked up from her phone. Her eyes landed, unfocused, on the pink visage of Vern's face. The hum from the dining room behind her became a steady ring in her ears. Her chest tightened.

VINE, an acronym for "Victim Information and Notification Everyday", was an automated alert system created to warn victims of violent crimes when their attackers were pending release from prison.

Troy was getting out.

The thought of his release—his early release—spawned a million other thoughts, a million what-ifs. All of them were varying degrees of awful, competing for attention, drowning out everything else.

Vern's question hung in the air and she latched onto that to keep the darkness pulling at the edges of her vision from dragging her into the black. Yes. Yes. She had to call someone. Who she had to call, she didn't know. And she was pretty sure she wouldn't like what they had to say, but she had to go make that call. Right now. Because not knowing would drive her insane. She had to get up, in the middle of her performance review for the job that took her three months to get, after the last restaurant she worked for went out of business. She had to get up and tell the man who held onto what little power he had in this world clenched in both fists like a club, that she had someone more important to talk to right now.

Vern leaned forward. "I asked you if you had to call someone?" It wasn't a question asked in concern. The annoyance in his voice was loud and clear. He couldn't stand being ignored.

His complete and utter lack of empathy stung like a slap in the face. Anger burned inside her, with no place to go. She fought back the tears and fell back to what became her default response to confrontation shortly after marrying Troy.

Avoid it at all costs.

"I can wait," she said.

2

Secret

"A week? You're telling me he's been out for a week?" Laney winced at the whine in her voice.

She sat in her car, a twenty year old Toyota Camry, outside of an apartment complex in Philadelphia that made her car look like a Porsche. The surrounding gray concrete buildings, stained by the blur of graffiti that wouldn't completely wash off, bordered a courtyard parking lot on three sides. A sliding gate stuck in the open position centered on a chain-link fence finished the square. She parked near the corner facing the street, sandwiched by a couple of minivans and tried not to melt as the air conditioning failed to fend off the heat.

It was just after seven, an hour before sunset. A handful of kids played outside in the still sweltering temperatures, bouncing a cheap rubber ball on the cracked asphalt of the parking lot. Her kids were likely in the apartment, eyeballs glued to screens. A fact that would make her feel like a terrible mom on most days, but today was a relief.

She tried calling the Lacroix County Sheriff's Office as soon as her disastrous review was over, but got bounced around. Eventually, she got a voice mail and left a message. Officer Miller called her back just as she pulled into the lot. It was perfect timing. She didn't want to have this conversation in front of the kids.

"I'm sorry, Mrs. Pierce-" the woman's voice on the other end started.

"Ellis. Ms. Ellis. I changed the name."

It was expensive, but Laney tried to cover every track she could after Troy went to jail. She cut all ties with the people she knew in Chicago. It wasn't hard. They were mostly Troy's friends. She moved around a lot, following work, then eventually found a restaurant willing to invest in her. They trained her to be a manager. Poised to take over one of their prime locations, things were looking bright for Laney, then the chain went bankrupt. Forced to move again, she tried to put even more distance between her and Chicago. But even with Troy in a federal prison three states away, she fell asleep most nights with the feeling of his breath on the back of her neck.

And now he was free.

"Ms. Ellis. No system is perfect. I'm not really sure what happened. Sometimes paperwork... You know what? Let's cut the bullshit." Officer Miller had a calm and sympathetic voice. "He's on parole. That means check-ins. It's illegal for him to leave the state of Illinois. If he fails to meet with his parole officer, we'll bring him in."

Officer Miller sighed.

"I know you've done quite a lot to distance yourself from your ex-husband and keep your family safe. This is the part of the call where I'm supposed to reassure you that the system works, and you'll be fine. But I've read your ex-husband's file, and he sounds like a piece of work. I want you to stay alert. I want you to stay careful. And I'll do everything I can to alert you if the system falls short."

"Thank you. I feel so much better now," Laney said, not trying to hide the sarcasm.

Officer Miller chuckled, a dry laugh that conveyed anything but humor.

"Sending good vibes is not really in my job description and you and I both know things don't always work how they're supposed to. I wouldn't have a job if they did. Goodbye Ms. Ellis. I really hope to not have to call you again."

"Good bye." Laney pressed the end call button. "I hope not too."

The odds of Troy playing by the rules for the first time were slim to none. Laney suddenly felt vulnerable sitting in her car. She grabbed the bags from the restaurant and got out.

Laney climbed the few stairs to the center building security door, and shifted the bags of takeout to one arm, avoiding her reflection in the door's glass. She clenched a metal spike the size of a cigar, her self-defense key chain in her fist.

The door opened before she could reach for it.

"You've been keeping secrets", Celia said, lips stretched in a mischievous smile as she held the door.

Laney steeled herself. Celia was her neighbor and her closest friend, but Laney didn't have the energy to deal with her today.

Pushing forty, a few years older than Laney, Celia was vibrant, outgoing, and comfortable in her skin. Everything that Laney wasn't. Always put together, she gave the impression of someone who floated through life, lucky and carefree. Laney knew the truth. Celia was a hardworking and dynamic force to be reckoned with. Laney had been on the receiving end of that force more than once, and knew firsthand. She could also be exhausting with her endless energy, but Celia was one of the kindest people that Laney had ever met.

"Thanks," Laney said, walking through the door. "What big secret am I keeping?"

"A tall, dark, and mysterious one. You never told me you were into bad boys."

Laney's blood went cold. She started for the stairs with an urgent need to check on the kids, but her knees buckled and she sat down hard on the metal step. She knew he would find her. *Knew it.* But didn't expect it to happen so fast. She should have left work the moment the message came through.

Celia rushed to her. "What's going on?"

"When?" It was all Laney got out.

Sitting on the step next to Laney, Celia put an arm around her shoulder, a worried look on her face.

"About an hour ago. I told him you weren't home from work yet and he left. Was that your ex?"

Wide eyed and pale, Laney nodded. "It had to be."

"Should we call the cops?"

"They'll be gone before he comes back."

Celia sat quietly for a moment, her lips drawn tight. She shook her head. "There has to be something we can do."

Laney didn't respond. What she had to do was run, but if Troy had already found them, it might be too late.

"You never talk about your past," Celia said. "How bad was it?"

Laney turned to look in Celia's direction, her gaze somewhere else. She started to speak a few times. Her mouth opened, but nothing came out. Then her eyes focused on Celia, and she found her voice.

"I have to go. Get away from here." Even as the words left her mouth, Laney knew she wouldn't get far. "But there's no way. I don't get paid for three days and my savings-" A hysterical laugh escaped her. "Oh, I forgot. I don't have any. Not after the brakes went. I don't know how I can-"

Celia took Laney's hands. "I have money. Just go. Go to a hotel or something until we can figure this out."

"I can't take your money-"

"You can and you will." Celia got up, but Laney grabbed her arm and pulled her back down.

"It won't be safe for you," Laney said. "He talked to you already. And he won't believe that you don't know where I am."

"Then I'll go too. I've got a friend to stay with." Celia punctuated the word "friend" with a sly smile and a quick raise of her eyebrows.

3

Home

The sound of cartoons struggling to rise above the whine of the of the window unit, fighting its own battle with the summer heat, greeted Laney as she entered the tiny, one-bedroom apartment. She quietly shut the door, bolted the lock, and hung her purse on the nearby hook, the only item on the empty, beige walls that she had never gotten around to decorating since they moved in two years ago.

Where did the time go?

The kids occupied either end of the sofa that dominated the neat, but sparse room. Ray wore headphones, turned up too loud, while swiping at the screen of his phone on one end, and Faith ate a bowl of cereal, engrossed in cartoons on the other.

Normal in tableau.

God, how Laney hated to destroy that completely mediocre but hard won state of normal. She would have been happy to stand there all night just soaking it in. Instead, she planned to drop a bomb right in the middle of it.

Or, as Ray would say, ruin it like she ruined everything.

She dropped the takeout on the small table that demarcated the border between kitchen and living room. At the sound of the bags landing, Faith, a blond-haired, bouncy seven-year-old girl, who shared her mother's blue eyes, jumped over the back of the sofa and rushed to Laney, her bright yellow t-shirt, the only streak of color in the room. Laney reached down, caught her daughter in her arms, swept her up off the floor and hugged her tight.

Ray, twelve, black-haired, handsome and gloomy, like his father, glanced in her direction. She barely glimpsed his gray eyes before he turned away with disinterest.

At least I have my Faith.

Laney clung to her daughter, not wanting to let go. The moment the hug ended, the shit would hit the fan. She needed just a few more seconds before she faced reality.

"Awkward." Faith said in a sing-song voice before letting loose a giggle.

Faith flinched when the bedroom door slammed, though she knew the bang was coming. The thin door barely muffled the stream of bad words Ray yelled from the other side.

"You're a potty mouth!" She yelled right back at him, tears streaking down her cheeks. She couldn't help crying when Mom and Ray fought. And this was a big one. Mom just told them they were leaving again and Ray hated moving. He hated it more than anything.

"Faith, honey, why don't you watch some TV while mommy packs the car." Her mother guided Faith to the sofa, wiped the tears from her cheeks, then handed her the remote and a bag of chocolate chip cookies, her favorite. The cookies were a bad sign. She knew they were supposed to distract her so she wouldn't ask questions. And that meant the answers were bad.

Faith dug her hand into the bag of cookies, pulled one out with only a couple of chips and threw it back, before reaching into the bag again. "Why are we leaving?"

Her mom, kneeling on the floor, pulled Ray's clothes from the small dresser that the TV sat on and shoved them into a big trash bag. "Think of it more like a vacation, hon," Mom said without looking up.

Faith sighed. She was seven, not stupid.

"Ray said we're leaving and you're blocking the TV." She pulled out another cookie. The chip count met approval, and she took a bite.

"Oops, sorry." Her mom ducked down, her head still blocking the bottom of the screen, but Faith let it go.

"Ray doesn't understand what's going on," Mom said.

Footsteps pounded from the bedroom, and the door swung open with a bang.

"I know what's going on. We're running away again because you're afraid he's here to take us out of this shit hole." Ray's eyes were red. Faith could tell he was crying before he came out. "You're afraid he's going to take us away from you. I hope he does."

The thought of the father she didn't remember taking her away from her mom threatened to bring fresh tears of her own, but Faith sniffed them back. Someone needed to be the calm one. It definitely wasn't Ray. He looked like he was going to explode.

And then he said the worse thing ever. "I fucking hate you."

Her brother had said a lot of bad things to their mom over the years, but that was the first time he ever used the "H" word. The hurt on her mother's face when he said it made Faith furious, and she couldn't be the calm one anymore.

"You shut your stupid jerk face, Ray!"

"Enough!" Mom bit her lip for a second, then said, "we have to-"

Bang. Bang. Bang.

Someone knocked on the door hard, so hard Faith could feel it through the floor. She really, really hoped it wasn't her dad.

Everyone froze at the bang on the door.

Ray hadn't expected his father to actually show up. He thought his mother was just overreacting again. Uprooting their lives because she heard someone say the name Troy in a crowd, or someone who kind of looked like him, or one of his friends came into the restaurant.

But still, a tingle of excitement ran through him at the idea. Ray hadn't seen his father in years and could barely remember him. There was a scent, an aftershave, that came rushing back to him and a faint memory of the sound of his voice, deep and gravelly.

"Rayban, my man."

But hearing that voice in his head made the hair on the back of his neck stand up. Without thinking, he took a step back and glanced over at his mother. She had pulled Faith behind her and just stood there, her eyes fixated on the door like it would burst open at any second, letting a horde of zombies rush in.

The unease that rushed through him a second ago, at the possibility of seeing his dad again, became disgust at his cowering mother.

What a fucking wuss.

Ray crossed the room. With each step, the buzz of adrenaline built until it coursed through him like electricity. This was his moment. Opening this door was him calling her out for everything she put him through. All the moving. All the crappy schools and shitty apartments.

Maybe with his dad around, he might get a normal life. No more babysitting Faith because Mrs. Porter had a doctor's appointment, or eating the shitty takeout Mom always brought home. If he smelled garlic bread one more time, he'd puke.

His mom spent years making his life miserable, and it stopped now. He had dreamed of his dad showing up like this, even though his mom always acted like his father was some kind of monster. Sure, Ray remembered some yelling from when he was little. But he knew his mom. She probably started it. After all, she was always bitching at him about something.

He turned to look at her as he reached for the deadbolt. He wanted to see the look on her face when he twisted open the lock.

But the sight of her stayed his hand.

He'd seen her scared before. It was practically her default state. But this was different. She stood pale, wide eyed, sucking in quick, shaky breaths, her whole body vibrating.

The knocking came again, shaking the door with each hit.

Ray yanked his hand back.

You are your father's son.

The thought jolted through Laney the second Ray turned to look at her as he reached for the lock, toying with her like a predator, like his father. The gleam in his eyes, the cocky smirk, he looked so much like Troy in that moment.

Part of her wanted him to open the door and let in the nightmare that he couldn't remember. It would almost be a relief to get it over with, like she'd been holding her breath for years and could finally exhale. And then Ray would see the truth of it. Everything he blamed her for, everything he hated about his life, were all necessary sacrifices to keep them safe. She could almost picture, with smug satisfaction, the remorse on Ray's face as he watched Troy choke the life out of her.

You sure he'll even care?

Guilt washed over her at the thought. Ray could be an asshole, but he wasn't Troy and never would be as long as she could help it.

Which probably wouldn't be that long.

After years of riding the roller coaster up the hill, the constant clack, clack, clack of inevitability reverberating in her head, she was about to reach the top. And she wasn't ready for the ride that came after. She stood there, not moving, pinned down by the surety that everything was about to go to hell unless she did something. But what that something was, she didn't know.

"Laney?" It was Celia's voice. "Laney, are you okay?"

The top of the hill would wait for now.

Ray twisted the deadbolt and opened the door. "Oh, hi dad." He locked eyes with Laney, making sure she couldn't miss the disgust on his face before he walked away.

With a no small measure of relief, her legs took her forward into her friend's waiting hug.

"You had me so worried," Celia said.

"Sorry." Laney stepped back. "We thought you were...someone else."

As if she could feel the tension in the room, and needed to break it, Celia looked over at the pile of stuffed trash bags and said, "this has all the makings of a white trash road trip. I'm getting you some luggage for Christmas."

Laney smiled, but knew that they'd be long gone from here at Christmas. Even if Troy went back to prison, she couldn't risk it. He knew where she was now and he had friends.

Celia slipped a thin wad of cash, wrapped in a piece of paper discreetly, into Laney's hand. "You get somewhere safe. The number where I'm staying is on the paper. In case you can't reach my cell."

"I can't thank you enough. I'll get this all back to you, every cent. You're a better friend than I could ever hope for." Realizing the truth of it for the first time, she choked up.

Celia hugged her, smiling. "Let's not get that started now. I think we have more than enough drama here at the moment."

After letting Laney go, Celia hugged Faith and waved to Ray, who sulked on the other side of the room. "Let me help you pack up the car. I can stick around until you leave." She reached for a bag.

"No," Laney said, wincing at the idea of Celia becoming collateral damage. "You go have fun with your friend. We're right behind you."

Celia turned to Laney and smiled. "We'll have some drinks and laugh about this in a few days. You'll see."

"Can't wait." Laney smiled back at her, ending their friendship with a lie.

Pole lights cast pools of illumination around the parking lot, but Laney didn't have the forethought earlier to park under one. In the dark corner of the lot, the light from the trunk of her car shone like a beacon designed to draw in any psychotic ex-husbands who might be lurking about. And she wasn't exactly being a ninja shoving trash bags full of their worldly possessions into the trunk of the Toyota. With all the rustling of the bags, she wouldn't have heard an ice cream truck come up behind her.

And she didn't hear him.

Laney turned to grab another bag from the ground beside the car and there he was, his gray eyes glinting in the light from the trunk. For a split second, Troy stood right in front of her. She jumped back, banging against the bumper of the car.

Ray rolled his eyes, a trash bag in each hand weighing down his arms.

Laney smiled, surprised and grateful that he got on board with the plan. "Thanks, hon."

She expected a glare, or some pissy comment in response, but to her dismay, he smiled back. His lips spread into a shy, earnest grin, like she hadn't seen in years. She melted, all the anger from earlier gone, replaced with a flood of warmth at the idea that just for a moment, she had her little boy back.

Laney wiped away the sudden tears distorting her vision, and her smile wilted. Ray's eyes focused at a point over her shoulder. That sweet smile belonged to someone else. And before she even heard him say it, with dread, she knew who.

"Dad?" Ray asked, his voice soft, hesitant and—the real gut punch—hopeful.

"Rayban, my man," said the gravelly voice behind her.

4

Garlic Bread

Laney was calm for a woman scared out of her mind.

Focused on heating the takeout, her eyes locked on the pot of spaghetti cooking on the stove. Not the microwave, because Troy hated microwaved food. The sauce bubbled and popped as the wooden spoon pulled the angel hair in a circle, tracing a spiral in its turbulence. She stared into the cone-like depression in the center created by the whirling pasta, the calm center of the storm, knowing that's where she stood at the moment—in the calm center of the chaos that was Troy.

Behind her, Ray chattered away, showing off his skateboarding videos to his father. It had been a long time since she had seen him this animated. He had said more to Troy in the past twenty minutes than he said to her in months. She worked two extra shifts to get him that skateboard, and quite a few more to get him the phone.

Troy sat with the kids at the kitchen table a few feet away from her, with his back to the front door. From that seat, he could watch Laney at the stove and anyone trying to leave would have to go past him.

He wasn't a big man, but he was strong and wiry, with a lean, muscular build. He wore his dark hair pulled back in a short ponytail, and had added a tightly trimmed beard and a scar on his left cheek since last she saw him. His gray eyes, that Laney found soulful once upon a time, shone hard and cold.

Ray sat in the middle seat. And Faith sat across from Troy, closest to Laney, hugging a teddy bear to her chest. The little girl eyed her father with suspicion and hadn't said a word to him yet, not that he tried much to engage her in conversation.

"That was grinding." Ray said, pointing to his phone as the video finished. "It's when you-"

"I know what it's called, son. They had skateboards when I was a kid too." Troy smirked.

"Oh, I wasn't sure if you knew. Mom doesn't know anything about this stuff. So, I thought I should explain."

"There's a lot your mom knows nothing about," Troy said, loud enough to make sure Laney couldn't miss it, daring her to deny it.

Ray laughed. The little shit.

Troy tapped a cigarette out from a pack of Camels, and slid his chair back, screeching across the linoleum with slow deliberation. He got up, took three steps to cross the short distance, and stood inches away from Laney, his back to the kids. Laney looked down, her eyes locked on the spaghetti in the pan, stirring it like it would explode if she stopped. He just stood there breathing at her. Hatred radiated off of him. Behind them, the room got quiet. Laney could feel the kids watching.

He was baiting her. She knew it and let the awkward silence build until she couldn't take it anymore. She looked up into those hateful gray eyes that bore into her like jagged spikes and averted her gaze to his chin almost immediately.

"What?" She tried not to flinch in expectation of what might come next.

He stared her down, as if savoring her fear. "It should be obvious," he slipped the cigarette into his mouth. "I need a light."

Laney backed until she hit the wall, all the while patting her pockets as if she expected a lighter to appear. She choked back the tears at the thought of her kids seeing her like this again.

"I don't really have a lighter or matches or anything. I don't smoke. Maybe in the drawer-"

Troy reached out. She had nowhere to go. If she pressed up against the wall any harder, she'd become one with the beige. He wrapped his hand around the wooden handle of the spaghetti pot.

Laney got ready to move, trying to anticipate what would come next. Would he try to burn her with the pot, or finish what he started and bash her head in while her kids watched? To her surprise, he moved the pot to an empty burner and leaned in towards the flame. The tip of his cigarette flared to life. He straightened, blew smoke in her face, and leaned in close, cheeks almost touching. The mixture of menthol and cheap cologne churned her stomach.

He whispered, low enough so that the kids couldn't hear him, "I owe you seven years of pain."

Laney flinched as if he roared.

Troy moved the spaghetti back to the lit burner and turned to the kids. Face transforming from psycho deadpan to shit-eating grin mid turn. He rolled his eyes and said in a falsetto imitation of Laney, "I don't have a lighter. I don't smoke".

Ray let out a nervous laugh.

Troy sat down. "Let's see some more of those wicked-cool, skater vids dude," he said in a surfer voice, throwing a hang ten sign.

"This is a no smoking building." Faith's quiet voice pierced the room like thunder.

Please don't.

Laney willed her daughter to just sit quietly and be forgotten.

Troy looked at Faith as if he just realized she was there. "It can't be," he said.

"It is." She glared back at him, a little girl, clutching a teddy bear, fearlessly stoking a sociopath.

Ray shot his sister a "shut the hell up" look. But Faith didn't notice. She was too busy staring down the man who tried to kill her when she was three months old.

"It isn't," Troy said, leaning in towards her. "Do you want to know why?" He didn't wait for her answer and leaned in closer. "Because I'm smoking, honeybun."

"Spaghetti's done," Laney called out in an attempt at a cheerful voice that came out high-pitched and manic. Trying to hide the shaking of her hands, she plated the food.

"Extra meatballs for you, as usual", she said to Ray when she put his plate in front of him.

Laney moved to Troy next. Leaning back, keeping her distance, she stretched her arm out to place a hefty plate of pasta in front of him. Out of nowhere, Troy slapped the table hard with the palm of his hand. The slap rang through the kitchen like a gunshot. She jumped and only years of experience working crowded restaurants kept the steaming pile of spaghetti off the lap of the ticking time bomb, just waiting for an excuse. She thunked the food down on the table with a shaking hand and stepped back.

Eyes cartoonishly wide, Troy looked past his meal and made a show of searching the table. "I thought there was garlic bread."

"It's in the oven," Laney said, her voice tight, letting slip a hint of annoyance. She knew it was a trap. As if the entire kitchen didn't smell of garlic from the garlic bread, he watched her put in the oven.

Here we go.

The roller coaster reached the crest of the hill, and the shifting gravity tilted the cart forward.

"You really gonna serve the spaghetti before the garlic bread? I thought you worked in a restaurant. What do you do there? Wash the dishes?"

"She's a manager," Faith leaned forward, her blue eyes fierce. "Honeybun."

Ray choked out a laugh, spraying bits of pasta, and tried to cover it with a cough.

Laney held her breath.

Troy looked at Faith, his face blank, as he sized her up.

"Well, maybe, just maybe, she can *manage* to serve the bread before the spaghetti's cold." Troy said, his voice low and calm. Not the calm that belied the maturity of an adult talking to a precocious child, more like the kind before the storm.

Trying to deflect the coming hurricane, Laney opened the oven door, its hinges squealing on the way down.

She slid the drawer next to the stove open, pulled out the oven mitts, and sucked in her breath when she saw the small, dark object underneath. Laney forgot she had put it there. Pulse pounding, she slipped it into her pocket, shoved the oven mitts on and took out the baking pan full of steaming hot bread. She nudged the oven door up with her foot, and it sprang closed with a bang.

"Finally," Troy said, inhaling deeply as the wave of heat that wafted from the oven carried the powerful aroma of garlic through the kitchen. His focus shifted to Faith, and he leaned in towards her.

"You know, *honeybun*, it's not okay for a little girl to be a smart mouth to her daddy. We'll have to work on-"

SMACK.

Garlic bread flew. The hot metal pan sizzled against the side of Troy's face. He let out a scream of rage and smacked the pan from Laney's hands, sending it clanging to the floor.

He jumped from his seat and shoved Laney. She flew back, hitting the stove hard. A plastic burner knob cracked as it dug into her back. She barely felt it. The oven mitts slipped from her hands. Her world imploded in on itself until all was a blur, except for the rage coming at her. Even the pounding of her heart was distant, as if it came from under ten feet of water.

She screamed for the kids to run, not knowing if they were even still in the apartment, hoping they were already out the door. Hands frantically searching for anything she could put between her and Troy, found a pot handle, and she wrapped her fist around it.

Troy charged as she swung the pot forward. Metal met cartilage crunching his nose, sending vibrations ringing up her arm.

He staggered back, and bent over, clutching at his mangled nose as blood poured through his fingers. Rage emanated from him.

At least he'll kill me fast.

He looked up at her through blood-soaked fingers, the measure of hatred in his eyes assuring her how wrong she was.

"Mommy!" Faith's voice flared through Laney's panicked fog like a beacon.

She turned and saw her little girl at the open door. Ray tried to drag her out, but Faith clung to the doorjamb, tears streaming down her face.

Laney ran for it, Troy right behind her.

She grabbed for her purse hanging on the hook by the door as she went past and slipped one strap over her shoulder as she followed the kids down the hall.

Footsteps thundered behind her. Troy closed the distance and lunged. He got a hold of the dangling purse strap and dug his feet in, stopping hard.

The floor went out from under her still pumping legs, and she got air time. The cheap, stained carpet covering the concrete did little to soften the impact when she landed.

Shrugging off the strap, Laney rolled to her knees. Troy stood over her. The blood dripping from his nose adding to the carpet stains. The contents of the purse spilled out on the floor between them.

Troy dropped the strap and closed the distance, fists clenched at his sides, just as her neighbor opened his door. "The fuck is going on here?"

No, Ronny, don't even try.

She knew Ronny's story from when she sometimes brought him left over meals from the restaurant. Twenty years ago, a smart man would have shit his pants at the thought of going up against Raging Ronny, an ex marine turned bouncer who considered making people spit Chiclets a hobby. That was before the emphysema. Now, he stood hunched and pale, forty pounds lighter than his glory days. An oxygen tube in his nose, a cigarette in one trembling hand, and the other hand dragged his tank behind him on a wheeled cart.

"Two packs a day for decades can humble a man." Ronny once told her.

Troy turned and leered a bloody grin at him.

"Fuck this psycho shit," Ronny said, slamming the door. But he gave Laney all the time she needed. The stairwell door swung closed behind her around the same time Ronny was deciding maybe the deadbolt wasn't enough and he'd do the chain lock too.

Feet hitting metal steps reverberated off the walls like gunshots. Three flights of barely controlled descent, and they reached the landing.

"Hey!" Troy yelled from above her. "Wherever you think you're going, you won't get far without these."

Without looking, Laney knew Troy held her car keys, but she wasn't concerned about that. She had grabbed the spare key from the kitchen drawer while Troy ranted about garlic bread.

It was the thought of the cash Celia had given her that sat heavy in her gut. Without that, she knew they wouldn't get far. And right now, that cash was lying on the hallway carpet three floors above her.

The door slammed behind them as they rushed into the deserted parking lot. Her car hunkered in the shadows across from them, still sandwiched between the two minivans. The street traffic on the other side of the metal fence bordering the lot might as well be miles away. Not that it mattered. This wasn't a neighborhood where people got involved in a stranger's problems.

Laney hit the button on the key fob, and the car chirped out a beep as the doors unlocked and the lights flashed. The security door squealed open behind her and Laney found she still had some adrenaline left in reserve. She picked up Faith and sprinted for the car.

Ray reached the car first and opened the passenger side door before Troy locked the car from across the lot, with the set of keys he took from Laney's purse. With wiry, teenage speed, Ray threw himself across the driver's seat, unlocked the door and pushed it open before Troy could hit the lock button again.

Faith let out a whimper as Laney ducked in, squeezing them both past the steering wheel. Troy's pounding footsteps closed in. She pushed her daughter off, passing her to Ray—rougher than she would have liked—then pulled the door to close it. But Troy got a hold of the top of the door frame and held fast. She braced her legs, threw her weight back, and forced Troy to let go or lose fingers as the door slammed shut.

Laney hit the lock button, and four simultaneous clicks responded with the illusion of safety. "In the back. Seat belts now."

Ray helped Faith climb over the seat and they both buckled in.

Laney put the key in the ignition.

Troy leaned down close to the glass. His face, illuminated by the dashboard lights, was a monstrous sight. Not because of the blood that still leaked from his nose as he showed Laney his teeth, like a dog ready to rip her throat out. It was his eyes. They weren't full of hate or anger. Instead, they shone with a promise of pain. She had seen that look before, but tonight, Troy dialed up the intensity. She half expected the glass to crack under his glare.

"If you even think about starting that car, I will make you suffer."

Laney didn't doubt it, but she started the car, anyway.

He held her keychain up, the metal spike dangling. She couldn't help but picture the damage he could do with it. Pointing the key fob at her like he was aiming a gun, he hit the unlock button. His other hand must have been waiting by the handle. The door yanked open before she could grab it.

She threw the car in reverse and hit the gas. Troy jumped back, flattened himself against the minivan, triggering its alarm. The Camry's door just missed him as it swung wide from momentum, catching the side of the minivan and leaving a trail of sparks in its wake. The car squealed out into the lot. Laney cut the wheel hard, swerving right into a ninety-degree angle to avoid the parked cars behind her, and her door slammed shut.

The lot, alive with flashing lights, clamored with the rhythmic blare of the minivan's alarm. The smell of burned rubber hung acrid in the air.

Troy walked out of the darkness and into the smoke from the tires, illuminated by the chaos of lights, like the MC at a wrestling match. Laney switched gears, panicked at the thought of him getting in front of the car and blocking their path, afraid she wouldn't have the guts to run him over if it came to it.

She hit the gas. The engine revved, but the car went nowhere. It took far too long for her over adrenalized brain to register the glowing "N" on the gear shift panel. She shifted down into drive and looked up as she hit the gas again.

Troy stood, fuming, in the headlights' glare as the Camry bore down on him. Laney hit the brakes, stopping hard.

"Are you crazy?" Ray screamed. She couldn't tell who Ray was yelling at. Her or Troy?

Troy threw his head back and laughed like a lunatic. Until he looked down at her, locking eyes. A garish grin stretched across his bloody face. "That's my girl."

The seismic shift of Troy's smile. That's how she knew.

It was the way his expression altered so grotesquely that made Laney realize she was out of the seat, bearing all of her weight on the gas pedal. It was the first time she had ever seen fear on him. She almost didn't recognize it.

Troy dove to the side as the car tore by, but not fast enough to avoid getting clipped by the fender. There was a sickening pop, and he hit the ground, rolling.

Laney didn't look back.

Five miles later, Ray's mother pulled into a Wawa parking lot and cried.

Ray expected tears out of his sister too, but Faith sat, dry-eyed, watching their mother. He had a sudden sense of déjà vu. Everything back at the apartment was a blur. But this part, the aftermath, felt all too familiar.

He didn't understand what happened back there. Ray knew there was tension between his parents, but he didn't see the twist coming. One second he was shoving a meatball in his mouth and the next all hell broke loose when his mom whacked his dad with a baking pan. It was totally out of nowhere. And he didn't understand why she did it. From the look on her face when it happened, maybe she didn't know why, either. But when it all went down, spurred by instinct, he grabbed Faith and tried to run for it. He needed to put distance between them and his parents.

Just get Faith and get somewhere safe.

That had a familiarity to it. Get Faith. Get safe. He had a flash of him holding Faith when she was a baby. They were somewhere dark, surrounded by softness and the clean smell of fabric softener.

Like someone hit a switch, the exhaustion came in an instant. Sitting there, next to Faith, in the semi-darkness of the car, the tide of adrenaline ebbed away. He closed his eyes and drifted off to the sound of traffic and his mother crying, the scent of fresh laundry in the air.

Ray didn't know how long he had been sleeping when his mother gently shook him awake. Disoriented, he sat up, wide eyed, trying to place his surroundings. With a knot in his gut, it all came back to him.

His mother's eyes were red, with dark circles under them, but she wasn't crying anymore.

"Please tell me you brought your phone," she said, her voice low and desperate.

Ray nodded and pulled his phone out of his pocket, unlocked it and handed it to her. He pulled it back at the last second before she took it.

"No snooping."

She nodded her head in numb agreement, and he gave her the phone.

5

Philip

Philip Haines, a soft faced man with blue eyes and blond hair like his mother and his sister, was still at his office despite the late hour. It was not a corner office, but it was on the 30th floor and had a decent view of the Manhattan skyline.

He sat in an overstuffed leather chair near the window, a bound document in his lap, and a glass of whiskey in his hand. The office was dark except for a Tiffany lamp on a side table next to him and the lights of the city through the window.

He had court in the morning, and it was his ritual to spend the night before in preparation. It was not as if he didn't already know the case inside and out. He certainly put in the hours. Like a craftsman of fine furniture readying a piece for delivery, he took this quiet moment of study as an opportunity to appreciate the work, to reassure himself of its soundness, to run his hand along its smooth finish.

Across the office, his cell phone rang silently, lighting up his desk. If it was urgent, his wife would call the office line next. If it wasn't his wife, it wasn't urgent.

Later, he'd look at the phone and see the three missed calls from his sister Laney and be glad he ignored the ringing. The last thing he needed the night before court was more of her drama.

$$6$$

With a Bang

They had nowhere else to go. It was a four-hour drive and they should have just enough gas to get there. Laney had never told Troy where the farm was, and he never asked. Thinking of that place had always given her a sense of unease. And though she hadn't been there in almost twenty-five years, anxiety crept into her chest.

But it wasn't like she had a choice.

She moved the car to an open spot near the glass doors of the Wawa. So, she could see it from inside the store.

Hoping she wouldn't regret not having the change for gas later, she scrounged enough from the car to grab a cup of coffee for herself and a bottle of water for the kids. The coffee was a necessity. She could already feel the remaining adrenaline leaving her body and knew from experience that a bone deep exhaustion would come next.

She got out, hit the lock button, and pushed the car door gently closed until she felt it catch. The kids didn't stir.

The crowded store gave Laney both anonymity and protection. It was too busy for anyone around her to notice the state she was in, and too crowded for anyone to miss an assault if Troy somehow tracked them down. She went straight for the coffee island. Not wasting time or valuable cup space on cream or sugar, she filled the largest cup to the brim and grabbed a bottle of water on the way to the register.

From her place in line, Laney watched the police car pull into the lot and park next to her car. The young officer who got out on the passenger's side noticed Ray and Faith sleeping in the back seat. He took a moment to glance in at them before following his partner into the store. Had the police gotten her location from Ray's cell phone when she dialed 911 earlier? She didn't think so. She hung up before the call went through.

Did it even matter if they did?

Laney ran her hand through her hair, her fingertips sliding over the bumpy texture of the scar. She tried going to the police before. It didn't work out for her, or for them.

Seven years ago, Laney walked through the doors of a police station in the middle of the night, an infant in her arms and a five-year-old walking close behind. Ray held her hand in a tight, sweaty grip.

The empty lobby didn't convey a sense of sanctuary, more a place where the business of suffering was dealt with efficiently and practically. A place where every surface was designed for the ease of cleaning bodily fluids. Hard plastic chairs sat bolted to the floor on long metal beams. The seats, more yellow than orange in the harsh florescent light, lined the cold white walls. The scent of industrial cleaning fluid, underpinned by vomit and cheap alcohol, filled the air.

Their footsteps echoed as Laney lead them to the front desk, a long counter in front of a window of one inch thick safety glass. Ray planted his feet and pulled at her hand, crying. "Lets go mommy. I don't like it here."

"It's okay. This is a safe place." She pulled his shaking body tight to her, and he looked up at her with big, trusting eyes. "These people will protect us."

God help them, they tried.

The desk officer was a hard-looking man. He didn't need the lines on his brow, or the gray in his hair as proof of his experience. Though he attempted to convey concern, the look of shielded indifference in his stoic eyes betrayed him.

She stood before him, one eye red and freshly swollen shut, the other still bruised a green and purple from an argument the week before. She had missed the crust of dried blood on her earlobe when she tried to get herself together in the car before coming in.

He sighed, pulled his keyboard towards him and ran through a standard list of questions without taking his eyes off the screen. Name? Nature of your visit? Do you need medical attention?

The station door opened behind her and determined footsteps slapped hard on the linoleum tiles, heading in her direction. It never occurred to her those steps might come for her. Not here.

She was in mid sentence, describing the fight with Troy, when he grabbed the back of her head. His fist tangled through her hair, and he yanked her head back, swift and hard. There was a wrench of tearing pain as chunks of hair ripped from her scalp at the root. But his grip did not loosen.

That was just the wind up.

Troy pulled her ear to his mouth just long enough to say, "there's only one way you're leaving me". Before he shoved her head forward in an arc, heading straight towards the counter.

Though from shove to impact was less than a second, Laney had time to notice that the officer was looking at her now. His face wore an ill-fitting mask of shock as he lunged towards her helplessly, blocked by the glass.

This felt like it.

The moment Laney had feared for years. She didn't expect to survive Troy's violence this time. If he was attacking her here, that meant he was long gone from the point of self preservation. He was all in. But she didn't have time to let her life flash before her eyes. Laney had only one thought.

The impact would crush Faith.

Her infant daughter, nestled against Laney's chest in a fitful sleep, was between her and the counter rushing at her. Somehow, Laney twisted her body enough, just before she hit, to keep her daughter safe.

The crack was far away and muffled, like thunder on the horizon, and the force of the impact sent her brain knocking around her broken head, banging up against the sides of her skull. The last thing she saw before the world turned off was the look on Troy. His leering grin split a face, sweating and flush with excitement. Small gray circles stood stark against the bloodshot landscape of his gaping, frenzied eyes. She got the sense he was savoring the moment, sucking in every last bit of her pain and enjoying the hell out of it.

That was the end of her life with Troy.

He always said they would go out with a bang.

They sentenced Troy to ten years for assaulting her and the two officers who tried to pull him off of her. One of which lost an eye in the encounter and had to retire early. Troy would have gotten longer, but prosecutors sweetened the plea deal to discourage him from suing the county for the beating he got on the way to holding.

Ray and Faith went to live with her brother Philip and his wife Ellen for months while Laney recovered. She often wondered if they would have been better off if she left them there. Ray would probably say yes to that question. Live with rich Uncle Philip in New York City, or be dragged from one rundown apartment to the other with loser Mom? She was sure Ray would call that a "no brainer".

It turned out the police were also there for coffee, which worked out because Laney left the store without a word to them. She was done, drained, empty, and didn't have the energy to talk to the police or anyone. She just wanted to be somewhere else, far away. And every moment she lingered, Troy could close the distance.

She needed to be on the road.

7

Long Drive

Laney kept an apprehensive eye on the half full gas gauge while navigating the bottle necks exiting Philly. Pennsylvania was a big state, and she'd need every drop she had to cross it.

Once clear of the city, she spent the next three hours navigating through changing roads until she made her way to Route 80, heading west. The traffic dwindled along the way.

An hour later, when she exited the highway, the road became a dark and lonely place. Winding asphalt carved through the forest. A wall of dense trees waited beyond every curve. On open stretches, the Camry's headlights barely breached the black in front of them.

The coffee helped for a while.

When the caffeine left her system, and her eyes struggled to escape the pull of the double yellow lines passing by in a blur, she opened the window. Cool air blasted her face and arms, the wind fresh and invigorating, free of the heavy odor of the city that seems to go unnoticed until you escape it. The sudden breeze whipping through the car caused the kids to stir, but was no match for their exhaustion.

Between the fresh air and some stale Altoids she found in the console, Laney kept herself awake until she hit her second wind.

Watching the needle on the gas gauge fall as the miles passed didn't hurt, either.

In the drive's solitude, her mind kept wanting to return to what happened back at the apartment, but that was a dark path, easy to get lost on. She distracted herself by making a mental list of supplies the kids would need for the first day of school. Never mind that she couldn't afford the supplies, even before Troy showed up, or that the kids no longer had a school. Constant iteration over the now defunct list became a mantra against dark thoughts.

Her second wind close to spent, the GPS finally prompted her to turn, and guided her through country roads where farms, the occasional house, and the rare gas station interrupted the woods. The GPS stuck with her until the final turn onto a long stretch of road before it abandoned them to their fate, its signal lost.

Laney's best guess put her about thirty minutes away from the farm when the low fuel light went on. She didn't have to worry about a lack of caffeine, stale mints or tired eyes after that. They were in the middle of nowhere on a dark, two-lane road in the woods of Northern Pennsylvania. She knew she wasn't likely to find an open gas station this time of night. And even if she found a gas station, she couldn't afford the gas.

Her hands white knuckled the steering wheel, and she willed the fuel left in the tank to be enough, just enough.

That's all I'm asking for.

As long as she didn't run out of gas and didn't miss the sign to the farm, they would be fine. Nothing to worry about. Not a thing.

The rain came out of nowhere and hit the windshield like a thousand pebbles. Laney nearly jumped out of her skin. Despite the pounding rain pummeling the car, she could still hear the kids scream behind her.

She turned on the wipers and shut the windows, but not fast enough to prevent the left half of her body from getting soaked. Shivering, she slowed the car to a crawl and had to lean over the steering wheel. She squinted to see the road through the brief clearing on the windshield, carved out a second at a time by the overwhelmed wiper blades.

"It's okay." Laney struggled to sound reassuring, while also yelling to be heard. "We're almost there. Nothing to worry about, guys."

Even as she hunched over the wheel, eyes focused on the small patch of visible road ahead, the orange glow emanating from the low gas light stayed in her peripheral vision, a constant reminder that there was always something to worry about.

"What's that light?" Faith asked.

"Nothing, honey, just an indicator light."

"What's an indicator light?"

"It indicates that something bad's going to happen," Ray yelled.

"What the hell is wrong with you?" Laney glanced in the rear-view mirror to catch a glimpse of Faith, to see if she was okay, but it was too dark to see anything. Ray seemed to be his old self again. God forbid the trauma of the night cause him to repress his inner asshole.

Miles that should have taken minutes to cross went on for what seemed like forever through the never ending deluge. Finally, the woods gave way to a field on their right, thick with tall waves of corn. Stalks quivered with the impact of the rain. It was the farm. It had to be. She breathed a short-lived sigh of relief. Then a bolt of lightning split the sky and Faith let out a blood-curdling scream.

She spared another glance away from the road to shoot Ray a dirty look in the rear-view mirror and gasped when a face lunged out of the darkness. Faith scrambled over the console into the passenger seat.

Laney brought the car to a stop. "Never, ever take your seatbelt off when I'm driving."

Her daughter's face looked unearthly pale in the blue glow of the dashboard lights, and the little girl's shoulder's hitched with each gasping breath.

Faith looked up at her, eyes wide with fear and incredulity. "Why did you stop? He'll get us!"

"Who?" Laney asked, expecting the answer to be Troy, but unable to run a scenario in her head where he had somehow followed them.

I would have seen him on the road. It's not possible.

"The man in the corn. Go! Go!"

"Huh," Laney said. Not the answer she had expected, but it made sense for Faith's imagination to be in overdrive after the night she had. Hell, Laney had been seeing Troy on random street corners, in dark alleys and occasionally skulking in shadows of the back seat of her car for the past seven years.

"Go mom." Faith said.

"Okay. Okay. Get back in your seat with your seatbelt on and I'll go."

Faith stayed in the passenger seat and slipped her belt on. That wasn't where Laney had intended, but she wouldn't argue right now. She reached below Faith's seat and adjusted it back as far away from the airbag as it would go. They were more likely to run out of gas than have a head on collision, but better safe than sorry.

"Mooooom," Faith whined at the delay.

"Okay. Okay. I'm going honey."

Laney put the car in drive and creeped forward. Faith crouched down in her seat, leaning away from the rain splattered window, not taking her eyes off of it.

Without the buffer of the woods beside them, the wind had picked up. The rain pounded on the car with torrential urgency. Corn stalks swayed together, like the entire field was a single, undulating organism that could suddenly envelope them and swallow them whole.

There's a reason they make horror movies about corn fields.

Please, be enough gas.

Just on the edge of visibility, Laney saw something in the corn ahead that made her forget about the gas.

The shape of a figure, too dark to make out, taller than the corn, and not swaying with it, not moving at all except the brim of his hat fluttering in the wind. Faith saw it too and moaned.

The man in the corn. Of course, there's a man in the corn. Of course there is. Laney's gut told her to stop, turn around, do it now. But she recognized the figure for what it was and ignored her gut.

As they inched closer, the figure took form in the headlights, a wide-brimmed hat, broad shoulders, and a glint of metal in his hands. Wrapped in the figure's arms, that crisscrossed like a mummy, was an axe. Its rusted head was just clean enough for the blade to catch a glint from the headlights. The figure had no eyes, just dark holes in a burlap sack. Laney knew she should be relieved, but that was the creepiest scarecrow she had ever seen.

And since when are scarecrows armed with axes?

The moan coming out of Faith increased in pitch and intensity. She pressed down into her seat like she wanted to slip into the crack and hide there.

"Faith, honey, it's okay. It's a scarecrow. It's just a scarecrow," Laney said as they passed.

"Faith must be a crow then." Ray's voice came from the darkness of the back seat.

Laney looked in the rear-view mirror. "Will you please just stop?"

The car responded, shuddering, and she patted the wheel. "Not you, car. Not you."

When the shudder passed, and the engine remained running,

Laney mouthed a silent thank you, but didn't let herself relax. Her fingers ached from her grip on the wheel. Between the rain, the gas, and her imploded life, she felt like she could fuel the car with the stress emanating from her.

Through her hands, to the wheel, to the engine itself.

As if to dissuade her from having any delusions of control, the car shuddered again. She held her breath until the engine smoothed out, knowing that after the next shudder, they might not be so lucky.

Lightning flashed, illuminating the corn ahead of them, and Laney's mouth drew into a tired smile.

Flanked by well worn no-trespassing warnings, stood a large sign, its weathered wood pitted and cracked. Letters, painted a faded red, were barely visible, but she could make out just enough to see they had arrived at Killian Farm.

She turned onto the driveway carved through the cornfields just past the sign. She didn't even freak out when the car shuddered again for the last time. It was a long driveway, but it was smooth and slightly downhill. The car coasted for what seemed like forever down the narrow drive, with only darkness ahead and the corn on either side.

They rolled past another creepy scarecrow, this one armed with an old, rusty cleaver, before the road leveled out and they slowed to a stop. Faith's head turned on a pivot to watch the scarecrow go by. They didn't leave it far behind.

In the headlights, Laney could make out the rain blurred steps leading up to the wrap-around porch and the front door of her childhood home beyond them. After the day she had, hell, after the past few miles alone, this should have been a welcoming sight. But she wasn't feeling warm and fuzzies in the pit of her stomach, quite the opposite. For a moment, the dread was so overwhelming a small sob involuntarily escaped her. She covered her face with her hands and took a deep breath. When she had it under control again, she wiped her eyes and tried to pass it off with a fake yawn.

The kids didn't seem to notice. Faith craned her neck, looking at the corn behind the car where they saw the last scarecrow. Ray hid in the darkness of the back seat.

"I don't see any lights." His voice came from behind her. "Does he still live here?"

"Your grandfather will never move. This farm has been in the family for generations. It's a family legacy," Laney said.

"What happens to it when grandpa dies?"

That's a morbid thought.

"I guess it goes to your Uncle Philip, or me, or both. I don't know. But don't worry. You've never met your grandfather. He's too stubborn to die."

8

Knock Knock

Rain pelted the car in steady droves, turning the Toyota into an over-sized white noise machine. Laney couldn't see it from the driver's seat, but she could feel the house—her father's house—looming in the darkness, taunting her. She didn't drive four hours to sit in the dark waiting for the rain to stop, or slow, or just get it all over-with and drown them already. She needed to suck it up and go knock on the door.

Faith had either fallen asleep or passed out in fear of scarecrows, and Ray hadn't mouthed off to her in a while, so she was pretty sure he was asleep too. Without their expectant eyes on her goading her into action, the only person she could disappoint by cowering in the car was herself. Fortunately, she had lowered her expectations years ago.

She settled back in the seat and let her tired eyes drift closed. What was the point of trying to keep them open, anyway? She couldn't even see her own hand in front of her face. Besides, Troy couldn't find them here in the middle of nowhere. The kids were asleep. She could deal with her dad in the morning.

It didn't take long for her breathing to find the rhythm of sleep, for her mind to fall away. She let herself sink into the blissful quicksand of unconsciousness.

"That's my girl," a whisper in the dark, rough and splintery against her ear.

Laney bolted upright. Her breath sucked down deep in her throat. Clumsy, sleep addled fingers fumbled for the key already in the ignition. They found it, then twisted a half turn, engaging the battery. She pulled the knob for the headlights so hard her fingertips burned from the friction.

In the dimly lit interior, she twisted in her seat, ignoring the pain in her back. She searched for someone that logic told her wasn't there. Couldn't be there. But tonight, logic was not the boss of her. Ray slept in the seat behind her. The rest of the bucket seat lay empty, leaving only the footwell on the passenger side out of sight. Troy, being a grown man, couldn't possibly fit there. She leaned over and thrust her arm into the dark space anyway, swatted around to confirm it was empty.

Satisfied that Troy would not uncoil and spring from the shadows of the back seat anytime soon, Laney faced the front.

Outside the car, headlights pierced the night. Through the blurred distortion of rain running in thick meandering rivulets down the windshield, quivering rows of corn led the way to the large red door, a hellish portal twisting and writhing against the white paint of the porch.

She triggered the wipers. The blades swept in arcs across the glass, and for a split second at a time, the door was just a door.

Might as well get it over-with.

Bruised from her escape and stiff from the drive, Laney's muscles protested the very concept of standing. She groaned under her breath while climbing out of the car and gently closed the door behind her to avoid waking the kids. Her clothes soaked through within seconds and clung cold against her skin. An icy rill found the curve of her back and trickled down between her shoulder blades, sending a shiver down her spine as she ran for the porch.

Rain had transformed the entire dirt driveway into a muddy pond with large roots wound through, curving up from the water like sea serpents. The rain coursed off them, giving the illusion of movement, of serpents slithering through the puddles.

By the time her foot hit that first wooden step, her sneakers squished, ejecting muddy water with each footstep. A trail of dirty puddles tracked her over the planks, past the welcome mat. She pulled open the screen door and raised her hand to knock on the red painted door behind it.

With her fist poised in the air, about to re-initiate contact with a man who had been out of her life for decades, coming here suddenly felt like a stupid idea. She hadn't seen her father since she was seven, hadn't spoken to him since she was fifteen. Back in Philadelphia, Laney would have bet good money that if she showed up on his doorstep, he wouldn't turn her away, not with the kids. But standing on the porch, tendrils of doubt wormed their way into her brain.

Seven-year-old Laney adored her dad. He was her hero, a man with a kind smile who gave her piggyback rides home from the school bus in the afternoon, and was never too tired to read to her at night. If there was any one person she had expected to fight for her, it had been him. But he didn't even say goodbye.

On the morning their mother took her and Philip away, Laney sat at her bedroom window. In the driveway below, her mother packed the rest of their things in the car, the last-minute things like toothbrushes, and Philip's special sheets. Her father had packed their suitcases the night before. She heard him in the dark when she was meant to be sleeping. But Laney didn't watch her mother, didn't want to see the finality of it all. Instead, her eyes followed a cloud of dust in the field. The tractor's engine hummed in the distance, and she watched the dust gliding along the rows of corn, her father and the tractor hidden by the stalks.

That was her last glimpse of him.

During the years, when she felt especially low or alone, Laney would mail a letter, or a photo of the kids, with no return address to the dad she had when she was seven. Like a lonely little kid writing to Santa in the middle of March, just because.

She only knew that her real father, the one who let her leave without lifting a finger, the one she was a knock away from, hadn't died, or sold the house because Philip kept in touch with him. Knowing Philip, he did so for reasons that had more to do with the property value of the farm than sentiment. But at least Philip still had a father.

Laney rapped her knuckles on the door of a stranger and waited.

Nothing, no response she could hear. The rain pounding on the roof of the porch made it impossible to hear anything from inside the house. She checked the windows on either side of the door. Inside, both the kitchen and living room were dark, no lights, save the glow of the clock on the stove, no indication that anyone was awake.

He probably didn't hear me over the rain.

This time she pounded her fist against the wood, waited again. Nothing.

Laney couldn't remember if they locked the door when she was a kid, but wasn't this the kind of place where you left your door unlocked as a point of pride? She grabbed the doorknob to try it, but stopped short of turning it. She imagined herself just walking in. To what? How would he react to waking up and finding them in his house? Or what if she startled him, and he shot her? That was why people never locked their doors around places like this, wasn't it? The home armory?

A sudden darkness shrouded the porch.

Something passed in front of the headlights, something big. Had to be big, to eat the light like that.

Laney turned into the glare, threw her arm up to shield her eyes. But even squinting through slightly spread fingers, she couldn't make out anything. Whatever it was, had run off.

Or waited in the corn.

Or stood by the car, on the other side of the lights, watching her children sleep.

The first thought that popped into her head was of a well-armed scarecrow skulking about, an axe in its hand, hungry for human blood. The absurdity of that idea should have broken the tension, but it only upped it.

It had to be an animal, a deer? Or her imagination? Or even delirium, at this point.

Or Troy.

The kids slept in an unlocked car, keys in the ignition.

She dashed to the Camry, deliberately not looking anywhere but at the ground in front of her. She knew if she looked for them, she'd see threatening shadows everywhere. Troy shaped shadows.

Laney breached the wall of light. Eyes still adjusting to the dark, she cupped her hands against the glass of the driver's side window. Streams of rain flowed past her hands to either side, then down her arms, until they poured off the points of her elbows like waterfalls. She leaned in, her head against her hands, and could just make out the kids sleeping by the dim light of the dashboard.

Relieved, she reached for the handle, but something moved behind her... a wet hiss barely discernible above the noise of the rain. She turned her back to the car and faced the corn, breaking her rule about not looking for threats. But it didn't matter, she couldn't make out anything. The spill of light from the car brushed the outer edges of the cornfield. Beyond them, a thick, muddy darkness smothered the world.

She strained, listening for the hiss of motion that got her attention in the first place, but all she could hear was the rain impacting everything around her.

Lightning lit up the sky, forking into spreading branches above the field before exploding into a ball of energy, illuminating everything in its cold, white brilliance.

At that moment, she saw it. Straight ahead, about twenty-feet in. Droplets of water flew from the corn, falling up, not down. Something rushed at her through the stalks, fast enough to kick up a wake behind it. She caught a sharp glint of metal, then as fast as it had spread, the lightning retracted and was gone from the sky. But the harsh glow of the burst imprinted on her eyes, refusing to be blinked away.

She heard it then, despite the still pounding rain. The rushing hiss of stalks displaced by the thing plowing through them. Getting closer.

Laney reached down for the handle, and pulled, opening the door as she stepped aside, refusing to turn her back to the corn. She must have pulled it too hard in her panic. The door flew open wide, hinges squealing. She grabbed the inside handle as she shot into the car and yanked the door behind her, almost pulling her arm out of the socket when the door didn't budge. Not even an inch.

From the field, the corn buzzed as the thing tore towards the wide-open door. The stalks edging the field shook from the coming motion, shuddering with a violent resonance. Shredded leaves fell to the ground.

Her panic building, Laney leaned back and braced her legs against the frame of the car, bent her knees, then pulled with her whole body. Like she was about to pull a sideways stroke on a rowing machine. The hinges didn't even groan.

Any second now, it would burst from the field.

She backed away from the door, sliding over the console as far as she could go without squishing Faith. The little girl whined in her sleep as Laney's cold, wet clothes pushed up against her.

Laney held her breath, waiting. Her pounding heart counted down the seconds, drowning out the sound of the rain, but not the building rush from the field. Stalks vibrated so fast, the falling rain dispersed into a cloud of vapor around them. Then all at once, just when she expected the corn to erupt outward...it stilled. The stalks, once again, stood passively quivering from the impact of rain. Like someone hit an off switch.

Like it never happened.

Carried by the wind, a torn piece of leaf hit the window of the open door, stuck to the glass.

She sat there frozen until a stale breath gushed out of her burning lungs. Her eyes remained pinned to the darkness beyond the gaping hole in their defenses, waiting for sudden motion. The jump scare she had been trained to expect from too many horror movies. Between the dark and the rain, it could come from anywhere. What *it* was, she didn't know.

It's nothing. Just wind.

Yeah, wind. Every nerve in her body buzzed like a live wire. A big red *DANGER* sign practically blinked in her face.

What would she even do if there was something out there? The only weapon she could think of was the tire iron in the trunk, buried under mounds of trash bags. Solid plan. Take a little stroll to the back of the car to dig through trash bags while serving your sleeping children up, like an open buffet, to whatever hid in the corn.

Nothing hid in the corn.

She had to close the door. Maybe even had to get out of the car to do it. Her legs were already turning to jelly at the thought of pushing even a toe through that opening, but what choice did she have?

Slowly, quietly, she shifted her weight forward, slipped into the driver's seat. Her breath came in and went out in trembling gasps, stuttering loud in her ears. She waited at the precipice of the open door for her eyes to adjust to the shadows on the other side. When she could just make out the streaks of falling rain, she took a deep breath, leaned out-

SLAM.

The door shut an inch from her nose, rocking the car with the force of it.

Laney froze. Condensation from her breath formed on the window as rain poured down its outer surface in sheets glistening with light from the dashboard.

Beyond it lay nothing but the writhing shadows of corn against the dark of night.

Wind. Had to be wind.

But Laney knew it wasn't.

A voice pierced the darkness behind her. Her muscles, too wired to pull off a proper startled jump, gave a violent twitch, sending a shooting pain through her back.

Ray leaned forward in his seat. He had asked her something. She shifted herself around to the front so he couldn't see her face. "What?"

"Are we going in?" Ray asked again, sounding like he just woke up.

With a shaking hand, Laney hit the lock button.

"I guess not." Ray sighed and leaned back. "What's the deal? Is he not letting us stay?"

"He didn't answer."

"Did you try the door?"

"It was locked," she said. "Go back to sleep."

Ignoring the screaming voice inside her head, she turned off the headlights to preserve the car battery in case *it* came back again.

The wind, that is.

Laney shivered, eyes wide open in the dark, and settled back in the wet seat to wait for morning, sleep now the farthest thing from her mind.

9

Old Man

Laney woke up to the scent of petrichor and the sweet summer wind coming off the corn in a faint pre-dawn light. The rain had stopped. Shadows still blanketed the world, but shadows were an improvement over the pitch black of night. She sat pretzeled in her seat, half twisted to face the door, half leaning on the backrest. Her head laid on a harsh right angle against the headrest. Her muscles were stiff and exhausted from shivering through the night in wet clothes that still hung damp against her skin. Slowly, she gritted her teeth and untangled herself, every part of her body complaining, her back the loudest.

The tentative calls of birdsong from the woods beyond the farmhouse, warblers and starlings getting ready to start their day, came through the open door behind her.

The open door?

She turned, ignoring the pain in her back, and saw an empty seat where Ray should have been. Twisting back the other way, muscles screaming in protest, showed an empty passenger seat. Faith was gone, too.

Pain be damned, she opened her door and staggered out of the car on clumsy limbs. At once a rustling came from the field, and her eyes shot to the wall of corn she faced last night. But unlike the wet, green field from last night, the stalks were tanned and dessicated, leaves brittle and cracked. Something moved within them, parting the stalks that swayed with a rattling hiss as it passed. The shifting shadows of dry tassels twitched against the dim light cresting the sky. Then the corn parted, stalks pushed aside, and he stepped from the field. His features, cloaked in shadows, weren't discernible, but somehow the metal of the scythe in his hands caught a glint of light racing across its sharpened edge.

The man stalked towards her with slow, deliberate steps.

Laney fell back into the seat, pulled the door closed, and hit the lock button, as if he couldn't just come in through the open door behind her.

When he got closer, and his form took on definition, she could make out baggy overalls hanging from a lean, bony frame. It wasn't Troy. But that realization brought no comfort.

He leaned down close to her window, just like Troy had done last night when he warned her not to start the car. Trapped between moments in time, the terror filled her all over again. It wasn't Troy, but she'd seen this face before. Though she couldn't place him. Which made no sense, because he was anything but forgettable.

Greasy hair, combed back, hung down to his shoulders, revealing a long forehead, furrowed with deep grooves across its expanse. Pale, dry skin, cracked with lines and wrinkles wrapped his skull, clinging tight around the bones and muscles of an ancient, emaciated face. Like some mummified corpse, found preserved in a long forgotten tomb. But his eyes, a deep rich brown, shone bright and clear, and held her in their gaze for what seemed like forever. They did a slow pivot in their sockets and came to rest, first on the empty back seat, then the front passenger seat. They lingered there, where her little girl should be, before snapping sharply back to meet Laney's eyes.

Unable to look away, her heart beat faster and faster. And when she felt like it couldn't take anymore, like the fibers of her heart muscle would rip apart from the exertion, his mouth parted. His dessicated skin threatened to split, stretched taut by the cruel smile fracturing his face as he raised the scythe. Until it blocked his smile from her and all she could see was the honed edge of the blade clad in fresh blood.

No. Not the kids. Not them.

He took a step back, raised the scythe high over his shoulder, and swung hard. The blade smashed through the window, shattering the glass, before piercing her-

Laney woke with a start, her arms instinctively thrown up to protect her face, but there was nothing to protect it from.

She brushed away at the broken glass—that didn't exist—with shaking hands, before the sharp reality of the pain in her back overtook the residual fear of a nightmare already fading fast. Confusing bits and pieces of the dream haunted her waking mind— blood, the kids in danger—but the more she tried to focus on them, the faster they slipped away.

The rain had stopped, and the sun hung bright above the horizon. The kids stirred, stretching and yawning.

An old man with a familiar face leaned down to her window, and she flinched.

It was a hard face, and a lot more wrinkled than last time she saw it, but the brown eyes were kind, creased with laugh lines, and squinted in confusion. He held up a cup of coffee and gestured with his head towards the house.

For the first time in a long time, like she was seven all over again, Laney felt safe.

10

Hot Coffee

Pete Killian placed a hot cup of coffee on the table in front of his daughter, watched her wrap both hands around it and drink with reverence. She took a long sip, then sighed, her relief palpable.

When people say "it's the little things in life", they mean coffee.

The smell of sizzling bacon hung in the air. The morning sun coming in the windows filtered through sheer curtains dancing gently in the summer breeze, and filled the kitchen with a warm, welcoming light. Laney and the kids sat around the kitchen table, a green laminate oval, rimmed in aluminum. It was the same dinette set Pete ate at as a kid, the same his children ate family meals at. After she came downstairs, having changed into some dry clothes, Laney had gravitated towards her usual seat like no time had passed.

At his age, it was hard to surprise him. It certainly didn't surprise him when he stepped out on the porch to drink his morning coffee in the rocking chair and saw a car in his driveway. Pete supplemented his income by repairing just about anything with an engine. He formally trained as a mechanic in the Army, but he had been working on engines for years prior. There was always something in need of repair on a farm, and the work came naturally to him.

Pete converted his barn into an auto shop, complete with a

refurbished lift for engine work, when he stopped keeping livestock. Being too out of the way for most people, he wouldn't be putting Clevenger's Auto Repair in West Mills out of business anytime soon. But he had core customers who kept him busy. The beat up red Toyota was not a car he was familiar with. But it looked to be in a desperate enough state to be sent to the old guy who fixed cars out of his barn for cheap.

When he got closer and looked at the face of the sleeping woman leaned up against the window, though—that was something he never saw coming. In the last photo he had of her, she was a happy young woman in a modest white dress on her wedding day. She had sent him that picture along with a short letter announcing her wedding with no return address and a Chicago postmark. It was the first he had heard from her since she stopped writing to him when she was fifteen. After the wedding letter, he'd get occasional cards with pictures of her kids, and once, a terse letter informing him her mother, his wife—ex-wife—Janice, had died of cancer. But nothing else.

He knew a little about her life from Philip. His son got back in touch with him three years back, but Philip avoided the subject of his sister as much as possible. When he did talk about her, the tone of his voice implied little patience for his sister's life choices. As Pete understood it, Laney had married a cruel man. They had a rough break up, and she had taken her children and distanced herself from him.

Good for her.

Pete knew that type of man all too well. He wished things had been different. Maybe if he was in her life, he could have helped her avoid that situation. Hell, if he was in her life, it would have been an isolated incident, not a situation. He would've taught her husband why a man never lays a hurtful finger on a woman by kicking the ever loving shit out of him. And if that didn't work, well, Pete had learned the hard way, it was tough as hell to find a body on his property.

But wishing changed nothing. Things were as they were for a reason.

In the car, even while sleeping, Laney had looked exhausted. The kids looked like they had been through the ringer, too. Looking at them now, sitting around his kitchen table, Pete realized that, whatever brought them, coming here must have been their only option.

That's going to make it so much harder when I tell them they have to leave.

Pete turned back to mind the bacon sizzling on the stove. A small voice behind him said, "Grandpa, can I help?"

Grandpa.

He swallowed the lump in his throat.

"Sure Faith. Get the eggs for me, will you?"

"From the chicken coop?" Faith's voice rang with excitement.

"From the fridge. Sorry to disappoint."

"What kind of farm is this?" She looked up at him, eyebrows arched.

"The kind without chickens."

Her shoulders sagged a little, but Faith got the carton of eggs from the fridge and carried it to the counter with extra care, like they were precious cargo.

By the time she reached the counter, she had found her enthusiasm again. "Can I help crack them?"

Pete stopped fussing with the bacon and squatted down to her level. His knees popped like popcorn, but he didn't make a sound, or let the pain show on his face. He looked her in the eyes, an earnest look. "I got a bigger job for you, you and your brother, actually. It's a bit of a hike, but it's really important."

"Ooh, an adventure." Faith's eyes brightened.

"Yeah, an adventure, if you make it one. All the way at the end of the drive, is a special box," he smiled and waved his hands in the air. His voice turned deep and mysterious, "a *mail* box..."

He watched the light dim in the little girl's eyes as they turned to the cornfield through the open window. "I know I'm asking a lot, but I'm waiting for something really important in the mail, and you're a big girl. I know you can do it."

Her mouth tight, Faith nodded her head in agreement.

"Yep, she's a big girl. She doesn't need me to walk her to the *special box...Grandpa*," Ray said.

Pete turned his head back over his shoulder and looked askew at Ray. He didn't say a word, didn't need to. Pete had the kind of face that could send a clear "I'm not fucking around" message with just a glance. Ray rolled his eyes, slid his chair back, and got up.

"Stay out of the corn," Pete said. "And mind the road, because the trucks won't mind you."

Ray mumbled something under his breath while holding the kitchen door for his sister. Then shut it a little too hard behind them when they left.

Pete chuckled, watching the kids walk down the porch steps through the front facing window. "That boy is willful."

"He's like his father," Laney said.

Pete turned to his daughter. "He's like you. They both are."

Laney looked up at him, eyes narrowed.

"You were always my strong one," Pete said. "Philip has done well for himself, big shot lawyer and all, and he's worked hard to get there, but he's never done well with adversity. When the shit hits the fan, well…. let's just say he's always been soft."

Better to get it done with.

Pete opened the cabinet next to the sink, took out a coffee can. He turned and put the can on the table in front of his daughter.

Her eyes drifted to the can.

He turned back to fuss with the bacon. He had never been a weak man, but, god help him, he couldn't look his daughter in the face while he did this. Only one other time in his life had he been this much of a coward. It was the day he said his goodbyes to his sleeping family. Then, snuck away so he wouldn't have to watch them leave.

"I know you've dealt with some tough…situations, and I know if you showed up in my driveway this morning, it's because you had nowhere else to go. And I wish I could make things better for you. I really do. Best I can do is give you what's in that can. That's about eight hundred dollars plus change. It's not much, but I know you'll make it work. From what I hear, you always do. But you can't stay here. This house, it ain't fit-"

"I need gas," Laney said, interrupting, her voice flat. "Ran out last night. Barely made it here."

"I've got some in the barn." Pete expected anger, maybe tears. He wasn't expecting to be let off the hook this easily. The tension in his shoulders eased. He turned to look at her, "hell, I can even give you an oil cha-"

The look on her face shut him up. That wasn't a desperate woman sitting at his kitchen table. That was a woman who passed desperate fifty miles ago.

Laney stared into her coffee, face slack, unblinking. She was close to her limit when she got here, he realized.

And I just pushed her over it.

11

The Corn

It didn't make any sense.

When Faith reached the first scarecrow along the walk, it looked way different from last night. Kind of pathetic. Its hat and clothes, torn and dirty, hung loose like it didn't have enough stuffing. Its arms, stretched out and tied up to a wooden beam, hung limp. White stains that looked like bird poop covered the arms and shoulders. Tufts of straw, where hands should be, held nothing. No weapons. But its face, though not as scary as last night, was still pretty creepy with its eyes just dark holes cut out of the sack, staring dead ahead.

"Still creeped out by the scarecrows? Even in broad daylight?" Ray picked up a pebble from the drive, then side armed it, sending it sailing over the corn. "You're just like mom."

Faith didn't understand what it had to do with mom, but why wouldn't she find them creepy? "It's like their eyes are following us."

"They don't have eyes,"

"It's like their eye holes are following us."

"You're pathetic."

Dragging her gaze away from the scarecrow as they left it behind, Faith turned to her brother. "Do you think he'll find us here?"

"We're in the middle of nowhere. God couldn't find us here. Besides, what difference does it make if he does? The only one acting psycho last night was Mom. Everything was fine until she smacked Dad with the garlic bread."

"You should use your eye holes," Faith said before stomping off ahead of him.

"What the hell does that even mean?" Ray called after her.

Ray knew what Faith meant. He saw it last night, that look on Dad's face, like he was ready to kill. But he didn't see any reason to freak Faith out anymore than she already was. Especially not if they were going to be stuck here, surrounded by creepy corn fields.

Besides, nobody could be that psycho. Could they? Mom never talked about why his dad went to jail, and Ray didn't dare ask his dad last night, but he heard Uncle Philip talking behind Mom's back once. Something about some cop losing an eye and that his mom had shit taste in men.

If his dad actually took out a cop's eye, then maybe he was dangerous. Maybe they were lucky they got away last night. Who knows? All Ray knew for sure was that his mom had started it when she went to town on Dad's head with the garlic bread pan.

This family is so fucked up.

He watched Faith walk away. Except in the tire track depressions where puddles still lingered, a watering hole for hovering insects, the dirt driveway had absorbed the previous night's rain. His sister stomped down the middle, between the treads, a dust cloud following her. Her feet slowed as she approached another scarecrow. This one was in the corn a ways, but she edged to the opposite side of the driveway, not taking her eyes off it as she walked past.

He'd better catch up to her before she freaked out again. If anything happened to her on their super important mission to fetch the mail, he would get shit for it. Hell, his paranoid mother was probably watching them from the kitchen window right now. He turned to check, but the window was empty.

Something was off, though. Something other than corn surrounding them in the middle of nowhere. His stomach soured, like it did when he showed up for school and remembered his homework was still on the kitchen table back at the apartment. Only now, he had no idea what triggered the feeling. He took in the scene, trying to pin it down. Empty porch. Way too much corn. Their broken down, piece of shit car near the ancient family farmhouse. The scarecrow—the scarecrow looked at him. Its head, that had been looking straight a minute ago, had flopped on its left shoulder, and rolled to face down the driveway.

Empty eye holes glared right at him.

He knew his mother would drive him crazy, eventually. It only took a visit from Dad and five hours in the car on a family drama road trip. Now he was seeing threats where there were just coincidences. Maybe a stitch came loose in the thing's head or something? Maybe a stitch was loose in his head, that he's even burning brain cells on it.

Ray rolled his eyes, a little disgusted with himself, and turned to catch up to Faith. But the driveway lay empty, a dissipating dust cloud the only evidence his sister had been there. His stomach dropped. He did a slow jog up the middle, looking side to side for any sign of her.

I swear, if she jumps out of the corn at me...

"Ray! Help me!", her panicked voice came from ahead and to the left. From inside the corn.

What was she thinking?

Ray ducked into the field, roughly in the area where her voice had come from. Without a precise idea of the direction he should go, he pushed through, sweeping stalks out of the way with his arms, hoping it was taking him closer. The long leaves that jutted out from the stalks whispered a soft hiss as they brushed against him. The tight gaps in between rows left little room for him to pass and made it impossible to see more than a few feet ahead. His eyes darted between the stalks, hoping to glimpse his sister.

"Faith!"

"Ray. I'm here." Her voice came from a distance, and completely in the wrong direction. Somewhere back towards the house, but angled deeper into the corn. Fuming, he pivoted, and pushed his way through the stalks towards it.

He had one job. Walk Faith to the goddamn mailbox so she could do the stupid, fake errand *Grandpa* sent them on in a totally obvious attempt to get some privacy with Mom. If he went back without her, he'd look like a fucking idiot, not that he cared what some random old guy thought. But still, her running off like that pissed him off.

"Faith?" He had intended it to put some authority into it, but the word left his mouth in a twang of desperation.

"Ray!" Faith called back, her voice faint.

God, she sounded so far away. Her voice came from somewhere back towards the road, opposite the way he just came. Did he pass her? Ray stopped in his tracks, and spun, listening for the sound of her voice, or her movement through the corn.

"Ray, wh-where are you?"

Was she crying? It sounded like she was crying. Jaw clenched, he changed course again, stalks slapping at him as he plowed through the corn towards his sister.

"Stay where you are. Don't move. I'm coming." He yelled.

Carving a path through the stalks was hard work. The sweat dripped off of him, attracting thirsty insects that buzzed around him as he pushed through. He wondered if he was doing any damage to the crop. The old guy said to stay out of the corn, and was probably going to be pissed.

Thanks a lot Faith.

As he got closer to the area he estimated Faith's last call came from, the stalks started to spread out a little more and became easier to move through. He upped his pace to a jog. The rumble of a tractor trailer approaching told him he was nearing the road, and running out of corn.

"Faith?"

Ahead, he caught patches of sun bleached asphalt and faded yellow lines between the stalks, and turned to put himself on a path parallel to the road, heading deeper into the field.

"Faith. Answer me!"

Head on a swivel, his eyes scanned the sea of green around him, and landed on a dim blob of yellow in the shadows of the stalks up ahead. He broke into a run to catch up before he lost track of her again. Man, was she going to get an ear full whe-

Ray tripped.

His foot stopped abruptly, caught up in something on a weird angle. Momentum sent his body flying out to the side, and for a second when his head breached the corn at the edge of the road, the feeling of sun on his cheeks, and the wind in his hair gave rise to the relief of having escaped the field. Then, during his arc towards the asphalt, he saw it.

The glint of sunlight on chrome bouncing off the grill of the truck just feet away, bearing down on him. A shining grin of metal tines rushed at him, awaiting fresh blood.

There was nothing to grab onto, nothing to stop his fall except the pitted asphalt eager to meet his face. He crossed his arms out in front to protect himself. Skin skidded on the hot rough surface, and his cheek bounced off the top of his forearm with a meaty slap, just as the tire, tall as a mountain, treads a mile wide, loomed over him.

The ground beneath him rumbled. The air around him vibrated, before the growling hulk of steel reinforced rubber tore by his head with inches to spare.

His hair stood straight out, sucked into the slipstream, and waved with the passing of each massive tire until the truck left him behind. He laid face down, gasping for air and wondering if he had landed in a puddle or had pissed his pants.

He just laid there for a moment, too in shock to move, except to turn his head and watch the truck that almost killed him shrink away in the distance. Then he caught a sound on the road, coming from the other direction. His heart leaped into his throat and he pistoned his arms, pushing his upper body straight, until he was on his knees, tucked safely back into the corn, waiting for the threat to pass.

He watched it roll by.

The edges of a lone, crisp, dried leaf, scraped and scratched as it tumbled down the road, still caught in the truck's slipstream, and passed by the stalks in front of him.

Ray barked out a single hysterical laugh. Then the shakes hit him. His heart, still stuck in his throat, pounded against the side of his neck, and he sucked in deep gasping breaths of air, tinged acrid with lingering exhaust fumes.

Turning back towards the field, his eyes landed on the thing that had tripped him. A root, thick and ropey, protruded from the ground, forming an arch just big enough to catch his foot, and at just the right angle to redirect his momentum towards the road.

The craziest thought went through his head.

The corn tried to kill me.

Suddenly, the stalks hanging over him were too close for comfort, and he didn't want to spend another second in this field.

He stood on shaky legs to look for Faith. The scent of all that corn, musky and sweet, made his stomach churn. He soon spied the blob of yellow through the stalks, right where he had seen it before. And that bothered him. After this whole chase through the corn, direction change after direction change, the blob hadn't moved in the last few minutes, like not at all.

Ray made his way towards it and as he got closer, the blob of color between gaps of corn became more defined. The yellow blob became the yellow fabric of a t-shirt, which became a t-shirt covering a small frame, until he stepped out into a space between rows and found his sister, kneeling, unmoving, her back to him.

She didn't turn and acknowledge him, though it would have been impossible for her to not hear him coming. She just knelt there, too still. Ray froze for a second, watching, until he saw her shoulders rise and fall with breath.

"Faith?" He spoke softly, and took a tentative step towards her.

"Faith?"

She turned abruptly, one finger over her mouth, and shushed him. She fucking shushed him.

"Are you kidding me now?" Ray exploded.

"Stop yelling. You'll scare it," Faith said in a loud whisper.

He gripped the air in front of him, biting his lip as he squeezed his fists, then took a deep breath. "Scare what?"

A twitch of motion, a few feet ahead of Faith, caught his eye. A white, fluffy, rabbit butt, half stuck out of its burrow.

He rolled his eyes so hard he felt the twang of an ocular muscle. "I almost died trying to find you, and this had you screaming for help?"

Faith shot him a confused look, then once again put her finger over her mouth and shushed him.

Seemingly unconcerned by the noisy humans, the rabbit focused on its business in the burrow, its little cotton ball tail twitching as it chewed away. Ray had little experience with rabbits, but this didn't seem right. Aren't rabbits in the wild supposed to be skittish?

"It's so adorable," Faith said. "Maybe it will let me pet it." She slid forward, her hand reaching out.

Ray grabbed her shoulder and stopped her. "You don't pet wild animals."

"It's not a wild animal. It's a bunny."

"Rabbits are wild animals."

"Lions are wild animals. Bunnies are in petting zoos," Faith said, a whisper in pitch only.

"This ain't a petting zoo. It's a creepy cornfield," Ray yelled back at her.

A small, sharp cry squealed from the burrow, and they both turned to look.

Ray caught a strong whiff of something that he hadn't smelled before. Something coppery. He pulled Faith to a standing position next to him. She didn't fight him on it.

The rabbit wriggled, working its way out of the hole in the ground. Ray and Faith both took a step back in response, but curiosity wouldn't let them look away.

Its white, fluffy tail twitched, and the rabbit hopped back with a wet slurp. As if it suddenly realized it wasn't alone, the rabbit dropped what it was dragging and spun around to stare at them with unnerving pink eyes. Its white face, covered in blood and dangling bits of meat, twitched at them and Ray swore he heard a low growl escape its throat.

Rabbits don't growl. Do they? Do they?

Faith sucked in a sharp breath and squeezed back against Ray. He tightened his grip on her shoulder.

Pink eyes regarded them for a moment longer, then the rabbit flared its nose in the air, and turned back to its prey. When it turned to face them again, a bloody rag doll of stained white fur dangled from its mouth. The kit's head lolled and bounced as its mother took a hop towards them. Its stomach, chewed through, left a trail of pink intestines dragging along the ground beneath it. Its tiny mouth opened and closed, stretching taut strands of bloody saliva between its gums, and it let out a tiny, pitiful, gurgling whine.

The rabbit hopped again, then again. At first, it took one deliberate hop at a time, then its cadence increased with each hop. And with each hop, Ray and Faith took a step back, away from it. All the while, the kit cried as it jostled in its mother's mouth, intestines unspooling behind it.

Ray pushed Faith behind him. "Go!"

He threw his arms out wide and stomped a single step towards the rabbit, letting out a wild yell to scare it off.

It responded by taking a huge, equally aggressive leap towards him.

Ray turned and ran, soon passing Faith, trying to guide them towards the driveway.

Their feet pounded on the dirt. The swat, swat, swat of leaves slapping them as they ran through the stalks did little to drown out the kit's gurgling cries, that were getting louder, more desperate, and closer.

Worried they might be running towards the road again, Ray tried to jump above the corn as he ran, to get his bearings, but he couldn't clear it. He'd get a tantalizing glimpse of blue sky over the ears, but couldn't see beyond that. And with each step, the rabbit closed in.

Then a body hit the ground.

Faith ran as fast as she could, trying to keep up with her brother, but his longer legs kept taking him farther and farther away, and with each stalk between them, he became harder to keep track of.

She could hear the bunny right behind her. Each hop impacted the dirt with a sound that made it feel like something much bigger was chasing her.

Thump. Thump. Thump.

And with each hop, the baby let out a wet scream that sent tears streaming down Faith's cheeks. She wanted to help, but wasn't sure she could. The way its stomach had looked, she thought it was going to die no matter what.

Faith dared a glance back. A blur of white and red rushed towards her. Her foot got caught up, like something grabbed it, and she hit the ground sprawling. A weight landed on her back, roughly grabbed her shirt, and dragged her to her feet.

She screamed.

Hands grabbed her by both arms, human hands.

"Calm down. It's me," Ray said.

Faith opened her eyes and found her brother's face, flush with fear. She jerked her head around, looking for the rabbit. But she didn't see it anywhere, or even hear the baby's cries. Then she glimpsed something beyond Ray, and her eyes went wide.

She twisted, snaking out of his grasp, pushed past him running and not stopping till she dropped to her knees, panting, in the middle of the driveway.

"What the fuck?" Ray stepped out behind her. "No way we were this close unless we got really turned around there at the end."

"Why would she do that?" Faith asked, tears streaming down her face. "That was her baby."

Ray looked at her like she was stupid. "I got two words for you. Wild. Animal."

They kept to the middle of the driveway, away from the corn, for the rest of the walk to the mailbox. Ray never let his sister out of his sight, not even to glance at the corn, make sure pink eyes weren't looking back. After they escaped the field, Faith had just wanted to go back, forget the mailbox, but after all that shit, there was no way Ray would walk back into that house without some goddamn mail in his hand.

A distant rumble announced the pending arrival of another tractor trailer as they neared the road, sending a violent shiver down Ray's spine. Faith looked up at him, a question in her eyes, but he said nothing. They reached the mailbox just as the truck flew past. A gust of air hit them and kicked up a cloud of dust.

Waving his hand to clear the dust near his face, Ray looked both ways, then stepped out into the road to open the mailbox. The contents of the faded metal box triggered a justified eye roll. He reached in, did his best not to disturb the spider lurking in the back of the box, and grabbed the mail. When he looked up, Faith was gone. Again.

His stomach lurched, an all too familiar feeling lately. "What the fuck?"

The long driveway lay empty all the way to the farmhouse in the distance.

Gravel crunched behind him, and he spun around. Faith stood across the road.

"What are you doing?" He yelled, trying to erase the image in his head of a speeding truck bearing down on his sister as she crossed.

"I found this." She held up a wilting bouquet of wildflowers tied with a purple ribbon.

Ray checked both ways again, still no traffic, and jogged across.

Faith stood in front of a tree that looked like a tremendous force had cleaved it in two a long time ago. One part of the trunk reached skyward, the other leaned parallel to the road. Both parts of the tree flourished in their own way. The skyward trunk had continued the natural growth pattern of the tree and sturdy branches reached out for the sun. The leaning trunk grew short, stunted branches that curved up abruptly when they neared the road. Moss grew in the scars around the base of the tree.

"Just leave the flowers. I think someone put them there on purpose." He gestured to the split tree. "There was probably a car accident here a long time ago. Someone must have died, and now their family leaves flowers like it's a grave. C'mon, let's go."

Faith put the flowers back gently at the base of the tree. She kissed the tips of her fingers and touched them to the mossy trunk.

Ray tried to take Faith's hand to cross back, but she yanked it away. "I'm not a baby, jerk face."

They turned to face the farm. "Have it your way, dog breath."

A long walk past the corn awaited them. The house sat small, like a toy, in the distance. Faith grabbed his hand, and they walked back to the farmhouse together.

12

Cold Breakfast

Pete sat across from Laney, each with a cup of coffee in their hands, neither drinking, breakfast going cold between them. The scrambled eggs had dulled, their greasy sheen gone, and drops of fat congealed on the strips of bacon. Neither of them had spoken a word to each other since Laney shut down.

All these long years, Pete never once imagined he could have a relationship with his daughter again or be a grandfather. He was too pragmatic for self delusion. Those days were in the past for a reason. But in that moment, emptiness filled him at the loss of a second chance that he never thought he'd get, and the old wound opened anew. He wished it could be otherwise, but things couldn't change between them. There was too much to risk. He had accepted that long ago when Janice took the kids away, and it was too late to go back now. But the look on his daughter's face, the utter apathy, chilled him.

The kitchen door opened, and Laney turned to look, her first real movement since he placed the coffee can in front of her. Her eyes crinkled in worry, and he turned towards the door. The kids stood just inside the open door, both of them filthy. Ray had one hand on the knob, the other wrapped in his sister's hand. He had a fresh scrape down his arm, and the beginnings of shiner all puffy and pink, around his left eye. Tear streaks washed through the grime on Faith's face.

He expected there was a story there, but neither of the kids looked like they cared to tell it right now.

They paused at the door and looked from him to their mother. Finally, Ray let go of his sister's hand, nudged her forward, and closed the door behind them. Then the boy marched across the room, pulling something from his pocket. He looked Pete in the eye when he dropped the *important mail* on the table in front of him. Pete looked down at the rain stained postcard from a furniture liquidator a few towns away.

Pete shook his head and stood. "What took you so long? Breakfast is getting cold. Sit down. Dig in." He crossed through the open archway to the hall. "I'll go make up your rooms," he said without turning.

The words hung in the air behind him as he walked up the stairs, worried he was making the biggest mistake of his life.

After Laney's father disappeared upstairs to get the rooms ready, the kids ate. Ray like a ravenous dog, wolfing down the cold food, and refilling his plate. Faith pushed hers around, barely touching it.

Something happened on their walk to the mailbox, and Laney intended to find out what, but she didn't have the energy to deal with Ray right now. Her head still spun from her father's abrupt change of mind.

When they finished eating, the kids staggered into the living room, their ability to fall back into routine a testament to their adaptability. Eight apartments, a single wide trailer, and now the old family farmhouse. Location didn't matter. Natural gravitation pulled them to the same spot, regardless of where they were. The opposite ends of a sofa in front of a television.

Laney listened to Ray channel surf while she cleaned up the breakfast dishes. On a normal day, Faith would have lost patience with her brother after about five seconds. But this morning she laid curled up against the armrest, drowsing, barely able to keep her eyes open.

A warm breeze blew in through the window over the sink, and Laney realized, for the first time since she got here, that something was missing. Where was the scent of hay and the musky odor of the goats? She leaned over the sink, looking out the window towards the back. Looking past the barn, she could see the animal pen, overgrown with wildflowers, no animals in sight.

The red barn stood directly across from the house. Its big white double doors faced the window. The entire building wore a fresh coat of paint. She glanced around the kitchen. Not much had changed in here that she noticed, but everything was clean and well kept, quaint even. Did her father try to tell her earlier that the house wasn't fit for them? The exchange was muddy in her head. She had picked up on where he was heading with the whole "you're my strong one" bullshit, and it became hard to listen after that.

Laney didn't know what her father's problem was, but her gut told her the smart move was to accept the coffee can, the free gas and go. Her father had been right about one thing. She could make it work. She'd done it before.

But the kids hadn't.

They lived with Philip while she was getting back on her feet after the hospital. Ray may think he's had a shitty life, but he was living it up in New York for the worst of it.

The stairs creaked with her father's footsteps. Laney kept her back to the hall and busied herself drying the dishes. Ray wasn't the only one she wasn't ready to deal with.

Her father must have poked his head into the living room. "Get your mother's car keys and help me bring your stuff in," he said. It wasn't a shock to hear Ray groan in response, but he didn't put up an argument.

Between the two of them, it only took one trip to carry in all the possessions she and her children now owned, fully contained in a half dozen trash bags. For a split second, she wondered what her father thought of her showing up in the middle of the night, all their clothes stuffed in ten gallon plastic bags. He probably thought she was a total loser. Then she remembered she wasn't seven anymore, and she didn't give a damn what he thought.

When he and Ray came downstairs, her father went outside, and the wonders of satellite television lured Ray back to the sofa.

Through the window, Laney watched her father walk to the barn and open the double doors. He disappeared into the shadows inside for a moment, emerged with a red gas can, then disappeared again around the side of the house. A few minutes later, her car, washed clean by last night's rain, pulled around. Pete reversed it into the barn and killed the engine. It didn't take long before classic rock, and the whine of power tools drifted out.

Laney stared into the shadows of the barn, unable to see her father inside.

What made you change your mind?

13

The Mantle

Laney slouched next to Faith on the sofa in the living room.

Around lunch, her father had come in from the barn and announced he was going to town. "More people require more food" were the words he used. He enlisted a reluctant Ray to go with him by doing that thing with his face again. T*he Eastwood Eye,* as her mother had called it. The look that could make a grown man shit his pants. It was a skill Laney remembered well from her childhood, one that she always wished she'd learned. It commanded him respect from the other soldiers when they lived on the base, but Laney knew him better—or thought she did—and the look always made her giggle when he tried it on her.

Fresh from a bath and looking ready for a nap, Faith stared in the general direction of the television as bright colors and shapes reflected off her glazed eyes.

A fuzzy memory of Laney's own cartoon binges in this very room came back to her. Saturday mornings were the one time she didn't have to battle Philip for the television. He would be off doing chores. Laney had her own chores, but she didn't sulk and drag her feet like Philip did, and she got them done faster, giving her dominion over the remote. Life had been a lot simpler then. It didn't take much to be happy. A bowl of Corn Pops on the TV tray, the Smurfs on the screen in front of her, and her life had meaning and fulfillment. Sitting there, a long forgotten feeling of being safe and content danced close enough that Laney could feel a faint warmth coming off it, but stayed distant enough to keep any comfort from its heat out of reach.

The room had changed since she was last there. The brownish wallpaper, with some hazy pattern she couldn't remember, had been replaced with a calming shade of light green paint that complimented the wood accents. A well-worn leather recliner in the corner sat within arm's reach of a small bookshelf full of horror paperbacks with cracked spines.

But the starkest difference from the way she remembered the room, the entire house really, was the size. The palatial home, so different from the base apartments she and Philip had known before coming here, with space for running, dancing, and countless hiding spots for hide and seek, had shrunk over the years. In another home, this living room would feel cozy, but here, burdened by Laney's childhood memories, it felt diminished.

To be fair, though, it wasn't much smaller than the entire living space of her apartment in Philly. But that *wasn't* her apartment. Not anymore. Not for the first time today, a flash of sinking dread ran through her at the thought of being homeless in a heartbeat at the fickle whim of her father.

Laney wondered if this was what menopause felt like. Everything's fine, then bam, out of nowhere, a hot flash. Or in her case, a reality flash. She tried to keep the static in her head at bay. The thoughts of her job, the apartment, her hard earned credit score buzzed in her head like a cloud of mosquitoes. She knew the moment she gave focus to any of them, they would all swarm her and suck her dry, leaving a dried out husk of self pity and anxiety.

She got up off the couch. It was a simple act, but it gave her momentum.

The trash bags full of their clothing in the bedrooms upstairs called to her, but it made little sense to unpack. If her father changed his mind again, they might have to leave fast. There was only one thing for her to do—clean the already clean house.

She went from slouching in front of the television to a torrent of activity. The scents of window cleaner and lemon furniture polish soon overwhelmed the fragrance of sweet corn and wild flowers from the open windows.

As she worked her way through the living room, it gratified Laney to see a thin line of dust when she moved one of the many photo frames on the fireplace mantle. Finally, something that wasn't already clean, something she could make progress on, chalk up a small win. But the sight of familiar faces staring up at her distracted from her minor victory. The frame held a photo of Ray and Faith. Ray was five, his pudgy cheeks bursting in a huge smile. He held Faith, only a few months old, in his lap. She looked up at her big brother with a silly grin on her face.

Laney remembered that day. It was one of the good ones. Troy had been out of town on a hunting—meaning drinking—weekend with his friends, giving her a few days of peace. Her eyes swept over the rest of the frames.

All the photos were there. Every single one she mailed to her father over the years. They took up most of the mantle. She wondered what they meant to him, photos of grandchildren he had never met. Their place of prominence implied the kids were important to him. Why, then, was he so quick to turn them away this morning?

She found a picture of her parents. They were young. Her dad wore his uniform, her mother a brightly colored peasant dress. They stood in front of the Army chaplain, looking happy and carefree. That was how she remembered them together. Until the day her mother abruptly announced they were leaving, upheaving their lives overnight. What happened between them?

Before the melancholy of a life missed out on could sneak up on her, a black-and-white image, tucked away behind the other photos, caught Laney's eye. A smiling couple in front of a majestic oak tree peeked out at her. The man wore a suit and the woman a white dress, with a ribbon in her hair. They must have been her grandparents.

Laney picked up the wood frame to get a better look. Her finger brushed something soft on the back of the frame. She turned it over to reveal a faded purple ribbon pinned to the velvet backing. It looked like the one her grandmother wore in the photo. She flipped the frame back over.

Another wedding photo. A smiling preacher stood next to her grandparents, bible in hand. A young couple stood behind them to the right. They too had smiles on their faces as they gazed at the newlyweds. Then her eyes drifted to the left and Laney's breath caught in her throat. Between the tree, the woods, and the wedding party, it would have been a beautiful scene, if not for the lone figure invading the frame on the edge of the photo. He stood apart from the rest, and in their moment of celebration, he cast a hard eyed glare at her grandparents.

The man was older than the others. She guessed late sixties. But his age did nothing to soften his menace. He stood tall and straight. A muscular build filled out his black suit, more fitting for a funeral than a wedding. He wore his dark hair cut short and slicked back, a severe frame for his weathered face.

His presence changed everything about the photo. Where before Laney saw a happy couple, she now noticed a sense of unease in their smiles. The groomsman on the right no longer seemed to look at her grandparents. His wary eyes betrayed his smile as he looked past them to the man. The preacher, facing away from him, seemed to recoil, as if he had backed up too close to a lion's cage.

But the most disturbing part of the picture had to be that Laney recognized the man. One look at his eyes and the fuzzy memories of her dream crystallized and came rushing back to her. Despite the age difference, and the strength of his build, it was unmistakable. He was the old man from the corn, and likely, from his presence in the photo, her great grandfather.

14

Small Town Folklore

Ray said nothing the entire ride, just laid his head against the frame of the opened window, his hair blowing in the breeze as he watched the woods go by in a blur. His grandfather clearly didn't feel the need to fill the silence with conversation. By the time they had reached the end of the drive, Pete had the radio cranked up, blasting ancient rock from the truck's speakers. Ray acknowledged his grandfather's taste in music with a disappointed shake of his head.

Miles went by, the occasional house disrupting the tree-lined roads, but he didn't see a single person. Ray had never been anywhere so isolated. It felt like a place straight out of a zombie movie. Which, he had to admit, made it a little cool.

They passed a sign that read Welcome to West Mills, and house sightings became more frequent, but they weren't bunched together right on top of each other like in the city. Each house had some land between it and the next.

Houses gave way to small stores and cafes with tables on the sidewalk. Small, neatly landscaped trees grew in squares of dirt at regular intervals along the walkway. It looked like the set of a television show his mother might watch. Where the characters drank a lot of coffee and never shut up.

Pete kept driving until garages, run-down houses and grungy concrete buildings—more familiar territory—replaced the quaint main street shops. Add some trash and graffiti, and this could be any neighborhood Ray had lived in.

The truck made a left into a crowded parking lot, and pulled up right outside a big glass window. In the remnants of scraped and faded yellow paint, Ray could make out the words *Clevenger's Auto Repairs* on the glass.

"I have to talk to Henry about some parts for your mom's car. I'll just be a minute. Want me to leave the radio on?" Ray responded with a side-eye glance. Pete smirked, then shut off the truck.

Ray watched his grandfather shake hands with a tough looking old guy through the window. The two men talked for a bit, then Henry—he guessed—two-finger punched at some keys on a keyboard covered in a grease stained, vinyl overlay in front of an ancient computer.

Pete handed him some cash, then dropped some bomb on Henry that turned his face pale. Whatever it was, it must have really concerned the man because he looked to be peppering Ray's grandfather with questions. Most of which Pete answered with a shrug or a shake of his head. After a minute, the man leaned against the window, shielding his eyes from the glare with cupped hands. He gave Ray a weak smile and waved. Feeling like an animal in the zoo, Ray returned a half-hearted wave.

Henry turned back to Ray's grandfather, a serious look on his face. They talked for a bit. Or rather Henry talked, and Pete listened, his face clenched as he nodded along. Occasionally, the muscles in the corner of his jaw popped out. Finally, Henry patted his grandpa on the shoulder and smiled at him, but not a real smile. Ray could tell. Even with a windshield and an old, dusty store window between them. It was a kind of forced, everything will be okay smile. A sentiment Henry clearly didn't believe.

Seemed like grandpa wasn't thrilled about having house guests.

When his grandfather stepped out of the store, his eyes had a storm brewing behind them. The rest of his face wore a stern mask. Suddenly Ray wished he was back on that couch, back with his mom, instead of riding around town with a man who was essentially a stranger. A stranger in a bad mood, from the looks of it. Ray didn't know what to expect from him.

But when his grandpa got back in the truck, all that was gone. Slipped behind a hell of a poker face, maybe. He gave no indication that anything serious went down in Henry's shop. He just smirked and handed Ray a lollipop. "From Henry."

"Thanks, I guess." Ray shoved it in his pocket.

They went back down main street the way they came, then Pete pulled over and parked the truck in front of the smallest grocery store Ray had ever seen.

"You want to come in?" Pete asked before shutting off the truck. "I'm going to be a while. It's gonna get hot out here."

"Nah, I'll get out. Okay if I look around?"

"How would your mother answer that?"

Ray looked him in the eye. "She would totally let me."

Pete stared back at him, eyebrows raised.

"Fine." Ray slouched back down in the seat. "I'll wait here."

His grandfather smiled. "You got your phone with you?"

Ray perked up, cautiously hopeful. "Always."

Pete handed Ray his phone. "Put your number in here."

He punched it in, hit send, then held up his phone to show his grandfather the call when through.

Pete pulled out his wallet, opened it, slipped out a twenty, and handed it to him.

Ray's face lit into a surprised grin. "What's this for?"

"Well, I missed a birthday or two."

Smiling, Ray held up the twenty and waggled it. "You kind of missed them all."

His grandfather laughed. "Thirty minutes. Be back at the truck. Don't make me come looking for you."

Ray saluted, then crossed the street before his grandpa could change his mind. All plans of mindless wandering were cast aside. The twenty started burning a hole in his pocket the second he stuffed it in there. With thirty minutes on the clock and money to spend, he was a man on a mission.

He passed a bookstore, a coffee shop, an ice cream shop— promising—and a quilting shop—whatever the hell that was—before he struck gold. Almost hidden amongst the fishing rods and camouflaged hunting gear, a skateboard sat in the display window of Buckner's Sporting Goods. It wasn't anything amazing. He didn't even recognize the brand, but it was better than no board. His Santa Cruz sat abandoned back at the apartment he'd never see again.

A cold blast of conditioned air escaped when he pushed open the door, and a small brass bell overhead jingled. A thin old man, sitting behind the counter on a stool, racks of shotguns and rifles covering the wall behind him, jerked his head up from the magazine he was reading. His eyes, slits almost camouflaged by the many wrinkles surrounding them, snapped to Ray. "You here with someone?"

"Uh, I was just looking," Ray said, his hand gesturing in the direction of the skateboard.

"You from out of town?" The old guy's face scrunched, like he had a nasty taste in his mouth.

"Yeah," Ray said reluctantly.

The man stood up from the stool and gestured towards the door with the magazine.

Then a thought occurred to Ray. A small town like this, the guy probably knows Grandpa. Couldn't hurt to drop his name.

"Um, Pete Killian. That's my grandpa. I'm staying at his farm."

The old guy sat back down, like his knees went weak. "You Laney's boy?"

Ray's eyebrows shot up in surprise to hear the man knew of him. "Yeah. You know my mom?"

The man's face relaxed some. "Never had the pleasure. Tell Pete, I said hi."

"Sure." Ray turned away, smiling. Grandpa must have talked about him.

"And stay out of those woods round the farm," the old man said, deadly serious.

"Um, okay. Thanks." Ray said over his shoulder, then made a beeline for the board in the window. Seeing it up close, his initial enthusiasm took a hit. It wasn't a great board, plastic, not wood. The wheels sucked. He looked at the dangling price tag and rolled his eyes. Thirty bucks was way out of his price range, and way too steep for this crappy board.

He sighed. Can't ride it at the farm, anyway.

Not ready to give up yet, his eyes wandered around the store until they landed on a display of pocket knives. He always wanted a pocket knife, the kind where the blade flicked out. But mom, of course, shut that idea down fast. She said they were dangerous and asked him what he would even use it for, anyway. He tried explaining that you never know what you're going to need a pocket knife for, that's why you keep one in your pocket. That went over about as well as he should have expected.

But, on a farm, he imagined there were many justifiable uses for a pocket knife.

A wicked looking black and red folding knife, the pointed blade visible through the open metal frame of the handle, fell right into his price range, and even left him a few bucks for ice cream.

Perfect.

Ray made his way to the register to pay for it, keeping an eye out in case something better caught it. But he doubted he'd find something better that he could afford. When he stepped up to the counter, the old guy never took his eyes off the copy of Field and Stream in his hands. Instead he yelled, "Angela."

Nothing happened. Ray stood there waiting. His eyes went from the curtained doorway behind the counter, where he guessed Angela would come from, back to the old guy, wondering if he should say something. When Ray was just about to, as if the man sensed it and wanted to avoid any further conversation, he barked out the name again. "Angela."

Finally, the curtain parted and a young girl with long brown hair stepped through and rolled her hazel eyes at the old man. "Must be some article, gramps."

Ray let out a nervous laugh. The old man either didn't hear her or ignored her.

"Sorry for the wait," she smiled at Ray, her braces glinting under the fluorescents, a rainbow spectrum of rubber bands woven through the metal.

He smiled back, put the knife on the counter and slid it to her, half waiting for her to tell him she couldn't sell a knife to a kid, which would be super embarrassing coming from a girl his age. A *pretty* girl his age.

Instead, she rang it up. "That will be sixteen thirty-five."

He gave her the twenty. She put it in the drawer, counted out the change, then handed him the bills. Her pinky finger brushed his hand as she turned hers over to let the coins drop into his palm. He hoped his cheeks didn't look as red as they felt.

"Have a nice day," she said, flashing her braces again.

Ray nodded, started for the door, and somewhere between the tackle boxes and the rack of cheap sunglasses, his courage showed up. He turned back to say thanks or goodbye or anything, but Angela was already gone, the curtain flapping behind her.

Real smooth Ray.

He stepped out into the warm air and checked the time on his phone. Still eleven minutes before he had to meet Grandpa at the truck. He hoped there wasn't a line at the ice cream shop.

The door jingled behind him.

"Hey, I gotta ask," Angela said.

Ray turned back to her.

"Gramps said you're staying at Killian Farm?"

Ray nodded.

"Have you seen him?"

"Him who?" Ray looked at her, his brow creased. Was she talking about Grandpa? Angela took a few steps closer to him.

"Jeremiah." The name left her mouth in an awed whisper.

"Who's Jeremiah?"

Her face lit up, and the sparkle in her eyes said she had a tale to tell. "You seriously don't know?"

Pete waited at the truck for five minutes past the deadline, watching Ray talk to Angela, Kent Buckner's granddaughter. She was a good kid, and he'd be happy to give Ray a break after what he had been through, but he didn't spend good money on ice cream to let it melt in the truck.

He reached in the open window and laid on the horn. Ray turned, holding up one finger, telling Pete to wait a minute.

No, he didn't.

Smirking, Pete laid on the horn again, and didn't let up until Ray started back to the truck, red faced.

"Bye Ray." Angela called after him.

The boy almost walked into traffic, turning to wave back to her.

Pete greeted his grandson with a big grin when the boy climbed into the truck.

"Sorry," Ray said.

"Angela, huh?"

Ray smiled, blushing. "She's cool. You know, for a friend."

"Friends are good to have." Pete pulled the truck out of the parking spot, heading for home.

"Yeah. Maybe if we're staying with you for a bit, she can come visit me sometime?" Ray said.

The smile drained from Pete's face. "She tell you the haunted farm story?"

"What? The farm's haunted?"

"Nice try, kid. Farm's not haunted. It's all a bunch of small town folklore. People around here have been going on about Jeremiah since the day he died. They always get one thing right in all their stories, though. He was a mean son of a bitch until the stroke hit." Pete paused, his face hardened. "Then mean don't even begin to cover it. But dead is dead, even for a nasty piece of work like him."

Ray got quiet. He pulled out his new pocket knife and ran his finger along its metal frame before he spoke up again. "Is it true he once killed a man with his bare hands?"

Pete thought for a moment about which answer would be the most effective? The last thing he needed was the kid spooked, but he decided on the truth. It was common knowledge around these parts and he didn't want the boy not trusting him.

"Yeah, for trespassing."

"What about the kid, Victor something?" Ray asked.

Pete turned his face away from Ray and checked his side mirror. "The boy got lost in the woods and fell down a ravine." He looked back at the road, his voice thick as he tried to block the image of Victor's face, always accompanied by that god awful scream, from his mind. "It was...it was horrible. But it was just an accident."

"So, not haunted?"

Pete struggled to keep his voice casual. "No. It's not. And do me a favor. Don't mention any haunted farm stuff at home. Okay?"

15

The Door Under The Stairs

Designed to create a grand entrance, the wide hall, papered from floor to ceiling in the original wallpaper, a rich ocher color with gilt flowers and leaves, split the house down the center. It was bright and airy, with light spilling from the open archways of the kitchen on the left, and the living room on the right, and from the open bedroom doors on the second floor. Half turn stairs made of warm oak decorated by ornate balusters stood at the far end. What a visitor wouldn't notice, at first, was the dark stained oak door, lurking under the turn of the stairs in the shadows, shying away from the light. But if they stood in the hall long enough, it would draw their eye, the way the one crooked frame on a wall of perfectly hung photos would.

Laney sat on the steps, dusting the balusters, when the long band of sunlight along the floorboards of the hall caught her eye. Puzzled, she grabbed the rail, pulled herself to her feet, and went down the steps. The light spilled through the crack along the side, and out of the old-fashioned keyhole of the door under the stairs. She had forgotten about that door. And this was the first she noticed it since being home, maybe because it was getting later in the day. The light in the pantry must have shifted, casting light where before there were only shadows.

The door, simple, unembellished, solid oak with a bronze knob, always unnerved her as a kid. At some point, her father installed a deadbolt, the kind with only a keyhole. From the sunlight shining through the crack next to it, it appeared to be unlocked.

The pantry beyond that door had been strictly out of bounds to her and Philip. Not that she ever wanted to go in. Her parents gave the excuse that she or her brother would knock over the canning jars. Even at her young age, Laney didn't buy it. She always had the sense of something on the other side of the door, waiting, wanting her to open it. Now, she chalked those fears up to a childish imagination and wondered why the room was really off limits.

Only one way to find out.

She walked to the door but stopped short, hesitating. It was a strange juxtaposition, standing in a place she hadn't been in for twenty-five years, about to do something forbidden to her the last time she was there. It was hard to be in the house without feeling like all the old rules still applied. But that would be absurd. She was an adult now.

Laney reached for the doorknob just as the front door opened behind her. She turned to see her father staring at her, holding paper grocery bags in both arms. His face was hard to read. Her cheeks burned like a kid who just got caught.

"Can I get some help with these?" He held up the bags.

"Of course." Laney met him at the door, took the bags from his arms and into the kitchen. As she put the bags down on the table, the snick of a deadbolt sliding into place came from the end of the hall. She turned in time to see her father walk past the kitchen, sliding keys into the pocket of his jeans, before he went out the front door.

16

Old houses Make Noise

Outside, the setting sun cast shadows on the farm, as Pete placed big steaming bowls of hot food around the table. It wasn't a big spread, like the kind Janice used to make, just some chicken, mashed potatoes, and corn. But seeing Laney and his grandkids sitting there, the smell of comfort food in the air, triggered bittersweet memories of long gone meals.

The antique serving bowls he inherited from his parents, along with the farm, had been collecting dust for decades. He almost forgot where he kept them. Janice had loved those bowls. If she hadn't left in such a rush and he had known she was never coming back, he would have packed them up for her to take.

He put the bowl of mashed potatoes down in front of Ray. The second it hit the table, the boy grabbed the spoon and started shoveling a heaping pile onto his plate.

Pete smiled. That boy was a handful, but he was a good kid. And Faith, she made a place brighter by just being in it. It would be easy to underestimate how tough that sweet little girl was if she didn't remind him so much of Laney at that age. Warmth spread through his chest just looking at them. Pete hadn't been feeding his daughter a line that morning. She was his strong one, and these kids were the proof.

Not for the first time today, he felt his eyes tearing up and turned back to the sink so he could wipe them without being seen. Once he pulled himself together, he sat down to his first family meal in decades. The very thought of it almost got the eye faucets going again.

Ray passed him the bowl of potatoes, half gone.

"Thanks for thinking of us," Pete said.

"Huh?" The boy didn't even bother looking up as he started doing damage on the plate of chicken, spearing a big chunk of breast meat with the serving fork.

"Never mind." Pete served himself a small spoonful, then passed the bowl to Faith.

"Thanks," she said, taking the bowl in two hands. "How come you don't have chickens? Is it because we're eating them?"

"You're really stuck on that chicken thing, aren't you?" Pete asked, unable to keep the smile off his face.

"It's a legitimate question, Grandpa." She put the bowl down in front of her, looked up at him, and he couldn't help but picture a future journalist. "This is a farm," she said.

The kitchen timer dinged, distracting Faith in a way only a kid can be. Compelled by forces most adults unfortunately learn to overcome, she announced in her sing-song way, "the bread's done."

Pete slid his chair out, but Laney, who was closer to the oven, stopped him.

"Sit. I'll get it, dad." She stood, grabbed the mitts off the counter, then reached for the oven door.

"Wait!" Ray suddenly looked up from his overstuffed plate in panic and pushed his chair back with a screech.

Laney froze, startled. "What?"

Ray rushed to the stove and took the mitts from his mother. "Better let me do that."

She sat back down, looking perplexed until Ray opened the oven door, filling the kitchen with the smell of hot bread.

"Oh," she said and had the strangest look in her eyes when the giggling started, sad and maybe a hint of fear.

Ray moved the rolls from the hot pan to the serving plate with metal tongs and giggled, too. By the time he placed the rolls in the space Pete had made in the center of the table, the two of them were shaking with laughter. Laney covered her face with her hands. She laughed so hard Pete could see the moisture of tears on her cheeks.

Faith, focused on filling her plate, finally looked up at them, one eyebrow raised, but it seemed eye contact was all it took to spread the contagion. Her high-pitched laughter joined the chorus.

Pete had no idea what was going on, but he couldn't help but join in. Tears of laughter, though still tears, were allowed.

After dinner, her father insisted on cleaning up and Laney didn't argue. She went outside, sat on the front steps, and took in the night sky, a vast twinkling expanse unmarred by buildings or light pollution. The soft curves of treetops and rolling hills blackened the horizon, carving their shapes from the heavens. She couldn't remember the last time she had seen so many stars. It made her feel small, in a good way, in a humbling way. Because if she was so infinitesimally small compared to the universe above her, then so were her problems, at least in the moment.

Ray came out of the house carrying a bottle of beer.

"Un huh" Laney shook her head, but Ray cut her off.

"Relax. Grandpa sent it out for you. He said you needed it." Ray handed her the sweating bottle. "I told him you needed the whole case."

"Funny."

Laney took a sip and let the ice cold liquid slide down her throat.

Grandpa was right.

She took another sip, enjoying the moment. Laney knew that what had happened tonight—an actual pleasant family dinner, Ray's attitude change—was all the rubber band effect. The three of them were snapping back and overcompensating for the level of fear and adrenaline they experienced the day before. She expected things to go back to normal tomorrow, but for now, overcompensation was good. They all needed it.

Ray sat down next to her. His eyes were heavy, the day catching up to him.

"What happens now?" he asked.

"I honestly don't know, but I think we should worry about that tomorrow."

Ray feigned a look of shock. "Whoa. What's in that beer? You're passing up an actual, legit opportunity to worry? I thought that was your favorite hobby."

Laney smiled, but then a memory creased her brow.

"I have something serious to ask you," she said.

"Well, that lasted long. Quick, drink some more beer."

"This morning when you went to get the mail, something

happened-”

"Yeah, I was wondering about that. Did you and Grandpa have a fight?” Ray was the worried one now.

It seemed he had hit it off with her father during their trip to town. She was glad for it, but knew she should be concerned about how Ray was going to handle it when they eventually left.

Add one more thing to the list of reasons for him to hate me.

"No, I mean with you and Faith,” she said.

The color drained out of his face, and he looked down at his feet.

Laney didn’t want to press him, but was now concerned that there was something she really needed to know. "You guys looked like you took a mud bath. And it was obvious Faith was crying. What happened?”

"We saw something in the corn. A dead rabbit. You know how she gets about that stuff.” Ray shivered. It was a small motion, shoulders barely moving. He may not even have been aware of it.

There was more to this, she knew, but she let it rest for now.

When Laney and Ray came back into the house, they found Faith on the sofa, watching television, barely keeping her eyes open. Pete leaned back in the recliner, reading a book.

"Bed time,” Laney said, holding out a hand to her daughter. Faith groaned, grabbed the hand, and pulled herself to her feet.

"Wait a second,” Pete said. He put his book face down on the table next to him, saving the page, and straightened the recliner. "Sit down, please. Relax for a minute. I want to talk to you about something important.” A slight smile pulled gently at the corners of his mouth as he waited for them to sit.

Laney didn’t like it. Something about the tone of his voice contradicted his attempt to look casual.

He’s about to tell us to leave.

She sat on the sofa next to Faith, wanting to kick herself for allowing the kids, and herself, if she was being honest, to get comfortable. It would be one thing for them to move on after Laney figured out their next step, but for her father to reject them, reject Ray, it would be devastating. The look on her son’s face as he sat cross-legged on the floor, waiting for his grandfather to speak, said it all. In just the time span of a day, he had already grown attached to the man.

Her father looked at the floor like he was gathering his thoughts. After what seemed like minutes had gone by, Faith let out a long, dramatic sigh. He looked up at his granddaughter with one eyebrow arched and the little girl giggled. He chuckled at the sound of it.

"Alright." He took a deep breath, then began. "This is an old house. My grandfather built it in 1934, a man you'd never want to meet, not in a dark alley, not in broad daylight. But that's beside the point."

Laney's mind went to the old man in the corn.

Great granddad.

"The point is this," Pete went on, "old houses make noise. All kinds of noises. The kind that sound like house noises and the kind that don't, but they're still house noises." He paused, looking at each of them. "Questions?"

"So many," Ray said.

"Well, keep them to yourself." Pete smirked at the boy before continuing.

"You're going to hear stuff at night that sounds a lot different from when you hear it during the day. It's not different. With how dark it gets around here, the night can make a simple noise sound like something bigger. That's just your mind playing with you. Don't let it."

"Thanks dad," Laney said. At least they weren't getting thrown out. One less thing to worry about. For now. But what the hell was he talking about? "This is certainly... different from what we've been used to living in an apartment in the city. It's good to keep that in mind and be prepared for it." She stood, but her father gave her a little shake of his head, and she sat back down.

"That said," he continued, "this house can be dangerous at night if you don't know your way around. Except for the time I was in the Army, I lived here my whole life. I could walk this house from top to bottom blind folded.

"So I've never felt the need to change the bulb in the upstairs hall light. It's a pain in the ass to change. Got to lean from the top of a ladder with a big drop below you. Can't use one of those pole things, because it won't work with the fixture. Never seemed worth it."

He looked at each of them, maybe checking to see if they understood. Laney didn't know about the kids, but she had no idea where her father was going with all this.

"Until I get that bulb switched, I got this." He held up a night-light in the shape of a cartoon chicken.

Faith bounced in delight. "I thought you said no chickens at this farm, Grandpa?"

Laney watched his face light up at the word "grandpa" and her eyes glistened until she reminded herself that just twelve hours ago, he intended to send his grandchildren away.

"We'll make this one exception," he said, looking at Faith. "I'll put it in the upstairs hall. It's for emergency bathroom visits only. And don't worry if it's dark at first, it only lights up when there's motion."

"I think I'm good." Ray shined his phone light at Pete. "Like a boy scout, I come prepared."

17

Bed Time

Like the rest of the house, Laney's bedroom was smaller than she remembered it. Otherwise, nothing had changed. Nothing. Same white framed princess bed. Same flowered wallpaper, now faded with age. All the toys that she couldn't take with her were still there, piled high in her overstuffed toy box. It was as if a shrine had been erected to her childhood. She'd heard of parents who lost a child shutting off their room like this, unable to let the memory go. But Laney had been alive and never more than a few states away all these years, and he never tried to find her.

Faith let out an excited squeal across the room.

Her daughter sat in front of the window bench, framed by once bright pink curtains, their color now bleached away from years of sunlight. A white dollhouse with a black shingled roof took up most of the bench. Its interior was open wide, facing the room. Faith sat entranced. Her hands darted from room to room, touching tiny pieces of furniture, jingling the keys on the little piano. She opened the cupboards in the kitchen and giggled with delight at finding tiny bowls and plates inside.

"Was this all yours?" She asked, snatching up a small doll wearing a pink dress.

"Yeah, honey. When I was your age."

"Can I play with it?"

"Tomorrow. Sleep now."

"I'm too excited to sleep." She turned back to Laney, her eyes pleading.

"Tomorrow," Laney said.

"Fine." Faith slouched in defeat, then crawled into the twin bed they would share while here. Back at the apartment, Laney had shared a full sized bed with Faith, and she spent most nights with a foot in the small of her back. Still, she was grateful to not be sleeping in the car. Ray took Philip's room, thrilled to be finally getting some walls, instead of sleeping on a pull-out in the middle of the living room.

"Is this you?" Faith said, reaching over her to pick up a framed photo from the nightstand. "You look like me."

Laney looked down at her five-year-old self, staring up at her from the photo with a big smile on her face, taking in the forgotten memory. That year, they had been living on a base in Germany where her father had been stationed. On weekends and during vacations, they toured Europe, exploring different places and cultures, trying new foods, going to museums, hiking.

That was the life she pictured for herself after college. Travel. Adventure. Freedom.

In another life.

She pointed to the other people in the photo. "That's my mom, my dad, and Uncle Philip."

"What's that behind you?" Faith traced a finger along the structure behind the glass.

"That's the Eiffel Tower in Paris, France. When your grandpa was in the Army, we got to visit a lot of places. Then we moved to the farm to come take care of it after my grandma and grandpa died."

"Were they really sick?"

"No, they died in a car accident, honey."

Faith wrapped her arms around Laney in a hug. "That's sad."

"Yeah, it is." Laney left out the fact that she had never met them, and so had never really mourned them. "All right, slide over. You're hogging the bed." She snorted through her nose, making pig noises.

Faith giggled, then moved over a little so Laney could squeeze in beside her. The little girl fell asleep within minutes after her head hit the pillow, the tiny doll clutched in her hand.

Laney laid in bed, staring up at the ceiling she couldn't see. Nothing broke the darkness of the room, no glow of an alarm clock, or shine of street lights through the window. The sound of crickets and the wind rustling the corn like the soft shush of ocean waves, had replaced the noise of traffic, and muffled voices from neighboring televisions. Gone was the oppressive heat. Instead, a gentle breeze blowing through the window kept the room at just the right temperature to nestle under a thin cotton sheet. Even the mattress she laid on proved to be more comfortable than the one back at the apartment, despite the small elbow currently pressing into her ribs.

The room was perfectly conducive to sleep. So, of course, sleep eluded her.

She had crossed to the other side of exhaustion and, in the distraction-less vacuum of the dark room, her mind opened the floodgates to every random thought and worry. Thoughts of work, the apartment, where the kids would go to school all came crashing down on her, until she laid there, trapped under the rubble of her life.

She turned her watch to her in the dark, hit the light button, and the face emitted a soft green glow. It was almost three in the morning.

I'm seventeen hours late for work.

The thought induced a gut twisting panic, like waking to a blinking alarm clock with the sun low in the sky on a Monday. Tomorrow, she would call the restaurant to let them know she quit. Thank god she had direct deposit. She couldn't risk going back to pick up her check. Troy had, no doubt, figured out where she worked from the restaurant logo plastered all over the takeout containers. She'd have to give notice on the apartment, too. Though she'd lose her deposit for not cleaning out the place before she left.

Starting again wasn't impossible. It wouldn't be the first, or even the second, time she had to start from scratch. But the thought of the work ahead of her threatened to suck her down a hole darker than the room she lay in.

A long, drawn out screech came from downstairs, dragging her back to the here and now.

It's not Troy. Old houses make noise.

Troy's influence on her imagination when things went bump in the night, while never gone, had been waning for the past few years. Replaced by more mundane fears, like paying the rent, or her car breaking down, but after last night, he'd be a loud and hulking presence in the dark corners of her mind for the foreseeable future. She reminded herself they came here for a reason. He knew nothing about this place. It was just a house noise. Some random screeching house noise. That happens.

Laney rolled over to face the door, though she couldn't see it.

The sound came again, like metal grinding across metal, but it didn't fade out like last time. It began a repetition. The sound would get fainter, then stronger again, like something moving back and forth.

The old man.

She didn't know why her mind made that connection. It made little sense, but equating the man to the noise had a familiarity to it, and with it came a vague feeling of dread, like waking from a lingering nightmare she couldn't remember.

Suddenly, the dark took on weight. It became imposing, threatening, flush with danger. Like they weren't alone. Her wide, unseeing eyes stared into the black, and Laney held her breath to listen for movement within the room.

Crickets. Wind. Faith breathing beside her.

The creak of a floorboard.

Light skewered the room, and Laney jumped.

It was just a thin line of light from under the door, but it was blinding in contrast to the total darkness. Something had triggered the motion detector on the night-light. Meaning something was in the hall outside her bedroom door.

She froze, staring at the line of light under the door, waiting to see something break it, and give her an idea of what or where it was. Instead, the night-light eventually turned off, leaving her in the dark once again.

A bony lump punched into her back.

Laney sat up fast. Her hand fumbled in the general direction of the nightstand and banged up against the lamp. She ran her fingers along its neck until they found the switch and turned it on.

Getting kneed in the kidney when Faith jerked in her sleep wasn't an unfamiliar experience for her, but it had sent a jolt of panic through her, nevertheless.

The screeching continued downstairs and she would have been perfectly content to lie in bed with the light on, watching the door for the rest of the night. But something had moved in the hallway, and Ray slept alone in Philip's room.

Laney quietly got up and padded to the door, avoiding the squeaky floorboard that she intuitively remembered somehow. She gripped the knob, swallowed her fear and yanked open the door.

The night-light triggered, and the shape of her father sprang from the darkness. He stood at the top of the stairs, his eyes trapped, gazing down into the black pit below. It took him a moment to realize the light had come on. He looked around, confused. Until his eyes, at first glassy, found focus on Laney.

"Go back to bed. Old houses make noise," he said with a tired smile before starting down the stairs, like he had been on his way down the whole time and she interrupted him. Like he hadn't been standing in the dark, so still, the motion detector failed to detect him.

"Then where are you going?" Laney asked.

"Old houses make noise. Old men make sandwiches." He called back softly.

She watched him disappear into the darkness below. A few seconds later, the kitchen light came on, casting a warm light on the floorboards near the bottom of the stairs, and the strange noise abruptly stopped.

Whatever it was, her father must have fixed it.

Before going back to bed, Laney peeked in on Ray. He lay sprawled on his belly, taking up the entire bed, and didn't stir when she came into the room. Laney took the cellphone that dangled from his hand near the edge of the mattress and put it on the nightstand. She stood there a moment, watching him sleep, listening to the long, slow rhythm of his breathing, and realized she might finally be ready for sleep herself. She kissed his head, then slipped quietly out of the room, closing the door behind her.

Back in her room, Laney laid in bed, drowsing as she listened to her father move around downstairs. The refrigerator door opening, clanking of dishes, faucet running. Then nothing. She never heard him come up.

Why?

There was probably a perfectly good reason for it. It could be he stayed down there to read or fell asleep in the recliner. But she thought of him standing at the top of the stairs, almost in a fugue, and worried it was something else. Once the thought took root in her mind, she couldn't ignore it. Laney got out of bed again and made her way downstairs.

The dark hallway came into view on the third step down after the turn, and Laney froze at the sight of the figure standing in the shadows below her.

Her father, a specter, barely visible in the spill of light from the kitchen, stood unmoving, his eyes drawn to the door under the stairs.

"Dad, are you okay?"

Looking like she just woke him from a deep sleep, he squinted up at her and grunted. "Yeah. Let me get the light."

He reached into the kitchen and hit the light switch blanketing the hallway in darkness, then followed her upstairs. Laney watched him go into his room and waited until she heard the springs of his mattress take on weight before going back to bed.

18

Pancakes

"Do you want something to eat, honey?" said a voice in a loud whisper.

"Can you make pancakes mommy?" a falsetto whisper replied.

"Sure honey," said the first voice. "Chocolate chip or blueberry?"

Laney opened her eyes and squinted against the brightness of the room, finding her daughter exactly where she expected to. Faith sat on the window bench, a silhouette backlit by the morning sun. The tapping of tiny plastic feet sounded against the wooden floors of the dollhouse.

"I want some pancakes." Laney's voice cracked with sleep.

"Yay! You're up." Faith spun around to face her. "Now I don't have to be quiet."

"And you were doing such a good job of it." Laney sat up, but dropped back down when the muscles in her back erupted in fire. She didn't know if the pain was from Troy, sleeping in the car the other night, or Faith's knee. Probably all of them combined. Gritting her teeth, she sat up again, taking it slower now that she knew what she was in for.

She left Faith upstairs, and made her way down to the kitchen nice and slow, the smell of coffee dragging her by the nose. A full pot waited in the coffeemaker.

Thanks dad.

He kept the ibuprofen in the cabinet next to the coffee mugs. Seemed he had a morning routine. One that she could sympathize with right now. She filled a mug, shook out two pills, washed them down with a few gulps of hot coffee, then poured herself a refill. Standing made her back happy, so she drank her coffee, looking out the window over the sink.

The barn doors across from her were open to sunlight that angled in, only penetrating the first few feet of shadows. Classic rock from her father's radio drifted in through the open window on the breeze. She gave it a fifty-fifty chance Ray was still in bed, but her money—if she had any—would be on him being in the barn with her dad.

Out of habit, she looked at her watch. Her shift started in ten minutes, and yet she stood, leisurely sipping coffee with all the freedom of a kid on a summer morning. The debris field of her life left behind for the moment. She hadn't just escaped Troy by coming home to the farm. She checked out of reality.

The hair on the back of her neck prickled with the weight of eyes on her.

Think of the devil and here he comes.

She breathed in long deep breaths until the feeling diminished from menacing to nagging, wondering if she'd ever live a day untainted by Troy's presence, imagined or otherwise. If such a day existed, it would be far, far in the future.

On reflex, because it was in her hand, because hot coffee equaled comfort, she brought the trembling mug to her lips like a soothing balm, and retched. She jerked the mug away, sending a wave of dark liquid splashing down against the white porcelain sink, and gagged on the stench of the coffee. No, not the coffee, the air. The foul odor, a sinister melange of mildew and rot, filled the room.

Laney turned to where she felt the phantom eyes, but the hallway beyond the arch stood empty. The living room too. The stench could only come from one place. One place that made sense, anyway. She made her way into the hall, expecting to find the pantry door open, but found it closed tight. A slim crack of light from under the door struggled to breach the gloom of the hall. She walked towards it, her eyes watering from the reek that got stronger with every step she took.

A whisper of motion sent the hair on the back of her neck erect, and she froze.

She could feel the eyes again, now watching her from the dark corner under the turn of the stairs. And her eyes, still used to the bright kitchen, struggled to make sense out of the shadows lurking there.

A muffled tap, so faint she wasn't sure if it came from the dark space or her imagination, planted the idea in her head of a mouse, cowering under the stairs. She took a step closer, leaned in to listen, but could only hear her breath. Until the next sound came, a dry whisper, barely audible, maybe a draft of air. She held her hand out, palm up, feeling for it, and took another step.

The next tap, still muffled but closer, had a hint of an echo. Like it came from far away, not the dark corner just feet from where she stood. Followed, once again, by the whisper—no, the drag of something on the wooden floor.

For the millionth time, she wished she had her cell phone. The light would come in handy right about now. Was this what had her father so enraptured last night? Was he listening for mice? She liked the idea of mice better than the thought of her father having dementia. A thought that had nagged her ever since she saw the distant look on his face when she found him in the hall.

She inched closer, her hand still out in front of her, feeling for a draft that might indicate the mouse's entry point. Her eyes squinted against the murky shadows.

Slap.

No longer a muffled tap, but the slap of flesh on wood from far away echoed from the corner, reverberating up her spine. Laney jumped back and withdrew her hand, her heart suddenly racing.

The soft shush of something large being dragged followed. It resonated from a distance. As if the corner—darker than it had any right to be this time of day—wasn't just the joining of two walls, but the mouth of a long tunnel.

Then the slap again, and the drag, the pause between them less distinct. They came again. And again. The sounds repeated, looped in their motion, getting louder, closer, picking up speed.

She backed away, wanting to run, but stalled by her inability to comprehend what she would be running from.

With each repetition, the echo diminished until it was gone, as if whatever came through the tunnel neared the end. A stir of shadows in the murk, the motion of the sound taking form, lurched and wriggled in the dark, moving towards her. Coming right-

Thumpthumpthumpthumpthump.

The stairs erupted with pounding footsteps.

Laney jerked her eyes away from the darkness, turning in time to see Faith take the last few steps in a leap, her bare feet slapping hard on the floor when she landed.

Spurred by instinct, Laney rushed to put herself between her daughter and the thing coming for her, and turned back to face the… empty corner where the walls met in the dim light under the stairs. The stench had gone too, save for the faint trace that still lingered in her nostrils. She grabbed the baluster near her head to steady herself.

"Mom," Faith said behind her. "I have a great idea."

Faith's great idea was Laney lugging the doll house out to the porch so Faith could play outside. Laney agreed, despite the pain in her back, eager to get away from the hallway. Her mind reeled, trying to find logic to explain what she just experienced, or thought she experienced. It kept coming back to stress, and her mind playing tricks on her. It wouldn't be the first time her head had messed with her since she arrived. She thought of her car door, and the motion in the corn. The theory made unsatisfying sense, but sense being the priority, she clung to it.

To Faith's annoyance, when they reached the top of the stairs, Laney stopped to peek in Ray's room, and found his bed empty.

Good.

No way she was leaving him alone in the house right now, stress delusions or not.

Her daughter had clearly been counting on a *yes* to her proposal. Faith already had all the dolls and furnishings packed up into an old wicker basket. As soon as Laney folded the dollhouse and picked it up, Faith made a beeline for the stairs.

"Wait for me," Laney yelled, cringing at the sharp tone in her voice, but she didn't want Faith alone in the hallway right now, not even for a second.

Faith sulked back into the room. "But you're so slow."

Laney couldn't argue with that. She took her time going down the stairs, her back complaining with every step.

The dollhouse wasn't heavy, but its awkward size strained her back muscles, and she couldn't wait to put it down. Despite the strain, before heading out the door, she turned to look down the hall, somehow knowing what she would see. Stress induced hallucination seemed to be the winning theory, because nothing lurked under the stairs, not even a dust bunny. She left the house, unsure if that made her feel better or worse.

Grunting under her breath, Laney set the dollhouse on the wooden planks of the porch, and eased herself down next to it to help Faith set up the furniture. She grabbed a chair from the basket and placed it in the kitchen.

"Mom, no." Faith snatched the chair out of the room. "That chair goes in the dining room." Her daughter pulled out an oblong table from the basket, the same stain of wood as the chair, clearly dumbfounded that her mother could forget something so obvious about a toy she hadn't played with in twenty-five years. "See?"

Laney nodded. "When you're right, you're right."

Her dad was also right. Her kids *were* willful, but they didn't get it from her.

The moment Faith stood up to Troy back at the apartment came back to her in a rush, taking her breath away like she was right back there again. There were so many ways that could have ended badly, but Laney pushed through those thoughts, and allowed herself a moment of pride.

Her little girl was fearless.

Unless scarecrows are involved, of course.

Faith lay on her belly, her head filling the opening to the kitchen. She set the table for dinner, placing tiny spoons and forks next to equally tiny plates, lining them up nice and straight.

"Why would a mom hurt her kid?" Faith's question came out of the blue, catching Laney by surprise.

"What?" Laney asked. Questioning a dad she could understand after the other night with Troy, but not a mom.

Not me.

She leaned forward and put her hand on her daughter's shoulder. "Why would you ask that? You know I would never hurt you, right?"

"Not you." Faith twisted on her side to look up at her. "A different mom."

"Is this a mom I know?"

Faith shook her head, then stopped and tilted it to the side, brow creased in contemplation. "I don't know. Maybe. How long do bunnies live?"

"What?"

Her question hung in the air, unanswered, as a car turned down the long driveway.

19

Company

The black compact sedan tore down the driveway. Flames, painted on the sides of the car, blurred from the speed. Headlights glared like angry eyes. Its modified exhaust roared. Dust billowed out from behind the jacked up rear, like a cape.

Laney got to her feet, gripping the rail.

Pete stepped out of the barn, wiping his hands on a dirty rag. Ray followed him out, doing the same. Her father waved his hand for Ray to stay back.

As the car got closer, she could see there were two people in the front seat. It wasn't Troy, but from her father's gesture, she guessed he was expecting trouble.

"Faith, go inside. Now." Her daughter grabbed the dolls, ran into the house, then popped up on the other side of the living room window a few seconds later.

"Ray", Laney yelled, waving him towards her with her hands. Except for an eye roll she suspected was Pavlovian, he ignored her.

The car reached the end of the field, cut a hard left past the house, towards the barn, and engulfed the porch in a cloud of dust. It headed straight for her father. Pete stood his ground, still wiping his hands with the rag.

Laney white knuckled the porch rail, squinting through the dust. Until the sedan stopped hard, just a few feet away from her father.

Two men—overgrown kids, really—got out. One towered over the other, over her father, too.

She suspected size was how most people told them apart. From their similar faces, she guessed they were brothers. Both wore tight tank tops over gym rat builds, showing off their tattoo sleeves, and a white baseball cap, pointing backwards. Besides size, the smaller man's eyes were the only other notable difference. Even from the porch, Laney could make out his bright green eyes framed by dark lashes, giving him an effeminate, boy band look.

"Johnny." Pete nodded to the smaller man first, turned to the other. "Buster."

Buster hung back, leaning his bulk against the driver's side door, chewing a hangnail on his pinky finger, as Johnny swaggered towards Pete.

"Hey, Pete." Johnny nodded a greeting, then pointed to what must have been a pickup truck, from the size of it, covered with a tarp, next to the barn. "I need my wheels. Is she ready?", he said.

"Its been ready since I called you last week."

Johnny took a small wad of cash out of his pocket, then counted off some bills. "Sorry, been busy. We said two hundred, right?"

"Three fifty, and you know it."

Buster took his finger out of his mouth, and spit out some nail. "You calling my brother a liar?" He stood up straight. The car's shocks eased up with relief.

"Sounds about right." Pete said, his voice casual, like they were chatting about the weather.

"Um, dad?" Laney didn't like the direction the conversation was taking. Her father ignored her. She gestured for Ray to come over to the house again. He didn't even see her. He stood there with a big stupid grin on his face like he was ringside at a boxing match.

Laney worried he was.

"Well, I only got two hundred right now, and I need my wheels," Johnny said.

Pete shrugged. "Come back with three fifty and you'll get them."

Johnny coughed out a laugh, then held out his arms, palms up. "When have I ever stiffed you?"

"Never, because I only take cash on delivery."

The smaller brother leaned in closer to Pete. "I'm going to overlook the insinuation because we're friends. I've got a hot date and I really need her.”

“Take Buster’s car.”

“I can’t. I’m going to need some room to spread out, if you know what I mean. Well, maybe you don’t remember,” Johnny laughed and pointed to Ray, “but he gets it.”

“He’s twelve,” Pete said.

“Almost thirteen”, Ray said, quick to correct.

“I remember when I was his age,” Johnny said with a big smile on his face. “I was-”

“Still wetting the bed, from what I heard,” Pete finished for him.

Johnny’s cheeks burned red, like painted circles on a porcelain doll, really making his eyes pop.

Buster let out a belly laugh that wound down to a smirk when Johnny shot him a look filled with venom.

“You are trying my patience, old man.” Johnny threw the cash on the ground at Pete’s feet. “Get me my keys.”

Pete ignored the cash. “Or what?”

“I don’t want to say in front of the kid.”

“It’s okay.” Pete shrugged. “He’s almost thirteen.”

Johnny stepped up into Pete’s face, his fists clenched at his sides, chest puffed out. Buster stepped away from the car, took a few steps closer to the pending action, ready to join the fun.

Ray went pale, the big grin he wore a minute ago gone.

Laney held her breath as she watched her father lean forward until he was almost nose to nose with Johnny. He looked the younger man in the eyes, unblinking, unflinching.

The showdown lasted all of five seconds before Johnny crouched down and picked up the cash off the ground. He stomped back to the car, got in, and slammed the door.

Buster watched his brother go, then turned back to Pete, his mouth pursed like it had a nasty taste in it. “Not cool Pete. Not cool.”

Johnny blasted the horn, and Laney jumped. Buster sauntered back to the car. When he got in, he said something to his brother before starting the engine, and throwing the car in reverse. Johnny’s face clenched like he was holding back angry tears.

Buster drove backwards, clipped a few corn stalks as he made the cut into the driveway, then accelerated the rest of the way, still in reverse.

Halfway to the road, Johnny rolled down the window, hung out of the car and double flipped them the bird until Buster drifted too close to the field on the passenger side. Johnny’s right arm got lashed by a stalk so hard it busted the ear of corn clean off.

Laney couldn't hear over the noise of the muffler, but she had an inkling of what the words coming out of Johnny's mouth were. He cradled his bleeding arm as he ducked back into the car. She doubted he was holding back the tears anymore.

The car reached the end of the drive, then reversed hard onto the road without slowing, moving out of sight behind the cornfield. A second later, it blasted past the driveway, taking out the mailbox as it went. The engine faded to a distant hum as mail fluttered to the ground.

Pete walked back to the barn.

It wasn't the first time the Hess boys tried to pull that, but it got a little heated this time. Maybe he should have left the bed wetting out of it. Especially since he knew it to be true.

He had overheard their mother, Margie, complaining about it when he ran into town for groceries years ago. It was the way she referred to her son as the "Super Soaker" that made it stick in his head. She had seemed more pissed off about it than concerned while relating the story to Francine at the register. Francine laughed so hard she cried, and she told Margie to stop before she pissed her own pants.

Laney walked into the barn, her face pale. "What was that?"

Pete shrugged. "The Hess boys are mostly harmless. They try to come off tough, but they're just trying to see what they can get away with. When someone tries to sell you a bucket of shit, you just have to let them know, in no uncertain terms, you're not buying." He handed a socket wrench to Ray, then nodded to the tool bench behind the boy. "You know where this goes."

"Do you think they'll be back?" Laney asked.

"You mean after they change their pants?" Ray returned from the bench with a grin on his face.

"Next time they come back, it will be with the three fifty they owe me, and they'll act like this never happened." Pete said, while loosening the clamp on the radiator overflow hose. Handing the screwdriver to Ray so he had a hand free, he reached in, then unplugged the fan.

Laney finally noticed the disassembled state of the Camry. "What's wrong with my car?"

"What isn't?" Ray said.

"You have a radiator leak, among other things." Pete gestured to the part in front of him. "Don't worry. We're not charging."

"Speak for yourself," Ray said, smiling.

"It's not that bad, really," Pete said. "These cars will run forever if you take care of them. I have a new part on order. Should be here tomorrow. In the meantime," he gestured to Ray, "After we replace the radiator, we'll tune it up, change the plugs, rotate the tires, give it the whole white glove treatment. The kid will even wash the car."

"Speak for yourself," Ray said again, his smile gone this time.

"Thanks guys." Laney patted Ray's shoulder, an impressed smile on her face. "I'll get out of your way, then." She went back to the house.

Pete watched her go, not sure he was doing the right thing here. Things had been quiet around the farm for years. Then last night…he swore he could feel it.

If he didn't keep things under control, it could get dangerous again.

He was, maybe naively, working on getting them a place to stay nearby, hoping Laney would want to. It would make sense for her to want to keep moving, but here people could watch her back. Small towns were good like that. Maybe he should use the Hess boys as an excuse to put her and the kids up in the hotel in town in the meantime.

"That one guy, Buster, he was pretty big," Ray said. "Are you sure you could've taken him? Like if he wasn't afraid of you?"

"He would've snapped me like a twig," Pete tucked his head down, immersed in the car's guts.

"How come you weren't afraid?"

"There was a time I would've been shitting my pants. I've just learned how not to be afraid of the little things."

Ray laughed. "The little things? I can't wait to see the big things."

"You don't want to see the big things."

"Whatever. How did you learn? Can you teach my mom? She's afraid of everything."

Pete detected a hint of disgust in the boy's voice and had to bite back his anger. The kid didn't understand and, god willing, never would. Ray should thank his mother for the privilege of that ignorance.

"That ain't the kind of thing you can teach somebody." He stood straight and looked Ray in the eyes. "The only way not to fear getting your ass kicked is if you don't give a shit if you get your ass kicked."

20

Phil

Troy leaned up against a pillar across from a silver Mercedes parked in a spot reserved for its owner, according to the sign. Trying to ignore the throbbing pain in his nose, he watched as Philip exited the elevator in the parking garage. Philip hadn't been hard to find. Mr. Important was a partner now. His name was on the law firm, and the parking spot.

Troy had met so many guys like him. Bastards so full of themselves, thinking their shit doesn't stink because they wore expensive suits and drove fancy cars. They didn't live in the real world. They bought themselves a fake life where, if they toss enough money around, people will kiss their ass and tell them whatever they want to hear.

The first time he met Philip, never Phil, Troy had to set him straight. Even back then, when he was just some cheap suit wearing, grunt lawyer, Philip thought he was better than him. He and Laney were visiting New York, and had gone out with Philip and his wife for dinner.

Every time Troy opened his mouth, Philip hit him with the smirks and the eye rolls, as if everything Troy said was stupid. He puffed himself up, thinking he was the big man at the table because he had a law degree.

When the check came, he had looked Troy right in the eye and put his hand over it, insisting on paying it.

Right in the eye.

Philip's look said, "Take it if you can afford to." Like paying for dinner made him the bigger man. Troy didn't argue with him. He sat back and let Philip pay that check with a gracious smile on his face.

Before they left the restaurant, Laney's brother excused himself for a visit to the men's room.

He had his back to the door. Standing at the urinal, he pissed out a stream of that twenty-dollar bottle of white wine he insisted they get at dinner because it paired well with the fish. Troy walked up behind him, wound up, then punched him hard in the back, just below the ribs, on his right side. Philip crumpled on the piss stained tile, sucking in air and writhing in pain, all the while still trickling out that wine.

If Troy hit him hard enough, it would be a red soon.

Pair that with fish, asshole.

Troy stepped past the man, unzipped, then unleashed a stream into the urinal next to him.

"Hurts don't it?" Troy said. "Got to love a good kidney punch, its like someone set off a hand grenade in your back. You know what hurts worse? Me stomping your face in while you lay down there pissing yourself."

Troy shook off, then zipped up. He stepped around Philip to the sink, ran some water over his hands, then squatted down, and dried them off on the man's cheap suit jacket.

"I'm glad we had this private talk, *Phil*. Hashing things out like real men. No more disrespect. No more bullshit. We're just two guys who understand each other now. Right *Phil*?"

Philip groaned.

"Glad you see my side of it." Troy said, standing, "Oh, and thanks for dinner, *Phil*."

He left his future brother-in-law crying in his own piss. As far as Troy knew, Philip told no one about what happened in the men's room that night. Laney never mentioned it. That was the last time he saw his brother-in-law until today.

Philip walked right past him, head down, absorbed in reading an email on his phone. Too important to notice the world around him. He was so close Troy could have reached out and grabbed him by the hundred dollar haircut.

"Hey *Phil*."

Philip turned and looked, his head bobbing around to locate the speaker like a pigeon looking for breadcrumbs. Troy stepped out of the shadows.

It only took a second for recognition to dawn on Philip's face and even less time for him to break into a sprint. Expensive dress shoes slapped hard on the concrete at a rapid fire cadence.

Troy broke into a grin.

Look at that fucker go.

When Philip passed the up ramp, before Troy even took a step, amusement quickly became alarm at the speed the distance between them grew.

Troy ran after him, limping as fast as he could. His knee was all kinds of messed up from when that bitch hit him with the car. Philip, already way ahead of him, gained distance every second.

Should have just suckered him. Fuck.

If he let Philip get away now, he might not get a second chance at him, even if he figured out where the little shit lived. Rich fucker like him will have a cop parked outside his house with the snap of his fingers. Then Troy would never get his son back. And that bitch would never get what's coming to her.

But luck was with him for a change.

Philip took a sharp right for the down ramp towards the exit at full speed. His shoes, his fucking black leather shoes that probably cost more than anything Troy had ever owned, were not made for running. They skidded out from under him with a hiss, and Philip went down hard. His face hit the concrete floor with a wet slap that echoed off the garage walls and bounced into a skid before lying still.

Troy slowed to a walking limp, shaking with laughter. Bum knee or not, he was really going to enjoy kicking Philip's teeth in.

If the concrete left any.

21

Creeping Darkness

The roach infested one bedroom walk-up resounded with Ray's screams. Laney held her infant son to her chest and rocked him. She attempted to make soothing noises through a clenched jaw and waited for the explosion to erupt from the bedroom.

Troy got in at five in the morning, stinking of cheap whiskey and beer. A recipe for a hangover that kept Laney walking on eggshells all day.

She paced from the living room to the kitchen, bouncing as she went, wishing she was anywhere but this shit hole apartment. There were water stains on the ceiling, nicotine stains on the wall, and god knows what stained the carpet that crunched underfoot.

Home crap home.

The ancient pram stroller sat in the middle of the living room. It was funereal black, trimmed in lace once white, but now stained a dirty beige. She hated trying to drag that thing up the stairs, but it was all thirty-dollars would get her at the thrift store. Besides, it doubled as a bassinet, saving space. She reached inside, and felt around, checking it for anything that might hide in its dark corners before tucking Ray in.

As soon as he left her arms, he turned up the volume, his cheeks going from pink to red before she even tucked the blanket in. His little legs kicked, tiny clenched fists jerked, punctuating the air with each scream. Her eyes shot to the bedroom door, expecting it to fling open and slam against the wall, sinking the doorknob into its matching hole in the drywall. But it remained closed. For now.

She bounced the stroller as she pushed it, doing laps around the kitchen table. She'd probably logged more miles around that table in the past month than she did around the high school track that led to her college scholarship.

College.

That word seemed like the name of some far off magical land now. A place that she had read about long ago, in a book she no longer remembered the ending to. She didn't recognize it as a world she lived in less than a year ago, in a different life.

She choked down the familiar regret snaking its way up and focused on her son. Ray's cries finally wound down to some pouty whining barely audible over the traffic outside the window. He gazed up at her, teardrops drying on his cheeks, as he gave voice to his many woes. Her little drama king. His mouth worked overtime, struggling to form the nonsense sounds of a language she hadn't spoken in over twenty years.

The overwhelming love caught her by surprise, as it had so many times since she first laid eyes on Ray. Before the birth of her son, she never comprehended that an emotion could be so heavy and make her feel so light.

A low squeak came from one of the stroller's wheels. Too quiet to make a dent in Troy's whiskey coma, and nowhere in the same universe as the brakes on the bus that stopped outside their building.

"I know you want to talk, my stubborn little man, but you need to sleep."

Ray tried to fight it as she circled the table. He yawned. His gray eyes drifted closed, fluttered open, and drifted closed again. Laney lost count of the laps around the kitchen before he finally dozed off.

Her eyes followed the slow rise and fall of his chest as she eased her pace for a few more circles, not wanting to make the rookie mistake of stopping too soon. Holding her breath, she brought the stroller to a standstill, then let go of the handle, her grip leaving its mark in condensation on the metal.

She waited, her hand inches away, ready to go if he let out the tiniest of peeps. Ray had fooled her before. He'd be sleeping peacefully and as soon as she walked away, the cries would come like

Jason rising from the lake. Satisfied he wasn't faking, she padded to the sofa, careful not to step on the creaky floorboard near the coffee table.

As soon as her butt hit the worn cushion, the stroller shook with Ray's screams. Laney jumped up right back into the routine. It took three squeaky turns around the table before Ray calmed down. She didn't know what was wrong with him. He'd eaten, pooped and burped, the trifecta of a happy infanthood. So the pamphlets claimed. Meanwhile, Laney hadn't slept since... Oh, yeah. Yesterday. She should be the one crying.

The trouble making wheel let out a sudden shriek, loud and sharp, and for a panicked moment she thought it was a spring in the mattress Troy slept on. If this went on much longer, whiskey coma or not, Troy would emerge from the bedroom ready to share any pain left pounding in his head.

She eased up on the bouncing, then slowed to avoid the metallic whine as the rusty spokes went around, but like an infection, the noise spread to the rest of the wheels. They screeched, letting loose a disjointed cacophony of many fingernails on a chalkboard, and unlike before, the volume gave the bus a run for its money.

Trying to diminish the noise, Laney slowed her pace until the wheels rotated in seeming slow motion. Her head turned on a pivot, eyes locked on the bedroom door, sensing time wound down, as if the doorknob turned so slowly she couldn't track the motion.

But, despite her pace, the wheels complained.

She eased to a gentle break again, but Ray woke the second the wheels stopped turning. As if the incessant whine of metal was the only thing lulling him to sleep.

The force of his inhalation told her this next cry would be a big one. Laney lurched the stroller forward, and the wail caught in Ray's throat, cut off before it could begin. He looked up at her, his pudgy cheeks an angry red. Fat tear drops welled up in eyes that dared her to stop again. They made it a full rotation around when the wheels started shrieking.

She froze at the sound of it, and Ray screamed.

She pushed the stroller, and the wheels shrieked.

This is insane.

Laney reached in to pick Ray up, to take him outside, where his cries would disappear against the backdrop of the city. He thrashed in her arms, twisting his little body into contortions of rage, and threw his head back, letting out a warbling howl that rang in her ears. She gave up and got the stroller moving again.

The wheels screamed like the brakes of a subway train careening around a curve at full speed.

Ray looked up at her, still and content, his face placid. His tiny lips curved into a cruel smile as the keening screams of the wheels vibrated off the apartment walls.

Somehow, she still heard the pounding footsteps coming from the bedroom.

Laney woke up to pitch black, the faint scent of cheap cologne in the air, and angry butterflies bouncing off the walls of her stomach. The nightmare was already fading, but the adrenaline rush would last longer. She rubbed her eyes, then tried to focus on her watch. It was just after three in the morning and it was going to be a long night.

It took her a moment to realize the sound was back.

The high-pitched cry of metal on metal was louder tonight. She rolled to her side, facing the door, waiting for the night-light in the hall to come on when her father got up.

It never did.

Got to ask Dad what that is.

She could hear him now. "Old houses make noise."

Laney didn't have that much experience with old houses, but she was pretty sure that squeaking wheels weren't a typical "old house" noise.

Wheels?

Now that she thought of it, wheels fit the sound perfectly. The motion, the variation of pitch, could be caused by the rotation of something old and rusty turning. But wheels made little sense in the context of an old house. Maybe gears or a belt? Maybe the refrigerator, or an old water pump?

Definitely have to ask Dad about it.

She laid there listening until sleep pulled at her, calling her back to its passive aggressive embrace. Her eyes drooped closed and her breath evened. As she drifted off, ancient metal gears, pitted and weathered with age, turned in her mind's eye.

LANEY.

The disembodied voice shouted in her ear and she jolted awake, half sitting, filled with the urgent sense she was missing something important. Faith stirred in her sleep next to her.

Sighing, she laid back down. As soon as her head hit the pillow, a shiver ran up her spine. Chilled, she pulled the sheet up tight under her chin, despite the summer night. She wondered if she was coming down with something. A wave of nausea washed over her, and her stomach roiled audibly in response. She was definitely coming down with something.

Laney pulled the covers back, then sat on the edge of the bed, trying to decide if she needed to make a dash for the bathroom.

Better safe than sorry.

She reached for the lamp and froze when a floorboard near the door squeaked. Squinting against the expected glare of the night-light that never came, her breath caught in her throat when she realized why.

It was inside the room.

Her eyes strained, trying to focus on the dark space where the door stood. Hand shaking, she reached for the lamp again. Another creak, this one closer.

Laney held her breath, trying to hear over the increasing thud of her heart. The only sounds were Faith's breathing, and the squeals of metal from downstairs. The songs of crickets that she had drifted off to earlier in the night were now silent.

She moved her hand another inch towards the lamp and the creak came again.

Louder.

Closer.

Her hand shot out, fingers fumbling for the switch.

Charging footsteps vibrated through the floorboards beneath her feet, barely audible over the thrumming in her ears. Her free arm blocked her face defensively against the threat rushing at her.

The lamp clicked on, bathing the room in warm light.

The empty room.

Laney lowered her shaking arm. Her eyes, adjusting to the light, flitted from corner to corner, searching for any sign of Troy. But there was no one there. She yanked her feet up off the floor to the safety of the bed, just in case.

Downstairs, the pace of the metal cries increased.

Her eyes went to the closed door. The white painted wood seemed less a guardian of her childhood space, and more the promise of a looming threat.

Cramps twisted her gut and her mouth filled with saliva, but she fought the urge to run to the bathroom.

No way in hell I'm going out there.

She leaned over, arms hugging her stomach tight, determined to stay put. She didn't care if she splattered all over the Strawberry Shortcake throw rug.

Then came the creak of a door. Ray's door?

She shot out of bed, into the hall, triggering the night-light. The light threw long shadows of the open railing balusters, stretching them up the wall like bars on a cage, trapping the shadow cast by Laney behind them.

Ray's door was closed.

Out in the open hall, the metal screeching blared from downstairs. Laney quickly pulled her door closed behind her to avoid waking Faith.

Hunched over, she padded across the hall, giving the stairs a wide berth. Then she leaned her head against the heavy wood of Ray's door, listening, but between the screeches and the thumping in her ears, she couldn't hear a thing. Laney grabbed the doorknob, desperately wanting to check on him. He wasn't safe until she could see him with her own eyes and confirm it. But she fought the urge. The last thing she needed to do was wake him and drag him into whatever was going on downstairs.

The pain came again, nearly doubling her over. Cool, white tile past the open bathroom door called to her, but she found herself at the top of the stairs contemplating the murk below, a mimic of her father from the night before. Her stomach spasmed painfully and bile rose, burning the back of her throat.

She took the first step down, and her gorge settled. The nausea was gone as quickly as it had come.

Laney had no phone for light, but she knew there was a switch for the living room ceiling lamp at the bottom of the stairs. She took each step down, with the trepidation of someone entering an alligator filled swamp.

Halfway down, the night-light shut off. With nothing to keep it at bay, the darkness swallowed her whole. She froze as if her body had forgotten how to move without the light. Below her, the sound came closer. Ancient wheels turning. She tried to stifle her harried breathing by clamping her hands over her mouth. From where she stood, the sound's location was unmistakable. The middle of an empty hallway. This was no old refrigerator or overworked water pump. It couldn't be explained away as an "old house" noise.

It moved of its own volition.

The metal cry reached the bottom of the stairs and paused, as if sensing her. A vein in her temple pulsed with the beat of her pounding heart, making her eye twitch. She stood trapped in the cessation of the sound's motion. Until, finally, a screech cut through the darkness, turned a half circle, then started back down the hall.

Laney wanted to turn, too. She wanted to run upstairs, go back to bed and cower under the covers.

It will follow me. It will follow me right to the kids.

She had no choice. With a shaking hand, she hit the light button on her watch face. It cast a dim green glow that petered out a foot in front of her. She worried the light would draw whatever made the sound's attention, but she didn't care. She couldn't take another step without it.

Trembling, Laney stepped down, afraid her leg wouldn't take her weight, that it would just collapse out from under her, spilling her into the ether. But she refused to grab the rail. Instead, she hugged the wall, keeping the railing between her and the noise. Her foot landed on the step. Clenched toes clung to the grain of the wood. The muscles in her thigh shook, but held. She took another step, then another, and so on until the floor lay firm beneath her.

Down the hall, the sound was turning towards her again, but from her new vantage, it had evolved. It wasn't just the screech of metal turning. It was fuller, more fleshed out, more threatening. There was weight to it, rumbling on the hardwood floors beneath it.

Laney held her watch near the wall, and hurried. The light it cast illuminated the golden wallpaper, turning it a pea soup green. She almost screamed when she reached the arch to the living room and an inky blackness stole the light. She darted forward, knowing the switch was on the other side of the arch.

Come on. Come on.

The opening stretched out in front of her. She walked, lost in a featureless desert of night. Nothing was within reach of the dim watch light and its sickly green glow found no place to land.

All the while, the sound got closer. So close now, the screeches ran up her spine like tingling fingers.

When the gilded leaves and flowers of the wallpaper came back into view, she let out a gasp of relief. Turning, she planted her back to the wall, then slid along it, searching for the light switch. Pointing her wrist towards the sound, she caught motion teasing at the fringes of the dim light in front of her. One step forward, and she would see it.

Laney stepped back.

She continued sliding as the screeching paced her, always on the cusp of crossing into the light.

Where the fuck is it?

Was there really a switch? Maybe she misremembered, or had conflated the layout of this house with one of the many other places she had lived over the years. The wall went on forever and the hope that she might find the switch began to feel naïve. Then a hard nub protruded from the plaster and poked her shoulder. She turned, slapping like a drowning swimmer trying to stay above the water.

Her hand hit a pair of switches. Light erupted from the living room arch. She turned back to face the shrieking metal.

And for a split second, she saw it.

An amorphous shape formed inches from her. It's breath, cold and fetid on her face. Then her eyes adjusted to the light, and it was gone.

The hallway in front of her stood empty.

She waited for minutes, listening. But it was really gone, vanquished by a pair of forty watt bulbs in an overhead light fixture one room over.

For all her fear, all the buildup, she was left standing in an empty hallway, dripping sweat, exhausted and wondering if she finally cracked. She knew what it felt like to be toyed with. To be wound up to the point of snapping, so Troy had an excuse to blame her for what came next. But this was just a house.

Old houses make noise.

Laney bit back the cackle of hysteria trying to escape her throat. If she let it out, she might really crack.

She was done with this.

She walked up the stairs while her legs would still carry her, not bothering to turn off the light.

Halfway up, a new sound came from the hall. No shriek of metal this time. Just a simple click. Then a creak. It was the unmistakable sound of a door opening.

The pantry door.

The slow, drawn-out groan of the hinges revealed it didn't just open a little. It stood wide open.

She let out a ragged breath. Then forced herself to lean over the rail and look, but the stairs eclipsed the light from the living room, shrouding the door in shadows.

Knowing this wouldn't end on her terms, she made the trip back downstairs on shaky legs. She found herself in the hall again, staring at the open door nestled in the shadows under the stairs and the dark room beyond it.

No. Not just dark. It was a void where light went to die.

Laney's legs were jelly, but they listened when her brain told them to move. They didn't run. She was incapable of running right now, and every instinct told her not to. Something primal waited in the darkness, and running, she knew, would trigger its instinct to pounce. Without taking her eyes off the doorway, she backed towards the foot of the stairs.

But the room wasn't done with her yet.

A creeping darkness followed, spilling beyond the confines of the pantry. It flowed like pitch over the trim of the door frame, spreading along the walls, the ceiling, the floor. Everywhere it touched, it consumed the light. Saturated shadows blackened to coal. A thick and nebulous fog bled from the opening, overtaking the surrounding air, corrupting it.

She couldn't tell if the darkness was real, or if her consciousness was leaching away and soon she would find herself free falling into the void. But she knew beyond reason something was coming for her.

"What do you see?" the voice asked from behind her, and she screamed.

22

What Do You See

Laney spun and staggered back from the figure on the stairs. She didn't recognize him at first, sure it was the old man. Then her father stood in front of her in his pajamas, eyes creased with worry.

What do I see? Isn't it fucking obvious?

It wasn't. A look down the hall showed a closed pantry door nestled in the shadows and not the creeping, malevolent kind.

She struggled to find her voice.

"Nothing. I saw nothing." Her eyes locked on the door, avoiding him, as she lied through her teeth. "I heard a noise and wanted to make sure there was no one here. But, I guess, I mean, there's nothing. Just...nothing."

"You're right." Her father placed his hands on her shoulders, turned her to look at him. "There's nothing there, unless you make it something. Do you understand?" His eyes locked with hers, filled with a desperate need for confirmation.

"Ah, yeah. Totally." she said, not understanding at all.

He broke eye contact and looked away. "Great. I'm glad." His voice was flat. She knew he didn't buy it.

He walked down the hall, removed a key from his pajama pocket, then looked back at her. Gears turned in his head as he tapped the key against the palm of his other hand, undecided. Finally, he put the key in the deadbolt and turned it.

Click.

He turned and looked at her expectantly.

Laney stepped back. "I'm good. I'm just going to go back to bed."

"Please." His eyes pleaded with her. "I just want to show you what's in there."

"Okay." She nodded, but didn't move.

"C'mon. It's okay. Pinky swear." He held out his pinky, crooked in the air, waiting for her.

Laney couldn't leave him hanging.

It took all her will to walk to him, as if she walked towards the open door of a plane without a parachute. She sighed, wrapped her pinky around his, and gave it a halfhearted shake, like she hadn't done since she was seven.

He smiled and nodded towards the door. "Go ahead, open it."

She wrapped her hand around the cool brass knob and looked back at him. Now would be the time for him to stop her. Psyche. Just kidding. Don't open the malevolent door of creeping darkness. You'll totally die if you do.

But he gave her an encouraging nod, eager for her to turn the handle.

Too eager.

A thought occurred to her, and she pulled her hand back. "Why?"

Laney had the sudden mental picture of him shoving her in the pantry, locking the door behind her, feeding her to the darkness. She hadn't seen this man in decades, not since she was a child. How much of her father did she really remember and how much was the wishful memories of a naïve young girl?

His face sagged. Her father grabbed the knob and Laney took a big step back reflexively, like he just pulled the pin on a hand grenade. He opened the door and entered the room without hesitation. She lost sight of him in the dark, but heard his slippers scuff on the hardwood floor as he stepped deeper into the room. Seconds later, the light came on with a click. A string danced from the light fixture over his head.

From where she was standing, she could see shelves lined with canned goods, paper goods, boxes, glass jars full of fruit and jams. All things you would expect in a pantry.

She took a tentative step into the room. Shelves covered the walls, except for a gap on the outer wall of the house where the window was, and where bifold doors covered the wall on the left. Her father stepped to the doors, then slid them open, revealing a washer and a dryer. To her right, in the corner, a fold-up ladder leaned against the shelves. No doubt used to reach the top ones.

It was a perfectly sane and reasonable pantry with no creeping, sentient darkness anywhere to be seen.

"I don't know what you've been through," he said, looking down at his hands, each taking turns massaging the swollen joints of the other. "Philip told me some, but I doubt it was the complete story, and I don't want you to tell me unless you want to. Which I can't imagine you do right now. You probably don't remember, but this house it's...." He looked around the shelves as if he would find the right words sitting next to a can of peas.

"I just want you to be safe. And I missed you and the kids, even though I never met them before." He laughed. "Feels like I knew them forever. Anyway, it's late, but I wanted to tell you I called a friend. She has a place down the road. There's a cottage on her property. It's not much, but she's willing to rent it out pretty cheap. It will be ready in a week or so. Maybe by then the situation with that-" His jaw clenched. He took a deep breath, and unclenched it before starting again. "Maybe you'd want to stick around."

He finally looked her in the eye.

"You know, it might be good to be near family."

Laney crossed the room, and wrapped her arms around her father's neck, hugging him tight, like no time had passed between them. She didn't want to get her hopes up. But the idea of someone being there for her, of not carrying the weight of everything alone for once, was overwhelming. In that moment, having her father back meant everything.

Laney went back to bed feeling hopeful, but as soon as she turned out the light, thoughts of creeping darkness invaded.

If there's nothing in there, why does he keep the door locked?

She turned the light back on and didn't sleep until the sun peeked over the horizon, filling in the shadows of the room that the lamp on the nightstand couldn't reach.

23

Laundry Day

Laney took a greedy sip of coffee from the mug in her left hand before flipping Faith's grilled cheese with the spatula in her right. She was on cup number three, still struggling to wake up, despite it being close to noon.

Cartoons blared from the living room, today's location for the dollhouse. She glanced in there for the millionth time to check on Faith. Her daughter seemed content, splitting her attention between the television, and re-arranging tiny furniture for the umpteenth time.

It made her nervous to have Faith play so close to where she experienced...whatever last night was. Finding the right label proved to be difficult. In the light of day, her logical mind leaned towards delusion. But Laney knew better. The things she'd been experiencing since she got here were...well, maybe not real, but really happening.

Her dad all but confirmed it. She took his whole "nothing until you make it something" to mean they somehow manifested from her and weren't just stress induced hallucinations. To be fair, he had tried to warn her from the get go.

This house ain't fit.

But he hadn't told her everything yet. What was in the pantry? Had it always been there? Was that why she and Philip weren't allowed in there as kids? That would make sense, she guessed.

And most importantly, exactly how dangerous was it? So far, the kids had shown no indication that they'd noticed anything strange, and she wanted to keep it that way. But she needed to know if whatever caused her experiences since she arrived was a threat to them.

Laney turned off the burner, then plated the sandwich cut into triangles. She might have thrown a few carrot sticks on the plate if she were home, but her daughter had to settle for some potato chips. She poured out a glass of juice, then took both the plate and the glass into the living room where a TV tray had been set up since breakfast. In any other place, she would feel guilty about letting Faith spend a beautiful summer day in front of the TV with all that space outside to play, but she wasn't convinced the Hess Boys wouldn't show up ready for trouble. And there was still a matter of the man in the corn. Another thing she intended to talk to her dad about after the kids went to bed.

The door under the stairs called to her as she crossed the hall back into the kitchen, but she ignored it. She forced her eyes to stay straight ahead, denying the hungry door even a glimpse.

She cleaned up the grilled cheese mess and finished the pot of coffee, pouring the last into cup number four. Though her back had finally loosened up, she drank that last cup, leaning up against the arch of the kitchen while watching Faith play. Sitting meant dozing, despite the caffeine infusion she'd been imbibing.

The pull of the pantry door waned, and she found her mind slipping to the cottage her father had mentioned. She'd have to find a local job, of course, but if she could make that work, Ray might actually forgive her for all the moving in the past. Faith would be thrilled, too. Maybe they could even get some chickens. A warm buzz of excitement stirred in her as the plan came together in her head.

Her last pay check would be in her account tomorrow. She'd need to pay Celia back and use the rest to get a new phone. She could start filling out on-line applications as soon as she did. Her interview outfit still hung in a dry cleaning bag back at the apartment, but she should be able to dig up something presentable from the trash bags once she did laundry.

At the thought of laundry, she finally let her eyes drift towards the door.

There's nothing unless you make it something.

It was just a door.

A door with a washer and dryer on the other side.

With a trash bag full of dirty laundry swung over her shoulder, Laney walked to the pantry door without giving herself time to reconsider. She took the knob in hand, twisted it, and pulled, expecting the deadbolt latch to catch. But her father must have forgotten to lock the door last night, because it swung wide open, creaking as it went. She glanced back towards the front door, like he might walk in and catch her in the act again. But he was busy in the barn, and they were beyond that now.

Dust motes, set in motion by the breeze created when she opened the door, danced in the light from the small window across from her. Canning jars on the shelves, filled with fruits and vegetables, glowed warmly where the sunlight hit them. But the time of day, with the sun at high noon, left half the room deep in shadow, the half she had to walk through to get to the overhead light.

There's nothing unless you make it something.

Trying not to overthink it, she took the first step into the room, into the shadows. Nothing happened. No anxious need to fill the room with light propelled her to rush to the pull string. No unsubstantiated fear sent her running from the room. None of the dread from last night returned. Like it was any other room, she walked to the middle, reached for the string, and pulled it, vanquishing the shadows that really weren't that menacing at all.

Laney dropped the bag of laundry on the floor, then opened the bi-fold doors. The washing machine, an older model, had knobs instead of buttons. She turned the knob to select the full wash cycle, then pulled it out until it clicked. Water gushed into the drum. She found a box of powder detergent and scooped some in. It foamed in the turbulence almost immediately.

While the washer filled, she went through each item of clothing, checking the pockets, before putting it in the machine. A habit she picked up when Ray got old enough to color. Nothing like drying a load on high heat with the nub of a purple crayon in the pocket of a toddler's hoodie. When she turned out the pockets on Ray's cargo shorts, something red, about the size of a lighter, fell out, hit the floor and bounced under the washer.

He better not be smoking.

After Laney finished going through the remaining items and shut the lid, she laid belly down on the floor to look for the lighter. The gap under the washer wasn't that big, not quite as tall as her forearm, and no light reached there. She'd have to feel around for the lighter and hope it didn't go too far under. Sliding back until her arm extended flat on the floor, she squeezed her hand under the washer, but not much farther than her wrist.

Cobwebs engulfed her fingers. She slid her hand along the length of the machine, plowing up a pile of them until her finger brushed up against something metal. Laney pinned the object between her fore and index fingers, taking in the shape of it. A pocket knife. Not a lighter. He must have gotten it from her dad. Happy to be wrong, she slid-

Shit.

Her watchband snagged on something, and she couldn't pull her hand out. Trying a side-to-side motion didn't help either. The band was caught tight. She tried to push her hand in further to slip loose, but her skin could only compress so much, and the bones of her arm, not at all.

Dammit, she liked that watch.

With no choice but to break the band, Laney struggled to find leverage while lying flat on the floor, pulling her hand as hard as she could.

Finished filling with water, the washer switched cycles, and agitation kicked in. The machine vibrated against her forearm, its weight pressing then releasing over and over again. The shift in weight was minimal, but with her arm already wedged so tightly between the metal of the machine and the hardwood floor, the discomfort of the repetitions grew fast. She doubted it would cause any actual damage, but didn't plan on finding out.

Feeling like an idiot, she sucked in a breath to call for Faith, to send her for help, but held that breath. The hair along the length of her arm prickled and stood as the temperature of the air around her suddenly plummeted. When she finally let the breath go, it came out in a fog.

Her next inhale was a shallow gasp. The frigid air weighed heavy on her back, pressing her against the floor.

So fucking, fucking stupid.

She had let herself walk right into a trap, baited by a fucking washing machine.

Gritting her teeth, Laney twisted her body to the side, levering her arm up against the unmovable machine. White hot pain shot up her arm as she waited for bones to crack. All that pain for just a half an inch, but she twisted her hips enough to get her knee braced against the washer, and pulled with everything she had.

The watchband snapped, and her hand broke free for a brief second. Before something else snagged it, encircling it tight.

Panic rushed in, ice cold in her gut.

Dry roots, dusty with dirt, twisted around her wrist. No, not roots, fingers, gnarled bony fingers bent at swollen joints gripping her wrist like a vise.

"Mom?" Faith's voice came from down the hall, getting closer. "Where are you? I'm still hungry."

A faint light grew from beneath the washer, from far beneath the washer, and a form took shape. The floorboards were gone. A jagged hole, lit from below, took their place.

Nothing. There's nothing. Nothing unless you make it something.

It took everything she had to inject some semblance of calm, to keep her voice from shaking when she called to her daughter. "Don't come in here."

"Why not?" Faith asked, her voice too close.

Before her eyes, the form became a man, thin, emaciated. The light underneath him glowed yellow through the edges of his paper thin skin.

There's nothing.

"Glass, hon." The words came out hitched and breathy from the pressing weight on her back. "Broken glass. Stay out."

The man from the corn, her great grandfather, stood with the side of his head pressed up against the bottom of the washing machine. He smiled, pulling the taut skin of his face beyond its limits, splitting it open. Rivulets of a dark red liquid, too syrupy thick to be blood, oozed down in grisly laugh lines.

"Don't worry. I'll stay right here." The voice came from behind her. Close behind her.

Laney's heart pounded so hard she couldn't feel the beats, just one long, sustained percussion.

Faith was in the room.

"What are you doing? Is the glass under the washer?"

His dark eyes turned, looking past Laney to where Faith stood. The bones in his face cracked. Slow-moving rivulets became languid rivers, as his grin stretched far too wide. His mouth froze in that impossible smile, but his voice sliced through her brain, whirling razor blades hissing out his words. "Ah, fresh blood."

"God dammit, Faith!" Forced out through the constricting weight pressing her down, the words ripped the air from her lungs. "I told you to stay out!"

She pulled so hard she felt the bones of her wrist and hand begin to pull away from each other, threatening to split apart. And she didn't care. She didn't care if the whole damn hand ripped off. She pulled until his grip loosened, and he had to dig his long, dirty fingernails into her flesh to hold on. Still, she pulled. Until his nails left trenches in her skin and his grip fell away.

Laney laid on the floor, cradling her arm to her chest. She panted, trapped in his gaze, as Faith's footsteps echoed down the hall.

His smile disappeared, replaced by his lower lip jutting out in mock sympathy. Deflated cheeks sagged to folds of ruptured skin, still oozing red.

The blades tore through her head one last time. "I'll see you soon," they hissed.

And then he was gone, cobweb covered floorboards, a broken watch and a pocketknife in his place.

Laney didn't know how long she laid there, at least as long as the wash cycle, and then some. When she finally got up, she pulled the pantry door closed behind her, and walked into the living room, dazed and wondering if she was going insane. If the bloody gouges in her wrist were somehow of her own doing?

She found Faith on the sofa, staring listlessly at the television, the dollhouse forgotten, and plopped down next to her daughter.

Without looking up, Faith said, "you really hurt my feelings."

"I'm sorry, baby." Laney didn't feel the words that tumbled out of her numb lips.

"That's okay. I guess." Faith looked up with a smile stretching her tear stained cheeks. "Can I have a peanut butter and jelly sandwich?"

24

QBT

The dollhouse family made their way through treacherous waters floating on a blue sofa in a sea of bubbles. Faith pressed her lips together and blew motorboat noises in the water, while sending them careening through the frothy white suds. Laney turned off the tub faucet, careful not to get the bandage around her wrist wet. She picked up a copy of *Car And Driver* off the back of the toilet at the foot of the tub, and put the seat cover down, got comfortable. Words and images merged into a blur as she flipped the pages, her mind stuck on the pantry.

She made up a story about burning herself when her dad asked her about the bandage over dinner. Laney had every intention of talking to him about the events in the pantry, but not in front of the kids. She planned on leaving as soon as her car was ready. Ray would throw a fit, but she had no choice. She only hoped the coffee can offer was still on the table.

"What are you doing?" Faith looked up at her, somehow appearing unamused, while also wearing a bubble beard.

Laney held up the magazine. "I'm reading."

"This is my bath time," Faith said. A white glob of bubbles dropped from the chin of her very serious face.

"Oh, are you taking a bath? I didn't notice."

Pete finished putting away the leftovers while Laney started the bubble bath for Faith. Then he grabbed a couple of cold beers and took them out to the porch. Ray followed him out, sat on the steps, his face stuck in his phone. The boy had been his shadow all day, and he didn't mind that at all, not at all. But he needed to talk to Laney alone.

"Aren't you tired of me yet?" Pete asked.

Ray didn't take the hint. "Nah, grandpa. You're okay."

"Thanks, I guess, but why don't you skedaddle for a while? I need to talk to your mom about something."

"What's up, dad?" Laney asked, opening the screen door.

"That was a quick bath."

"She's still up there." Laney gave a nervous glance towards the stairs behind her. "Apparently, I don't give my children enough privacy."

Ray grunted.

Laney sat next to Pete, angling herself on the step, so she could steal another glance through the screen. He handed her a beer, then shooed Ray with a nod. The boy sighed and left the porch, heading around the side of the house.

"Where are you going?" Pete had expected him to go inside.

Ray shrugged. "I'm skedaddling. Whatever the hell that is."

"Don't go too far," Laney said. "You don't know your way around here. And stay away from the farm equipment."

Pete couldn't see it, but was sure the boy just rolled his eyes at his mother.

"Listen to your mother. It gets dark fast around here." Pete called after him, watching him go. "And stay out of the woods." Thoughts of the last time he searched the woods for a missing boy invaded his head. He had to get them to the hotel sooner rather than later. "I mean it."

"We need to talk," Laney said as Ray turned out of sight.

Pete turned back to his daughter, shaking his head to clear the ghosts of the past.

"Yeah, we do," he said. "I've been thinking about our visitors yesterday. Maybe you should take the kids into town and stay at the hotel for a few days. There probably won't be any trouble, but I don't want to put the kids through any more."

"What's in the pantry?" Laney asked. "It's why we left, isn't it? Me and Philip and Mom. Are my kids in danger?"

Pete's eyes shot to the bandage on her wrist. Dragging them away, he looked down at his beer. He'd hoped this talk wouldn't be necessary. That it wouldn't come to this.

"How much do you remember about the time just before you left with your mother?"

"Not a lot. I remember our dog, Goldy. And Philip's friend went missing, right? Does this have something to do with him?"

It made sense that Janice never told her about it. He wouldn't have either. Laney was so young at the time. They tried to protect her from it all. And, ultimately, they decided there was only one way left to protect their children. Pete still loved his wife. He missed her every day, and never once blamed her for getting remarried. He only wished he could have gone with his family when they left and put this place far behind him. His chest got tight, thinking about the conversation ahead of him.

He opened his mouth to speak, but the shrill, mechanical ring of the rotary phone in the kitchen interrupted him.

"I better get that." Pete stood.

"Dad, I need to know—"

The phone rang again.

"I know. We'll talk, but this could be about the radiator." He said over his shoulder as he opened the screen door. It wasn't about the Radiator. He talked to Henry that morning. The part would be in on Friday. But he needed a few minutes to get his head straight. He wasn't sure either of them was ready for this conversation.

"Fine. Whatever. I'll go check on Faith." Laney followed him into the house.

He picked up the phone on the fourth ring. "Hello."

"Philip, he...he..." Pete barely recognized Ellen's voice. His daughter-in-law never called. The fist clenching his chest gripped tighter.

"Ellen, what's wrong with Philip?"

25

Whats Wrong

Laney heard Pete and came into the kitchen with the same question on her face that screamed in his head. He prepared himself for the worst, waiting an eternity for Ellen to answer.

"That bastard assaulted him. It's bad. He's in surgery now. His brain is bleeding, Pete. Bleeding! His face... oh my god his face...." Her voice cracked, then drifted off into silence.

Pete closed his eyes, relieved for a moment despite the gravity of the news. His boy was still alive.

"What happened?" he asked, holding the phone away from his ear so Laney could hear too and immediately regretted it.

"It wasn't enough for your daughter to mess up her life. She had to drag us into it too." Ellen's voice had a new energy to it, fueled by anger. Pete tried to pull the phone back to his ear, but Laney put her hand on his arm, stopping him.

"I told Philip we should cut ties with her after she finally came back for her kids, but he wouldn't listen. Now he's getting his head cut open with a saw all because she-"

"Oh, my god. Troy." Laney said. The blood drained from her face.

Ellen must have heard her. "Is she there?" Ellen asked, her voice rising hysterically. "This is your fault! Do you hear me? Do you-"

Pete turned away, shrugging off Laney's hand, and pulled the phone back to his ear.

A man's voice had joined Ellen's on the other end. "Mrs. Girard, calm down. Calm down. Let's get you a cup of tea." The voice drifted away, along with Ellen's sobbing. Someone new picked up the phone.

"Who am I speaking with?" a woman asked.

"Pete Killian, I'm Philip's father. Is he going to be alright?"

"He's in surgery right now, Mr. Killian." the woman said. "I can leave a note for the doctor to call you once he's out."

"Yes, please do. What hospital is this?" Pete brought the handset back to his ear, then grabbed a worn pencil stub hanging on a string next to the phone. He jotted down the information on a yellow pad stuck to the wall. Before he hung up, Pete had one more question.

"When was my son attacked?"

The woman told him. Pete thanked her, gave her his number, then tried to hide the shaking in his hand as he hung up the phone. He turned to Laney. She paced, her face pale, eyes unfocused. He could tell she was spiraling into guilt, all the ways this was her fault coursing through her head.

"Don't." his voice quivered.

"Don't what?" she asked. "Don't blame myself? Who else is there?"

"Don't wallow." Pete snapped, and he saw her flinch. She probably expected him to tell her it wasn't her fault, to console her. It wasn't her fault, but he didn't have time for this shit right now. Neither did she.

"Troy attacked Philip to find you."

Laney winced, his words cutting deep.

"Whether it's true or not, Troy attacked Philip to find you and Philip told him where you are. Do you understand?" He took her shoulders, stopping her mid pace, then looked her in the eyes. He needed this to get through to her. "We can't hope that he didn't. Our reality has to be that Philip told him how to find the farm and that you were coming here."

"Philip didn't know where I was going. He didn't know anything. He didn't even answer the phone."

Of course, he didn't. The self centered little shit.

The guilt came as soon as the thought formed. He turned away from Laney and wiped the beginnings of tears from his eyes. He loved his son even if he barely knew the man he had become. Philip had been the sweetest child, always gentle, always smiling. This place ruined him. Jeremiah had tested the boy and found Philip weak. Then he tormented the kid until Janice took him away. Pete never should've brought him here. He pictured him now—not the man, but the kind, intelligent boy—lying on an operating table, the bloody blade of a saw cutting through his skull. Pete clenched his fist until his swollen finger joints throbbed to force the image away. He didn't have time for his own guilt, either. "Doesn't matter. Don't try to apply reason to this. We can't afford to be wrong."

"What are you not telling me?"

Pete turned back to face his daughter.

"He attacked Philip last night", he told her, his jaw clenching as the words came out of his mouth. He couldn't help but imagine the violence of what this man had put both his children through. "We have to assume Troy is here already."

"We have to get Ray and get out of here," she said.

"No. We get Ray, but we're not leaving." Rage pushed aside all the reasons he had to send Laney and the kids away. "Let Troy come."

The sudden sound of heavy rain filled the hall. Laney turned to him, and he saw his own confusion mirrored back at him.

26

Cool Toys

A horseshoe shape clearing carved into the forest behind the house. Ray couldn't believe it took him two days to actually go back there and check it out. Just past the barn, a small fenced-in field struggled to contain an overgrown meadow of grass and wildflowers. He'd seen it a bunch of times going in and out of the barn, but he somehow missed the dozens of butterflies flitting around the field before. Faith would go nuts for this. He took a few photos to show her, but they didn't do it justice. He decided it would be better to just bring her back here and show her in person. Maybe tomorrow.

In the center of the clearing, a large angled roof supported by thick posts created what looked like an open air garage. It covered a tractor, equipment hidden beneath tarps, and something that looked like the tail end of a dump truck, combined with a machine that looked part wood chipper and part hair clippers from hell.

Supported by chunky tires on both sides, lay a row of yellow, claw like, tines. On top of the row of tines sat double stacks of circular toothed blades, the size of garbage can lids. The blades looked like they spun in opposing directions, tearing apart whatever was unlucky enough to get pushed through the tines and sucked in between the whirling blades.

"Grandpa has the best toys." Ray squatted in front of the machine, trying to get a low angle to make the blades look more menacing. Switching the camera mode on his phone, his face popped up on the screen with the machine looming large behind him. He forced his grin away and took on an exaggerated look of fear for the selfie. Then, he posted it with the caption, "Think I should get a trim?"

His mom would have a shit fit if she knew he was on social media, but only his friends knew how to find him.

He stood, turned in a circle, looking for the next cool thing to take a pic of, but it seemed the tour was over already. Lame.

Then his eyes went to the woods behind the house. Since he got here, two people had told him not to go into those woods. And according to Angela, Jeremiah, who haunted the farm, had once murdered a kid in those very woods.

The temptation was too much.

27

The Bath

Laney and her father rushed into the hall and looked up at the waterfall flowing down between the balusters of the railing upstairs. The water splattered into a growing puddle on the hardwood floor in front of them with such a force it left a fine mist hanging in the air. A second stream cascaded down the steps.

"Faith!" Laney took off, splashing up the stairs, her father right behind her.

A constant stream of water gushed out from under the bathroom door, covering the landing. The blunted clamor of muffled cries and chaotic splashing came from the other side.

Laney ran to the door, turned the knob and pushed in one move, but she bounced back when the door didn't budge. She twisted the knob again. It moved freely. The door wasn't locked, but no matter how hard Laney pushed, it didn't give.

Pete pushed her aside and slammed his shoulder up against the door. The hall resounded with the crack of splintering wood, but the door stood strong. He hit it again and again, grunting with each impact. The hinges creaked, but the hits had no effect.

He ran to his bedroom.

Laney stepped in to fill the space he left behind, hammering on the door with both fists. "Faith! Answer me," she yelled, her voice shrill with panic. The only response came in the form of gurgling and splashing as water continued to flow from beneath the door in waves. She backed up, giving herself room to kick, but the barrel of a shotgun swung down in front of her, like the barrier arm at a parking garage.

The gun caught her off guard, and it took a few seconds to comprehend what it was for. She shoved the barrel away, and spun, planting her back against the wooden door, blocking it with her body. "No. You'll hit Faith."

He shook his head. "Its not loaded. Move!"

With blind trust, Laney got out of the way. As soon as she moved, Pete stepped up, holding the shotgun with both hands. Then, he drove it butt first into the doorknob, snapping the handle off in one blow. He shoved against the door again. Still, it didn't budge.

Dropping to his knees, he peeked through the open hole where the knob used to be.

It happened so fast.

Like a bolt of lightning struck him, he flung himself backwards, hitting the railing so hard it shuddered with his impact. He sat there, eyes squeezed shut, hands smashed against his ears.

All at once, the bathroom went silent.

The ebb of water from under the door slowed to a stop, and the only sound came from somewhere deep within her father, a gut wrenching moan.

Laney's throat constricted, barely letting any air through, but she didn't care. She didn't need air anymore. Her heart was gone. The moaning coming from her father told her so.

When the door creeped open a few inches, she involuntarily took a step back. "No," she said, the word barely a whisper. The room she was so desperate to get into only seconds ago had become the last room she ever wanted to enter.

But she had to.

She pushed the door open, stepped into the room, a room with nowhere to hide, and found only Faith. A crown of blond hair poked up through the blanket of thick white bubbles. The blue plastic sofa floated nearby, overturned in the suds. For seconds that felt like years, she stood there, willing herself to move, but frozen by the scene in front of her. She knew that her next move would release time, and once timed marched forward, there would be no turning back. The nightmare in front of her would become reality.

A single drop of water finally lost its grip on the rim of the tub spout and splashed down, popping the tiny bubbles in its path with a soft hiss.

That was all the trigger she needed. Like a starting pistol went off, Laney lunged for the tub, shoved her hands into the water, and pulled up her daughter's body.

Faith came up with chipmunk cheeks and expelled a loud whoosh of air, flattening them, wafting bubbles around her head.

"Moooom," Faith whined, wiping the water from her face. "You ruined it. I was almost up to a whole minute."

Laney dropped to her knees, pulled her daughter tight against her, and hugged her hard, finally able to breathe again.

Afraid to tempt fate by shouting them, the words came out a whisper, "she's okay." Laney looked at her father, tears rolling down her cheeks, and nodded, reassuring him, and maybe herself too, that this was real. "She's okay."

Her father returned a weak smile, tears in his eyes. Then she saw it.

The floor in the hall, the bathroom, everywhere but the splash zone of the tub was dry.

28

The Woods

Ray stood at the tree line in front of a patch of undergrowth that didn't look too thick and glanced back at the house to make sure no one was watching. The porch was empty. Grinning, he turned back to the woods and marched right through the ferns. He made it about five feet before the vines, sporting half-inch long, needle sharp thorns hidden beneath the leafy plants, forced him back. He did a hopping trot out of the woods. The last few vines, reluctant to give up their prey, clung until the last step, then sprang back into the shadows under the ferns. Hissing air through his teeth, he wiped the blood from his stinging calves. Spreading blots of red bloomed on his white socks.

Maybe shorts and a t-shirt were not the best choice for exploring haunted woods.

But he wasn't ready to turn back. He didn't know what grown up conversation his grandpa wanted to have with his mom, but he knew those types of talks dragged on. Part of him thought he should be worried that Grandpa wanted them to leave. But he just couldn't reconcile that with how it felt hanging with him. He never thought he would have such a good time with an old man, but his grandpa was cool, like legitimately cool. Grandpa didn't try to be a tough guy like dad. He didn't have to. Grandpa *was* tough, but he was also chill. And it wasn't just that, Ray got the sense that Grandpa needed them, as much as they needed a place to crash.

Unless, of course, Grandpa decided he didn't need kids who don't listen to him, and sent them packing.

But Ray wouldn't have to worry about getting caught in the woods if he couldn't find a way in. He walked the curve of the tree line around to the other side, finding no path. The few semi-clear areas were carpeted with innocent looking ferns, but he wasn't dumb enough to fall for that again.

Stumped, he turned towards the house, ready to cut back across the clearing, a little relieved if he was being honest. But the idea of just giving up didn't sit right with him. He was the kind of gamer who found every ammo stash and left no inch of the map undiscovered. He spun back towards the woods and walked backwards. Maybe it was because the sun was lower in the sky, or because he looked at it from another angle. But Ray saw a path in the woods that he had missed before, not too far from where he had started. It almost directly lined up with the steps off the back porch, hidden behind a few feet of dense undergrowth.

Careful to not plow through thorns again, Ray made his way past the vegetation, using a stick to push any vines away, until he reached the path. About three feet wide, it was clear of underbrush, with the occasional root jutting out of the ground. After almost becoming a smear on the grill of a tractor trailer thanks to one of those roots, he made a mental note to watch out for them.

The path curved through the forest, trees on either side obscuring what lay ahead. It was darker under the canopy of leaves, but still plenty of light to see by. He was no boy scout, but thought he'd have at least an hour of sunlight left to explore. Worst-case scenario, he'd have the flashlight on his phone.

A quick chill ran up his spine at the thought of being alone in the woods after dark. He ignored it. He had no intention of being like his mom, and let every little thing scare him. After setting an alarm on his phone, a reminder to turn back, he started down the path.

Ray held his phone in front of him, recording as he made his way along the path. He bent his knees as he walked, trying to keep his head level to stabilize the video.

His friends were going to love this.

I bet they've never been anywhere like this.

The woods lining the path were dense with trees and thickly packed underbrush. Dappled sunlight poked through the canopy above him, its golden glow swallowed by the greenish cast of ambient light filtered through the leaves. The path itself meandered, but was an easy and inviting walk.

He flicked the selfie button with his thumb, swapping to the front camera. His smirking face filled the screen.

"Just your everyday creepy path through the woods in the middle of nowhere. Let's see where it gooo-" Ray's voice pitched high in surprise as his foot caught on a tree root and he stumbled forward, almost dropping the phone. Taking it in stride, he recovered his balance, then re-centered the camera on his sheepish grin.

"I totally meant to do that," he said, while shaking his head no. "Ah, I'll probably edit that out."

A practiced flick of his thumb and the camera faced forward again. He watched through the screen as he rounded a turn in the path that opened to a clearing.

"No way! This is awesome!"

Centered in the clearing was a massive oak tree. The trunk, bulging and gnarled, as thick as a roided up sumo, climbed higher than everything around it. Ridges, the size of smaller trees, bulged like permanently flexed cords of muscle. Dark branches stretched out thick and twisted in all directions, creating a canopy over the clearing. Enormous roots swelled from the ground, spreading out from the center, and disappeared into the woods, leaving only one patch of dirt unscathed. The tree owned the space. Nothing could grow beneath it.

But, as much as its size conveyed power, the tree looked sickly. Like its strength was just a front and its core was rotten. The leaves were a dull grayish-green, mottled with spots. Its bark was dark gray with amber patches of dead moss. Ray's nose wrinkled at the dank smell as soon as he stepped into the open space.

Lurking beneath the tree's shadow was the object of Ray's excitement. A large, ornate tombstone stood sentinel over the hard crusted earth, the only patch of ground not invaded by tree roots. Instead, the roots wound their way around it, cradling the grave.

But it wasn't just any grave. Angela was going to freak.

Aiming his phone at the headstone, Ray creeped towards it for effect. It was darker under the tree than the rest of the woods, and he had to turn on the light to make out the words carved into the stone beneath the engraving of an oak tree with the head of an angled scythe below it. Weathered etches of swirling leaves created a border around the words, and along the edges of the stone.

"Here lies Jeremiah Killian. Soldier. Farmer. Patriarch. 1911 - 1998. May he never be forgotten. Hi, great, great, grandpa. I heard all about you."

He couldn't wait to show this to Angela. He thought about the stories she told him, about the trespasser and the dead kid they found not far from here. Standing in this space, next to the man's grave, it was easy to imagine how the stories spread.

There was something off about this place, and it wasn't just the grave and the dank smell. He suddenly realized how quiet it was here. The woods were silent, as if his presence was unwelcome.

Like he was trespassing.

And we all know how you feel about trespassers.

He shivered as a chill ran up his spine.

"Someone must have stepped on my grave." He laughed until he realized his foot was planted firmly on Jeremiah's. He took a quick hop off to the side.

Wanting to get more footage before he had to go, he spun a slow circle, letting the camera take in the whole clearing, starting at the narrow path he had entered from, then turned towards the tree. The phone light reflected off of the dark sap, oozing through grooves cut by the grain of the bark. Then he turned towards the grave, half expecting to find it disturbed. To find Jeremiah's rotting hand jutting from the dirt as he clawed his way out. As the tombstone came into view, the phone alarm went off.

He jumped, almost dropping the phone again.

Ray laughed, feeling like an idiot. He wasn't sure what scared him more. Coming face to face with his long dead great, great grandpa—the boogyman of West Mills himself—or breaking his phone.

The alarm meant it was time to turn back if he hoped to make it back to the house before the sun went down, and hopefully before anyone noticed he was gone.

"Just one more pic, before I go."

Switching the camera back to selfie mode, he switched off the flashlight, then wrapped one arm around the tombstone in a half hug. Grinning, he held his phone arm out as far as he could to get as much of the scene in behind him as possible. The flash blinded him for a second and he had to wait for his eyes to re-adjust to the gloom before checking the picture.

"This is so cool."

His friends, stuck in the city in the sweltering heat, were definitely going to be jealous. Ray uploaded the photo, then labeled the post, "hanging with great, great grandpa."

He was about to put his phone away when he noticed something shiny in the picture's background. Like the glint of metal. Pumped at the prospect of discovering even more cool stuff, he zoomed in.

I might have to come back here tomorrow. Earlier though.

The glint was just a pointy shape shining through some leaves. A red circle stuck out above it. He pinched his fingers on the screen, and zoomed out a little, searching the surrounding leaves, trying to get more context. There was something not far below the circle, barely visible through a gap in the leaves. It looked like...teeth.

Heart thumping, he spun around, turned his flashlight on, and aimed the light into the brush.

There was nothing there, but Ray was all too happy to head back to the farmhouse.

29

Six Pack

Troy beaned the empty beer can off the hotel room wall. He watched the cans progress past the fleshy overhang currently invading his view. His mangled nose had darkened to an overripe shade of plum, and his eyelids, a shade darker than his nose, had thickened to the point they intruded on the edges of his vision. The can rebounded against the curtains, then hit the floor with a ding, joining the other empties.

How the fuck did everything go so wrong?

When that pussy ass Philip hit the ground, he knocked himself out cold. Troy couldn't bring him to. He tried to slap him awake, but Philip just laid there, blood streaming out of his nose. The blood in his mouth bubbled back up as Philip tried to breathe. Troy had to roll him on his side so the fucker wouldn't drown before he found out what he needed to know.

Philip had smashed his face up good. He must have skidded after he hit. A concrete rash had taken a couple of layers of skin, starting at the forehead, down to his chin, off the left side of his face and nose. Jagged edges of broken teeth shredded his lower lip. The blood and drool pouring out slowed as his face swelled right in front of Troy's eyes. Philip would be eating out of a straw for a long time, but that was no consolation. Troy needed info.

After the shit went down at the apartment, Troy took off before the cops got there, but he didn't go too far. When things calmed down, he watched the building, waiting for Laney's friend to show. Women tell each other everything. That bitch probably knew where Laney was going. Hell, she probably even gave his wife the wad of cash Troy found in her bag, something he would make her regret. But after a day of waiting around, the bitch never showed.

He tried calling the number on the paper wrapped around the cash. But Troy hung up after a deep voice spit out a gruff, "Hello".

He needed a new source of info.

No one from the old neighborhood had kept in touch with Laney, and he knew her mother was dead. Her stepfather too. That left big brother Philip. So, Troy stole himself a car, and had a little road trip to New York. Philip was Troy's next-to-last connection to Laney. And he was pretty sure his last connection had been cut by now.

When slapping Philip didn't wake the fucker up, Troy tried pissing on him for old times' sake. He couldn't hold back the smile, listening to Philip gurgle when he got some of the stream into his brother-in-law's swollen mouth, but it did nothing to bring Philip around.

Fuck.

Troy paced, his fists shaking. If Philip had been a man and faced him—he'd still end up on the ground, gurgling in a puddle of his own blood. But then Troy would know where his wife was and would've had the satisfaction of putting Phillip there.

On impulse, his foot shot out, connecting with Philip's head and sending a bolt of pain through Troy's bad knee on contact. He screamed. A guttural stream of nonsense echoed through the garage while he limped around in a circle, trying to shake the pain off.

As the throbbing in his knee died down, his fury grew. When he could put weight on the knee again, he used his good leg to stomp Philip. After crunching some ribs, he went back to work on Philip's head. Each blow made his bad knee flare up again, adding fuel to the fire. Troy probably wouldn't have felt satisfied until Philip was nothing but pulp staining the concrete.

He never found out. The sound of a car thumping over a seam in the concrete a few floors above was his cue to leave.

Limping his way down the stairwell, he got a good look at his clothes in the fluorescent light. Blood splattered his pants and shoes.

Could this fucking day get any worse?

He swiped some unattended clothes from a nearby laundromat, then hunted for another car. It was only a matter of time before his face got blasted out to patrol cars. And between the burn on his cheek and his mangled nose, he'd be easy to notice.

Troy had made it a point to confront Philip in a place away from cameras, but once his brother-in-law took off running, the thought of staying obscure went straight out of his mind. Chances were he was on camera somewhere, either in the garage or in the stairwell. He needed to put some distance between him and New York before someone checked the footage. Not knowing what else to do, he drove back to Pennsylvania, hoping that would put him closer to Laney. How far could she get without any money?

Troy ditched the car before burning some of the cash on a cheap hotel room. He bought a six-pack, ibuprofen, and some food at a convenience store nearby. Then he went back to the motel to lie low. When the following day came with no inspiration for where to look next, Troy got the room for another day. Another six pack, more junk food and cable TV. Compared to how he spent the past seven years, this was living like a king. But Troy couldn't enjoy it. Down to his last twenty bucks, he'd have to move on tomorrow, and he didn't know where to.

He swallowed four ibuprofen, washed them down with a mouthful of beer. It helped take the edge off his knee and manage the swelling of his face.

His unfocused eyes landed on the wall past the television, watching the show in his head instead of the crap on the screen. It was a good episode. All about payback and plenty of not so gratuitous violence. He was just getting to the scene where Laney got what was coming to her when a notification chime sounded from the phone in his pocket.

That could only mean one thing. Troy checked his phone, then broke into a grin.

His wife had cut all ties with Chicago, but Ray hadn't. His chest warmed with pride.

My boy doesn't cut and run on friends.

He busted out laughing at Ray's photo with the combine and couldn't help but admire what a good-looking boy he had become. Like father, like son. Ray would turn some heads soon enough. Troy had so many things to teach him before then. The first thing—window shop. Never buy.

Troy got his son's social media accounts from the son of a friend in the old neighborhood. Ray had re-connected with the boy last year when he got his first cell phone. That's how Troy found them in Philly. And that's how he'd find them now. He knew Laney lived on her family's farm in Pennsylvania when she was a kid, and that her real dad was still there, if he hadn't croaked yet. Now he knew she had taken them back to that farm.

The wind went out of his sails when he realized Philip was the only one who could tell him where the farm actually was. Pennsylvania was a big state and Troy didn't have a clue where to start, except that the farm was in the northern half of the state. He couldn't even look up her father. He had no idea what the man's name was. When Laney's mom got remarried, both Laney and Philip took their stepdad's last name.

Shit out of luck and beer, he wound up his arm, but stopped just short of throwing the phone against the dingy concrete wall. He settled on letting loose a string of obscenities instead.

The restraint paid off. A half an hour went by and Troy was thinking about spending that last twenty on another six-pack when the phone chimed again. His face split into a grin when he saw Ray's latest post—the photo of his son smiling next to the tombstone of Jeremiah Killian. The browser search for "Killian Farm" pulled up an old story about a missing boy in a town called West Mills. A town in North Western Pennsylvania.

"Rayban my man."

30

Skittish

Laney watched her father through the arches from the living room while she towel dried Faith's hair. The little girl sat on the arm of the couch, eyes glued to the television, the bathroom drama already forgotten. And why wouldn't it be? For her daughter, the drama ended at a missed personal best in bubble bath breath holding. Not the dread of losing a child.

Her father was a million miles away. He stared out into space while loading his shotgun at the kitchen table. Muscle memory guiding his hands, one by one, each cartridge, a white plastic casing with a brass head, slid smoothly into the chamber with a snick.

Laney handed Faith the towel, kissed her daughter on the top of her head, and joined her father in the kitchen. She nodded at the shotgun. "I don't want you to take that."

"It's just rock salt. It won't kill him." The corner of his mouth curled up. "Probably."

"I'm not worried about Troy. I'm worried about Ray."

Her father's face paled at the sound of his grandson's name, and he gave her a reassuring nod. "Don't worry. I'm not skittish." But his hand betrayed his words by shaking as he loaded the next round.

The incident with Faith shook him. Laney couldn't blame him. She

144

had to fight back tears every time the image of her daughter floating face down in the tub barged into her mind, and it did that a lot, without warning. There was something bad on this farm. Something worse than Troy. Whatever it was, her father had lived with it for years, seemingly without trouble. But today it got to him, and that scared her more than anything. He looked a decade older than he did just an hour ago. The facade of stern determination on his pale, ragged face couldn't hide his fear. It was such a stark difference from his normal state that he might as well be shouting from the rooftop that he was scared as hell.

Outside, the warm oranges of sunset had cooled to shadowy blues. Every second that Ray was out there alone gave her a micro panic attack. Her father wasn't up to this, and she couldn't wait any longer.

She grabbed the flashlight off the table.

"Keep my daughter safe."

Laney didn't look back. She didn't want to waste time arguing. She needed to find her son.

Now.

Grandpa was right. It got dark real fast. Ray could still see a faint blue above, in gaps between leaves, but little of that light survived the fall to the forest floor.

He made his way along the path, that was a whole lot more narrow than he remembered. He couldn't escape the suffocating smell from the clearing. It followed him, clinging to his clothes, and it was easy to imagine the branches of the oak trailing behind him. Bony fingers covered in oozing bark stretching along the path, reaching for him, ready to snatch him and drag him back to the clearing where Jeremiah waited fresh from the grave.

Something rustled behind him, and he spun, shining his phone light on an empty path that lead to darkness. Wriggling darkness. He could just make out the movement in the black beyond his light.

Stop it. Stop messing with your own head. There's nothing there.

He turned back, picking up the pace.

What seemed like an adventure in the daylight suddenly seemed like a really stupid idea in the dark. The woods felt like they were closing in on him. And, though he was sure he was mistaken about there being a man in the photo, he didn't bother to check again to confirm it. He just wanted to get back to the house.

The path made a turn through the trees, and he followed it,

pushing through the brush on either side. This couldn't be the same path he took earlier. It never got this tight at any point. He'd remember.

What if this path didn't lead to the house at all? What if it went deeper into the woods?

He wondered if he should turn around, but that dry rustling sound came from behind him again. And his mind's eye saw Jeremiah's long dead corpse, shuffling through the woods, hunting him down.

Just keep going.

Easier said than done. The surrounding woods got closer, the vegetation thicker. Thorny vines tore at his ankles, forcing him to disentangle himself every few steps. He ripped the vines away with bleeding hands, then stomped the plants into the ground in frustration.

This way will take forever.

He turned to go back the other way, and froze, a sudden weight sitting heavy in the pit of his stomach.

There was no path.

Thigh high undergrowth of withered vines and their sharp, glistening thorns wound through the rotting vegetation filling the spaces between the trees. Confused, he spun, trying to find the opening he had just walked through, knowing it had to be there. But the forest had closed in on him in every direction. Even the path forward.

The rustling came again, crackling and dry, creeping whispers all around him. Then the worst thing that could happen happened. His phone battery died, and with it, the light.

31

Revenge

The sun dipped below the horizon, casting everything in a murky blue glow. Johnny led the way down the driveway, doing a half jog, sticking close to the corn. Buster crouch ran behind him, keeping his head below the top of the ears. If someone in the house wandered out onto the front porch, they'd need to duck into the field, or they'd be spotted in the dim light.

"It's still kind of early. Shouldn't we wait until they're asleep?" Buster asked.

"I need to pick up Cheryl in an hour." Johnny said. "We'll be quiet. It will be fine."

"You know, you could just take my car."

"That would look great. Wouldn't it? Me showing up in my little brother's car."

Buster snickered at the word *little*. He'd been doing that every time Johnny referred to him as his little brother, ever since he turned sixteen and sprouted into a freak of nature.

Johnny shot him a look. "Don't even start."

They reached the end of the drive and squatted down to scope out the house. Voices came from the kitchen. Occasionally someone passed in front of the window, the daughter from the looks of it. Word around town was Pete's daughter came home. Just showed up out of nowhere. It was perfect timing, as far as Johnny was concerned. Nothing like a little family drama to keep Pete distracted while he and Buster liberate his truck.

They got real low, turned the corner, still sticking to the edge of the field, and made their way towards the barn. Johnny slapped at a mosquito on his arm, forgetting about the bandage where that stalk whacked him because his brother couldn't keep the damn car straight. He sucked in the pain with a hiss.

All this over money. That's what really pissed him off. Pete knew he was good for it, but he just had to show off and be the tough guy in front of his family.

When they got to the barn doors, Buster pushed the left door open a foot, cringing at the sharp cry of the hinges. They quickly squeezed in through the narrow opening, and Johnny hung back a bit, peeking out to see if anyone heard them. No one looked out the window, and the front door stayed shut. It seemed they were in the clear.

Johnny turned on his phone light and looked around for his keys. It didn't take long to find them. They hung on a nail over the workbench just inside the door.

So much for security. Any asshole could've come in here and stole my truck.

He tried to imagine the look on Pete's face when he heard the truck tearing down the drive to the tune of two hundred bucks, and realized it probably wouldn't look much different from Pete's normal face. It was like pulling teeth to get a rise out of that man. His eyes landed on a hunting knife, sheathed and hanging on the pegboard over the workbench. He pulled it down and unsheathed the long blade, admiring the glint of its edge in his phone light.

"What the hell are you doing?" Buster asked. "You got the keys. Let's go."

"Pete needs to understand he can't fuck with me," Johnny said. He crouched next to the front tire of Laney's car and jabbed it hard with the blade. The knife bounced right off the sidewall, and fell out of Johnny's hand, landing point down, inches from his boot. Buster covered his mouth with his hand and snickered.

Johnny's blood boiled. From the heat in his face, he knew his cheeks were bright red, and that pissed him off even more. He picked up the knife and stabbed again, this time pushing his weight behind it, driving the blade home with a gratifying hiss.

He moved to the next tire, and readied the knife, but Buster grabbed his arm before he could stab it into the sidewall.

"Stop!" Buster whispered. Grabbing at Johnny's phone with the other hand and blocking the light.

Johnny tried to shrug him off. "Get the fuck off of me."

"Shut up", Buster hissed through clenched teeth. "Someone's coming!"

Johnny moved to peek out the door, with Buster right behind him. They watched the woman they had seen on the porch earlier, Pete's daughter, walk past with a flashlight in her hand. She must have sensed them watching her with that woman's intuition shit that chicks have, because she swung her beam in their direction. Johnny ducked back fast, expecting to bump into Buster, but he wasn't there.

The woman took a step towards the barn and called, "Ray?"

He waited until the light swung away, then peeked out again to watch the woman walk towards the back of the house. Once she was far enough, he turned on his phone light and swung it around, looking for his brother. Pete kept the barn neat. A place for everything and everything in its place. That left little room for someone Buster's size to hide.

Where the hell did he go?

Motion—a disturbance in the shadows—caught his eye near the partition at the rear of the barn.

"What are you doing?" he asked in a low voice. The only response was the muffled sound of Buster laughing. "Knock it off! We don't have time for this shit!"

Johnny walked back there fuming.

"I swear to god, if you're actually trying to scare me right now, I'm going to kill you."

When he rounded the partition, he stopped dead in his tracks.

Buster hadn't been laughing at him. His little brother stood tall and stiff in the light from Johnny's phone. His shoulders pulled back, fists clenched, arms straight at his sides. The gnarled fingers of an emaciated hand covered Buster's mouth, stifling his shuddering gasps. Its sickly, mottled skin glistened in the light. Johnny couldn't see who, or what, it belonged to with his brother in the way. One name came to the forefront of his mind, but that was just a stupid ghost story.

Besides, it didn't matter who it was. Nothing could scare him as much as the look of pure fear on Buster's face. He could hear his mother cackling at him as the warm liquid spread through the groin of his jeans.

The Super Soaker strikes again.

"Whoever the fuck you are, you let my brother go", he said, trying, and failing, to keep the quiver out of his voice. Then he remembered the knife. He pointed it in front of him, trying to look threatening despite his shaking hand. "I've got a fucking knife."

An anguished moan escaped Buster. Tears streamed down his face and his back curled into an arch, like a bow pulled taut. Gristly, wet sounds crackled from behind him. A spot appeared on Buster's chest, then spread, turning his white t-shirt red with a Rorschach of blood. The point of the blade followed, crunching as it pushed through Buster's breast bone until the blood-soaked steel glimmered in the light.

All the while, Buster's agonized moans, muffled by bony fingers, flooded Johnny's ears, drowning out the sound of his own pounding heart.

"So do I," the whispered voice behind his brother rasped unheard.

32

The Path

Passing the old goat pen on her left, Laney let her flashlight pass over the combine under the pole barn across from it. Distorted by the moving shadows, the cutter blades looked like giant gnashing teeth.

What was I thinking letting him explore?

There wasn't much else of interest to a twelve-year-old boy behind the house except the woods, and her father explicitly told Ray not to go into the woods.

Laney cut across the yard, heading for the path that led to the old graveyard in the forest. She had been there once with her brother when she was a kid, and vaguely remembered an enormous tree, and Philip scaring the crap out of her with his ghost stories.

Her father didn't like them being in the woods at all, unless he was with them. He always said it was too easy to get turned around, or walk off a cliff if you weren't paying attention. And after Philip's friend got lost, her parents laid down the law. No woods ever.

Philip.

The thought of her brother stopped her in her tracks. She had to close her eyes and try to force the image of what Troy had done to him from her imagination. If she had gone straight to the cops instead of running, Troy might be back in jail right now. But her only thoughts that night were to get her kids somewhere safe. It never occurred to her Troy would go after Philip. If her brother didn't make it, that was on her head.

No time for thinking like that. She had to focus on finding Ray.

She reached the head of the path. Thin, white birch trees growing at the edge of the forest stood stark against the beam of her flashlight, like skeletal sentinels guarding the entrance. The trail led deep into darkness. The gullet of the forest swallowed the light and everything that went down it. Troy could be in there with Ray right now. But given what she had seen in the house the past few days, her ex was not her biggest worry at the moment.

Laney took the path at a run, calling out her son's name.

33

Old Screams Die Hard

Pete sat at the kitchen table, a hot cup of coffee sitting next to the shotgun in front of him. He positioned himself so he could see Faith on the sofa in the living room. The little girl hugged a pillow to her chest as she watched television. Her eyes kept darting to the window leading to the porch outside. Whether she was hoping to see her mother return, or afraid her father might be there, Pete didn't know. He guessed both.

Like his granddaughter with the window, he found his eye drawn to the phone, waiting, with both dread and anticipation, for it to ring. His son hadn't become the man Pete hoped he'd be, and Pete understood his complicity in that. He carried that guilt every day. But Phillip didn't deserve what that piece of shit did to him. Nobody deserves that.

And now Laney and Ray were out there in the dark, maybe in danger, too. Driven back to this farm—and into his life—by the same man who tried to murder his son.

But Pete knew he'd be bullshitting himself if he tried to paint a line from the danger his family was in directly to Troy and end it there. That line went back a lot further. All the way back to the day, he brought his perfectly happy family to Killian Farm. The same farm that he had escaped from in the dead of night, and promised himself he'd never return to.

At the time, all of his reasons for leaving the farm and staying away were gone, or so he thought. Jeremiah, the monster of a man who made his life on the farm a living hell, had died. And Pete's parents, whom he loved and may have forgiven for not protecting him from Jeremiah, had they lived long enough, followed his grandfather a few months later. Their truck, piled high with everything they needed for a fresh start, plowed into a tree not twenty yards from the farm's property line.

He should have seen that as a sign, but he didn't want to stay in the army forever, and Janice was more than ready to put down roots. Knowing he couldn't have given them anything like the farm on a mechanic's salary, he agreed to come back. He had hoped he could finally put the past behind him and find peace here. And for the first six months, he did.

Janice fell in love with the farm the moment they arrived. She found beauty in every corner of the prison Pete grew up in, and she made it a home. The kids, who had spent their lives until then, moving from base to base, thrived in their newfound freedom and stability.

And without the heavy shadow of Jeremiah hanging over the place, it didn't take long for Pete to see the farm in a new light. The work suited him, and evenings with his family suited him even more. For a time, it was perfect, or so he thought. Until the day the Pennridge boy went missing.

Pete had been working on the tractor that afternoon, when Philip came stumbling from the woods, wild-eyed and white as a ghost. The boy's t-shirt was torn. Deep scratches gouged his skin, as if he'd been running through the underbrush. He wouldn't tell them what happened, just mumbled about getting turned around in the woods. It would take hours to get the truth out of him, and by then it was too late.

Later that night, they ate dinner in silence. Philip, his hair still wet from his bath, angry red scratches welled on his face, pushed his food around his plate while Janice watched him. The boy had barely spoken all day. For every question they asked, they got a shrug or a grunt in return.

Pete caught his wife's eye and gave her a warm smile. She smiled back, but he saw the worried creases around her eyes.

Laney ate her mac and cheese, oblivious to the tension at the table. One of the many benefits of being seven, Pete supposed. She finished her plate and took a sip of milk to wash down her last bite. "Is there dessert?"

"Yeah, sweety. Apple pie," Janice said, "I'll get it when everyone's finished."

The little girl perked up. "With ice cream?"

A tired but genuine smile lit Janice's face, probably in relief to have a little normalcy at the table. "What do you think?"

Laney grinned and rubbed her hands together, doing a little dance in her seat. "I think you can't have apple pie without ice cream." She turned to her big brother. "Where's Victor? He could have stayed for dinner and had some…" she sang the last two words, "apple pie."

The color drained from Philip's face. His lip trembled, and he looked down at his plate, unable to meet anyone's eyes. A fat tear drop splashed down next to a congealing mound of mac and cheese.

"He took him." Philip said, his voice not much more than a whisper.

Pete looked at Janice, then back to his son, an icy chill spreading through his gut. "Who took who?"

Janice's eyes narrowed. "Wait. Victor Pennridge? From school?"

Philip nodded, the tears now streaming down his face.

Pete dropped his fork on his plate. He leaned over and took Philip by his shoulders. "Listen to me carefully, son. Tell me the truth. Is there a boy from your school in the woods right now?"

Tight-lipped, and unable to meet his father's eyes, Philip nodded again.

"Is there someone in the woods with him?"

Another nod.

"Who?"

The boy finally looked up, anger burning through the tears. "You know who."

Pete let his son go, and stepped away from the table, fists clenching, over and over at his side.

"Why? Why didn't you say anything?" Janice asked, her face pale.

"He told me if I said anything, he'd do the same to me as he did to Goldy," Phillip whined to his mother.

Laney cried at the mention of Goldy. Pete knew his daughter still kept the dog's collar under her pillow.

He grabbed the flashlight from the cupboard and headed for the kitchen door.

Philip jumped up, grabbed his father's arm, and dug his feet in against the hardwood floor, trying to stop him from leaving. "You can't go. He'll kill you. He told me he would."

Pete took a deep breath, then gently removed Philip's hand, but he couldn't keep the anger out of his voice. "Son, Jeremiah is dead. He's gone. It doesn't matter what people say. He doesn't exist anymore. And Goldy got hit by a car. It was just an accident. That's all. Now I have to go find your friend because it's dark out there, and I'm sure he's very afraid right now."

He left his family to search for Victor.

Three days later, they retrieved the boy's body by the dark of night, and the screaming ended. In the woods, at least. Many times over the years, Pete bolted upright in bed, gasping for air with that god awful scream ringing in his ears. And he wasn't the only one. Those three days of searching haunted Henry and Kent too, and Pete wouldn't be surprised to find that every single person who had heard those screams had similar nightmares.

After Henry spotted the boy, Kent had gone for help and returned with Shawn and Clarke Tompkins. Their family owned the farm down the road. Word had been sent to the Sheriff, and Pete could already hear the voices in the woods getting closer, as the searchers convened on their location. The brothers met him and Henry halfway up the ridge and took over guiding the big man up the steep slope. Pete told them he needed a minute to rest. That he'd be right behind them.

He lied.

Pete may not have been the only person tormented by the screams after the search, but he was the only one to see the single word carved in the trunk of the sapling over Victor's body that night. He made sure of it. After Shawn and Clarke took over with Henry, Pete scrambled back to the body.

He pulled his t-shirt off and gently draped it over the boy's face. Then he took a sharp rock to the bark of the tree, and scraped the word away, trying to make it look like damage caused by Victor's fall.

Only one man would have left that there, but he was dead and gone. Pete couldn't comprehend the how of it anymore than he could explain the screaming, but he knew one thing for sure. If anyone else saw it, the suspicions going around town would be solidified. In everybody's eyes, he would be a killer.

So he erased the epitaph from the tree, but couldn't erase it from his memory. Sometimes he thought that was the start of it. The sin that began his downfall. The moment he scraped *trespasser* from the bark, when he hid the truth of what happened to the boy, his whole life began to unravel.

A scream broke his reverie and brought him back to the present.

34

The Mud

The dark was absolute.

Ray pushed his way blindly through sickly vegetation that seemed more rotten and slimy with each hard won foot he gained. Rather than being weakened by decay, the underbrush was tough and rubbery. It slid and stretched around him, and when he finally ripped through, it bled a putrid smelling slime. He was covered in the stuff, and it burned in every scrape and cut it oozed into.

But not as much as his leg muscles burned. The deeper he pushed through the rotten underbrush, the muddier the ground became. His feet sunk deep with each step. And to take the next step, he had to pry each foot free with a slurping release of vacuum. Then he'd clomp that foot, encased in mud, forward, feeling like he wore concrete shoes. So far, he still had both sneakers, but they were getting so heavy, he didn't think he would for long.

He had no idea how far he had gone since the phone died, or even what direction he was going in. Or if any direction ended in escape? It was like the cornfield all over again, only so much worse. He pictured being trapped there until someone stumbled upon his moldy bones. Barbed vines and decaying leaves sprouting up through his rib cage and out of his eye sockets.

A Chia pet from hell.

Pushing his right foot forward, created an opening in the vegetation. Like a starving dog finally thrown a scrap of food, he devoured the progress. He leaned into it, forced his leg through the bending branches, and tore at the vines around his chest. It all gave way at once, and he fell forward.

His arms, outstretched to stop his fall, sunk into deep, viscous mud, right up to his shoulders, and kept going until his face smacked down with a wet slap, before breaking the surface and sinking. The muck oozed into his open mouth, up his nose, and a bolt of panic ripped through him as it started making its way down his throat.

Arching his back and neck, pulling his head back as far as it could go, just freed his face from the mud. He was still chin deep, choking and gagging to expel the muck from his mouth with each ragged breath. His hands searched fruitlessly through the sludge for anything to grab onto, any way to push himself up. There was nothing. No tree roots. No bottom. Only mud.

His left leg was still in contact with the underbrush. He tried to tangle his foot through it for leverage, but the slimy foliage, that fought to hold on to him before, now slipped away with every twist of his foot.

The muscles in his neck and back screamed at the effort of keeping his head free, as he slowly sunk towards the inevitable. Soon his mouth would be in the mud again. Then his nose. Then all of him.

He didn't see a way out of this. His earlier thoughts of someone finding his bones seemed like a pipe dream now. Once the mud swallowed him, no one would ever find him. His mother would never know what happened to him.

This will kill her.

A far off voice called his name, her voice. He thought he'd imagined it until it came again.

Mom!

He tried to yell to her. But with his neck muscles pulled taut, he barely managed a grunt, and the effort left him choking.

Something moved in alongside of him. This time, he managed a whisper. "Mom?"

A putrid, icy breath brushed his face, triggering a gag reflex, and his throat spasmed, shooting bolts of pain through his ears.

"Your mother can't hear you." It was an ancient voice, dry and cracked, and though it only whispered, the sound reverberated through his skull, leaving terror in its wake.

A bony hand grasped the top of his head. Long fingernails bore into his scalp with excruciating slowness.

The hand pressed down. The mud climbed.

His body shook with exertion, fighting against the pressure. He tried to yell, but clamped his mouth shut when the mud climbed his chin. He flailed his arms in a desperate doggy paddle, to no effect.

His lungs worked overtime as he took panicked, rapid breaths through his nose. His heart thundered. Every nerve in his body surged, conducting the same message.

Don't die. Don't die. Don't die.

The mud reached his nose. He held his breath. Soon, his body clenched against the urge to breathe. Fireworks exploded behind eyelids, squeezed tight against the mud pressing up against them.

A low roar filled his ears as the cold sludge slurped its way in. The pounding of his heart became muffled and distant, a tiny sound, barely audible. His exhausted limbs stopped thrashing as adrenaline seeped away.

Don't...

The single bubble breached the thick surface and held. Excess liquid rolled off the fragile dome until only the thinnest layer of film was left to protect its precious cargo. The dome's surface tension weakened, its water molecules evaporating. Until, finally, the bubble popped, releasing Ray's last breath into the world.

The mud took him.

35

What Now?

The flashlight lit the way as Laney turned the last bend of the path and reached a clearing centered by a massive tree. Gagging on the smell of decay, she painted the clearing with the light in a frantic search, but Ray wasn't there.

Taking a deep breath, she turned a slow circle, running the beam along the edges of the clearing, looking to see if the path continued anywhere, but there was only one way in and out.

A dead end.

She pushed down the rising panic and looked for the source of the smell. Her mind tried to torture her with the image of her son's decaying body, but that wasn't possible. He had only been gone less than an hour. And it didn't take long to realize the smell was coming from the tree. Shining the light on the massive trunk showed a dark, viscid sap, glistening in the light, covering the bark like sweat.

She swung the beam in a slow, sweeping motion below the tree, searching for any sign that her son had been there. Her light fell on the tombstone, marking the grave of her great grandfather, and a fresh worm of unease wriggled in her gut. She remembered the name carved into it from when she was a kid. She had heard it spoken in hushed whispers behind her back at school, and from Philip's ghost stories.

Jeremiah.

Footprints marked the ground in front of the stone. Ray's footprints. Hoping to find a continuation of his prints to indicate the direction he might have gone, she swept the flashlight around the grave. But roots permeated the ground around the clearing.

She got the sense something was watching her, and shone the light up into the branches, scanning the shadows in the thick canopy of mottled leaves. There was nothing there. Still, the tree pulled at her as if she missed something dangerous. Like an antelope that caught the scent of a lion but couldn't spot it. She worried the moment she looked away it would slink from its hiding spot, and make its move.

A grunt came from the underbrush to her left. She swung the beam towards it, ignoring the instinct telling her not to turn her back to the tree. The foliage rustled in the light.

"Ray?"

She took a tentative step closer, and as she moved towards it, something within the underbrush caught her eye, a dark wavy pattern that looked out of context in the ferns, because it was. Laney rushed towards the sneaker, and swept the underbrush clear until she found the shoe still attached to her son, who lay face down in the dirt, unmoving.

His stillness sent a wave of panic through her. She laid the flashlight on the ground, pointing at Ray. Then tore at the thorny underbrush, ignoring the damage it did to her hands, until she cleared enough away to reach in and hook her arms under his. Half dragging, half carrying, she pulled his body into the clearing, then rolled him onto his back.

Kneeling next to him, she grabbed the flashlight and shined it on him. With one hand, she wiped the dirt away from his face, relieved to find his skin still warm. She ran the light along the rest of him. His chest rose and fell. Except for a few scratches, there were no injuries she could see. That lead her to thoughts of injuries she couldn't see, spiking panic inside of her again.

Laney gently tapped the side of his face. "Please, baby. Wake up. Ray. Wake up."

"Mom?" His eyes fluttered open, then squinted, and he raised his arm to block the light.

The sound of his voice unleashed the floodgates. Laney pulled him up into a hug and he wrapped his arms around her tight.

The hiccups in his breathing told her he was crying, too.

"It was like a dream, I guess," Ray said as he and his mom made their way past the barn. "But it felt so real."

Though freaked out, he was physically fine. Like nothing happened to him. Because it didn't.

He had never had a dream so vivid. When the mud swallowed him, he felt everything. From the burning pressure of it filling his lungs to the intense desire to survive, he felt the mud on every pore of his skin, on his eyelashes, the pressure of it against his eyeballs, oozing wet and cold under his clothes.

And the voice...it inspired a fear, deep in his core, existing on a different level than the fear of the horrible death he was facing.

It wasn't a blind, heart pounding panic, though his heart did pound. It picked him apart from the inside out. And trapped in the mud, with no way to scream, or cry, no release at all, it felt like every atom in his body vibrated to the point he was sure he would literally explode.

The dull haze that surrounded him now felt like the actual dream. The thought made him shiver.

What if it was?

What if this was his brain trying to escape the inescapable, while trapped in a body still drowning in mud? What were the chances his mother would go all Sarah Connor? That she would wander through the woods in the dark looking for him while his father could be anywhere?

As if she could read his mind, his mother took his hand, gave it a squeeze. That didn't reassure him that this was reality. But the shotgun blast from inside the house went a long way in convincing him.

36

A Promise Kept

Pete jerked his head up at the high-pitched scream of hinges swinging open. His eyes shot to his granddaughter in the living room, but the sofa sat abandoned in the flickering light of the television. "Faith?"

He grabbed the shotgun and rushed to the hallway.

Just as he reached the arch—*BANG*—the pantry door slammed shut with such a force he felt the vibrations underfoot. He turned the corner, half expecting to see cracks radiating from the door frame.

Pete ran for the door and grabbed the knob. Locked. Just as it was when he checked it for the third time today before they sat down for dinner. He fumbled for his keys, found the right one. Metal scraped against metal as he clumsily guided the key into the deadbolt. Hands shaking, he turned it, rewarded by the snitch of tumblers falling into place. He twisted the handle and pulled. The wood creaked from the strain but held tight. Just like the bathroom.

Please god, no. Not like the bathroom.

He braced himself, one foot against the wall for leverage, and pulled again, finger joints wailing in protest at his desperate grip on the knob.

The wood groaned, but didn't budge.

Pete lifted the shotgun.

The rock salt shells weren't just handy to put the hurt on a man without turning him to hamburger. The real reason he kept a box of them in his bedroom closet had more to do with their less pragmatic capabilities.

All the crap he had read and watched over the years, while trying to find a way to deal with Jeremiah, had claimed a lot of things. Fairy tales, folklore, fiction, non-fiction, myths, and message boards, every source he scoured for help, failed him. Snake oil. All of it. Every single tidbit of so-called supernatural knowledge was worthless. Except salt. He had some small success with salt.

"Faith, if you can hear me. Get away from the door. Right now."

He stepped back, hoping he wasn't about to riddle his granddaughter with chunks of rock salt, aimed for the door handle, and pulled the trigger.

The blast of the shotgun echoed through the hall, drowning out the sound of the hinges, as the salt pocked door creaked open a few inches. An icy whiff of foul air escaped the open crack. Pete reached for the handle. The brass knob jolted against his palm like he grabbed a live wire, and a flash of what he saw earlier shuddered through him. His left arm clenched under the tight grip of dread.

Ignoring the numbing cold sliding up his arm, he took a deep breath and yanked the door open.

Faith stood there in the center, half draped in the shadows of the pantry. Behind her, etched in a darkness deeper than the gloom, stood a twisted and gaunt figure. The blades of his emaciated shoulders cut sharp angles against the coat dangling from his frame, as he loomed, hunched over the little girl. He raised his hand and caressed the top of Faith's head with long, gnarled fingers.

Pete reached for his granddaughter, but the fist clenching his arm slipped around his heart and squeezed. Trapped in a vise of agony, he staggered back, his muscles contorting, curling his arms against his chest. The crushing pain wormed through him, burrowing across his back, up his neck. His jaw clenched so tight against the onslaught that he cracked a tooth and barely noticed.

He dropped to his knees, eyes locked on Faith. Tears blurred his vision, but not enough to do him the mercy of distorting his sight beyond recognition.

Jeremiah wrapped his bony fingers through the little girl's hair and pulled back with languid ease. Dangling strands of still damp hair dropped away, parting like curtains as Faith's head tilted up towards the light. From somewhere in the pantry, a distant echo careened as if from a deep, dark pit of hell, and swelled into a familiar sound as Jeremiah fulfilled the promise he had made to Pete earlier that day. A promise made through the knob hole of the bathroom door.

A void shrouded his mind as Pete hit the floor like a rag doll, leaving the screams of a long dead ten-year-old boy, now gushing from his granddaughter's unhinged mouth, far behind.

37

Instincts

Laney rushed to where Pete lay unconscious on the floor in the hall. The shotgun lay next to him, reeking of gunpowder. The muscles of his face twitched under skin, slick with sweat, tinged blue in its pallor. She put her fingers to his neck to check his pulse. The arrhythmic beat, beneath his clammy skin, thrummed weak and rapid. She rose to call an ambulance, but a firm hand gripped her wrist.

Her father looked up at her through glassy eyes, brimming with pain.

"Dad," Laney wrapped her hand around his. "Where's Faith?"

"Gone. Couldn't stop him," he said, his breath hitching.

"That bastard!"

Her father shook his head. "Not Troy," was all he got out before he stiffened up, holding his arms crossed tight across his chest.

"Just breathe. Just breathe." She told him, wanting to grab him, shake him, demand he ignore the obvious heart attack, and tell her who took Faith. But she kept her head despite her rising panic.

Laney turned to yell for Ray, but he was already in the doorway, his face pale as a ghost. She waved him to her, but he didn't see it. He couldn't take his eyes off his grandfather.

"C'mon honey. Just sit with him. I have to call an ambulance."

"No." Pete struggled to get the words out. "No ambulance."

"You're having a heart attack. You have to go to the hospital."

"No. They'll...get in the way. You ha- have to...stop him."

Suddenly, Ray was kneeling next to her. He took Pete's hand. "It was him, wasn't it?"

Pete closed his eyes, then nodded.

"Jeremiah," Laney said, finding the name had been on the tip of her tongue.

"Great, great grandpa." Ray looked up at her, shivering. "He took Faith like he tried to take me."

Laney shook her head. "This is insane." And it was, but she stopped living in a sane world three days ago.

Pete tried to speak. "P...p...p.." He took a deep breath, then tried again. "Pantry. He was in the pantry. The bathroom. Victor. All him. This farm... He is... this farm. His roots...roots run d- d- deeper than the oak his grave is under. But the pantry, the root...root-"

Laney was on her feet, heading for the pantry. The door, unlocked and peppered with rock salt, stood open a crack. She yanked it open wide and walked right in.

"Mom, what are you doing?" Ray said, his voice pitched high with alarm.

Laney didn't answer him.

"Mom?"

She wished Ray would stop talking as she groped the air in the center of the room, trying to find the pull string. It would be nice to hear if something was in here with her. The string brushed the back of her hand. She grabbed it and pulled. Light filled the room. Aside from some jams that fell victim to the shotgun blast, the room was the same as when her father showed it to her the night before.

But was it the same as this afternoon?

She got down on the floor in front of the washer and plunged her hand into the darkness. Wispy tendrils of cobwebs stuck to her fingers, the solid hardwood of the floor beneath them.

"Ray, get in here." Laney got to her feet.

He hesitated at the door, his eyes questioning her.

"Help me with this," she said and started wrestling the washer out of the closet. Frowning, and with a questioning look in his eyes, he joined her. They alternated shifting the machine forward side by side until they had walked it out as far as the water lines would go. She unplugged the machine, turned off the water valve on the wall, then unscrewed the hoses. Then they each grabbed a side and pulled the washer all the way out, scraping a trail along the floor.

Cobwebs and dust outlined the space where the washer had been. Laney squatted, swept it clear with her hand, looking for a seam, a trapdoor edge, anything that would give her a way forward. But there was nothing. No notches. No hidden door.

It made no sense. She thought for sure she'd find a way to Faith here.

Laney fought back tears. She could feel her son's eyes on her, and Ray was already teetering on the edge. She had to be strong for him, for both of her kids. Reaching down, she picked up her watch and Ray's pocket knife.

She returned to her father's side, and dropped to her knees next to him, took his hand.

"Dad, I don't know what to do. Where do I find her?"

Her father was out of it again. Knowing she should probably let him rest, she put her hand on his chest and tried to shake him awake. He'd want her to. His granddaughter needed him. But aside from a hitch, in his already ragged breathing, he didn't respond at all. His eyes roamed fitfully behind pale eyelids as he fought his own battles.

Desperate for a next step, her mind snapped to something her father said.

The oak his grave is under.

That tree. It had to be the source of Jeremiah, his connection to the farm. It had been a beautiful tree in that picture with her grandparents. Now it was a corruption, unnatural, and the way it made her feel like it was watching her, like she was prey. It had to be him.

His roots run deeper...

She'd seen his gnarled roots all around the farm. Much farther than an oak tree's roots should spread. The tree is Jeremiah, or at least his anchor to the world.

Laney looked up at Ray, a primal voice of intuition guiding her. She knew what she had to do. Her path was clear now. It was an insane idea, fueled by pure instinct, but it felt right. Down deep in her gut, it felt right.

"What are you going to do?" He asked.

She stood and tossed the pocket knife to Ray.

"Stay with your grandpa."

38

Limbo

Faith had never been in a cave before, not even on a school trip. She wasn't really sure she was in one now, but it felt like one. She shivered in a dark so deep, her eyes ached from the strain to see. The ground was too cold, so she squatted and leaned her shoulder against an even colder stone wall because it was the only thing around. She needed to touch something real, or she was afraid she'd float away into the darkness.

The air around her stank like sewer grates, rotten eggs and diarrhea, all mixed together in an old sneaker. She made the mistake of breathing through her nose only once. The taste still lingered on her tongue.

For now, she was a mouth breather.

Sometimes she could see her breath in front of her, a ghostly plume of tiny ice crystals sparkling in the air. But she knew it was just her mind playing tricks on her. At first she thought the man was a trick of her mind too, but the sound of him didn't fade away like the ice crystals. She could hear him shuffling around in the dark. Sometimes he would get close. And once she swore, his hand was right in front of her face, reaching out for her, so close she felt the heat of her breath bounce back against her.

Faith didn't try to talk to him. She knew he was a bad man. Not the kind her mother warned her about. The kind who would try to trick her into a van with candy. He was more like the kind who wasn't really a man, but a monster. The kind her mother told her didn't exist.

She tried to be quiet, hoping maybe he would forget she was there, but it was hard to be quiet when her teeth were chattering in the cold. Then, over the clack of her teeth, sounds she hadn't heard before came from somewhere in the dark.

Voices.

Muffled and distant, but close enough for her to recognize them. It was her mother, and Ray, and maybe even Grandpa.

"Mommy!" Her yell pierced the dark. "Ray!"

"She can't hear you." The voice shot out of the darkness, close to her ear, harsh and raspy, like broken glass scraping against concrete. She flinched, and slid away from it along the wall, trying not to cry, but unable to help it. Her lip quivered, and the tears started rolling down her cheeks.

"She's not coming for you." This time, the bad man whispered into her other ear. "Do you want to know why, honeybun?"

"You're not my father." Faith said, as she slid back the way she had come.

But you're like him.

"Your mother's dead." Close again, from in front of her. "I tore her guts out myself and decorated my tree with them, like Christmas. You like Christmas, don't you?"

"Mommy, I'm here!"

"Her eyes dangle from my branches. They spin in the wind." Air and spittle blew into her face, cold and foul, even worse than the air around her. It went on and on, fueled by a never ending breath. For a second she saw him despite the dark. Rotten cheeks ballooned so wide they might pop and cover her in his nasty spit. She wretched at the thought.

He cackled, a sound somehow worse than his voice, then sucked in a huge breath to blow again.

No!

She lashed out before he could start. Swung with all her might, aiming at where his face might be. Her fist connected with bloated flesh that burst on contact, and kept going right on through, coming out the other side splattered with ooze and slime. Desperate to get the goop off, she scrubbed her hand in the dirt, imagining putrid green bits of flesh floating in the rancid blood jelly that oozed between her fingers.

"Ah, spunk. I forgot what that tasted like." He erupted into a laughter that tore through her head. She put her hands to her ears, trying to block it out, but they only contained it, made it louder.

"Mommy help me!."

"Her eyes spin and spin, looking for you. But they'll never find you." He was no longer right in front of her, but all around her. His voice came from everywhere—the dirt, the rocks, the air itself. "Because you're nowhere now."

The voice lied. She knew this deep down in her bones. The same way she knew it needed her to be afraid. The bad man needed her fear, the way a crying baby needed milk. And she was afraid, the most scared she'd ever been. But she knew she'd never be afraid enough to make him full. So she yelled again.

"Mommy!"

"The birds will come and peck at her. Eat her piece by piece. Until she's nothing but a bloody stain that the rain will wash away."

With each yell, something changed. A resilience, deep inside her, strengthened each time she braved the darkness. Fear slipped away little by little.

"Grandpa, please come find me!"

"Don't waste your breath." The voice was louder. It was the voice of an angry man. "Grandpa will be dead soon. I have his heart in my hand. I'm gonna squeeze it to a pulp."

She stood, no longer cowering against the wall, and let her voice rise from deep within her, yelling with everything she had.

"Mommy!"

"Mommy!"

It was only enough to make her hair flutter at first, her clothes gently flap against her skin. Then the suction grew stronger and stronger.

"Momm-"

Her hair stood straight out in front of her face. Her chest constricted, leaving her gasping for air. Flickers of light sparked along the edges of her vision and she staggered back against the wall, sat down hard. Her hands clutched at a throat that felt like it was collapsing in on itself.

One by one, the sparks died out.

"Enough." A simple word, plainly spoken by someone no longer amused. The air came roaring back into the room, pressing Faith against the wall, filling her lungs until she was sure they would pop.

"If I want you to scream," the voice said, a whisper in her ear now. "I'll make you scream."

39

Trespasser

Ray wanted to come with her, and she almost let him. Laney was already a raw nerve at the thought of Faith missing. The idea of Ray being out of her sight was agonizing. But, given what she intended to do, she thought he'd be safer if he didn't. Plus, she needed someone to stay with her father and be at the house if, no, *when* Faith came back.

Her father was right. Calling an ambulance would only complicate things. What she needed to do couldn't be explained to the authorities in any way a sane person would understand. And she needed to do it fast.

In the barn, she grabbed two cans of gasoline, then tied them together with some rope. There was a burlap sack filled with old rags hanging on a nail on the wall. Laney pulled it down and emptied it. She grabbed a headlamp and the propane torch from the workbench. The torch felt full, but she grabbed a spare tank just in case.

Laney strapped the headlamp on. Everything else, except the gas, went into the sack. She was about to leave when she noticed it.

The barn smelled like a mechanic's garage. The odor of grease and rubber permeated the air. It wasn't an unexpected smell and Laney paid it no mind the last time she was in there. But this time it was different. There was another scent mingled in. She took a deep breath, trying to place it, and the hair on the back of her neck stood up.

Blood.

The odor was strongest towards the back, near what used to be the horse stall. She paused at the partition, feeling like she was standing at the bathroom door all over again.

When she finally turned the corner, she found exactly what her nose told her to expect. Flies buzzed around the fresh puddle of blood illuminated in the circle of light from her headlamp. A trail led from the puddle into the darkness near the back of the stall. She forced her head to follow the trail, dragging the light along the dark liquid soaking into the dirt floor of the barn. Laney stopped when it landed on sneakers too big for a child and choked out a gasp of relief. She almost didn't let her gaze continue to see who the sneakers belonged to, but a small part of her mind hoped it would be Troy. There would be karmic justice in Troy tracking her down to kill her, only to meet someone worse than himself.

But it wasn't Troy.

The bigger of the Hess brothers sat slouched up against the wall, his chest covered in blood. A wound two inches tall cut a narrow line through his shirt, near the top of the stain.

Painted on the wall above him in blood was a single word. *Trespasser.*

In a disturbing way, the scene gave her hope.

Jeremiah tormented Ray, but he didn't kill him. He'd made her believe Faith had drowned, but she had been fine. But this man, this trespasser, he killed. Killian blood, it seemed, had its privileges. She hoped to god she was right.

Laney slung the gas cans over her shoulder, left the barn and started the awkward walk towards the woods. Liquid lurched in the heavy cans on every step, shifting their weight, banging the cans against her body, digging the rope they hung from into her skin.

She kept her focus forward, not letting the changing shadows, or the dry rustling of movement all around, distract her until she reached the path. It had only been a half an hour since she'd last been there, but during that time, the path had changed. It was wider, clearer, more welcoming than the last time she had come through.

Jeremiah's way of saying "Bring it on".

She took it to mean he understood what she intended to do, and was prepared for her. Laney realized that once she went down this path, she might never come back. Killian or not, she meant to end Jeremiah. She doubted her bloodline would get her a pass. And that could mean that she'd never find out if her plan worked. She decided it would. If she took this path, Faith would be safe. No matter what. She had to believe that.

Laney stepped into the woods.

40

Maybe Forever

Ray tried not to cry. He didn't want to look like a wuss in front of his grandfather, even though the man was currently unconscious. Before she left to look for Faith, he and his mother had gotten Pete to his recliner. Ray rested Pete's head on a pillow, then covered him in a blanket, trying to make him comfortable. He plugged in his cellphone to charge in the kitchen, feeling naked without it, then pulled up a chair next to the recliner.

"Don't be scared," Pete said, startling him. His grandfather's eyes were still closed.

"I'm not grandpa."

"Liar."

"I'm the liar?" Ray slipped into a gruff impersonation of Pete. "Farm's not haunted."

"Smartass." The ghost of a weak smile flitted on Pete's bloodless lips, then disappeared. "Faith?"

"Mom's still looking for her."

"Pantry? Under the- the-"

Under the washing machine?

He would have thought his grandfather was losing it if that wasn't

177

the first place his mom checked.

"No. Mom looked. She wasn't there."

Pete's face twisted in confusion. "Has to be…"

Ray scrunched his brow. "How does Jeremiah do…what he does?"

"Don't know." Grandpa got quiet for a long while, and Ray thought maybe he fell back to sleep. He near jumped when Pete spoke up again.

"He was a willful man." His voice was still weak, but his grandfather spoke more clearly than before. Like he had summoned all his will for this conversation. "The stroke couldn't take him. It weakened him, but made him so much meaner. And the things he could do… I think my parents… I think they finally had enough."

"They killed him?"

Pete managed a small shrug. "Near as I can tell. They killed him. But he… he didn't go. He's still here somehow. Maybe forever."

A chill ran up Ray's spine. Was his grandfather suggesting they couldn't stop Jeremiah?

"Maybe we could dig him up, burn his body or something? Works on TV." Ray said.

"Can't." Pete gave a slight shake of his head. "Grave's empty."

There was only one way he could know that. All these years, and his grandfather never figured out how to stop Jeremiah. What if he was unstoppable? What did that mean for Faith? Ray couldn't think about his sister out there alone right now, knowing firsthand what Jeremiah could do to her. He changed the subject.

"Why did you stay? Why didn't you just leave?"

"I had to. I thought I could… get rid of him. Save the farm. Bring back my family. Your grandmother waited for me. But I wasted years trying. Then it was…too late. Couldn't sell and…and…have him hurt a new family. Had to let her go, let them all go." Pete grimaced in pain, and Ray took his hand.

"Don't talk, Grandpa. Rest. It's not too late now. When Mom and Faith get back, you're coming with us."

Pete's weak smile returned. "That would be nice."

Ray didn't know how long they sat there. His grandfather's breathing became more steady and relaxed, and his own breathing mirrored it. Exhaustion overtook him, and he leaned his head up against the side of the recliner near his grandfather's, let his eyes close. He dozed until the sound of footsteps upstairs woke him.

41

The Breeze

Faith couldn't sit there in the dark one second longer. She had to move. She stood slowly, sliding her hand up the wall as she went. The bad man hadn't spoken to her since he sucked all the air out of the cave, and she hadn't heard him moving, or felt him near her for a while now. She listened, waiting for him to say something.

He didn't.

Eyes still wide despite the dark, she kept her right hand on the wall and took a tentative step.

The voice didn't say a thing.

She took another step, left hand out in front of her. Then another step, and another. Her right hand hit something rough against the wall, and she jerked it back in reflex.

Swallowing hard, she forced herself to reach out again, and laid her palm against the grainy surface. Wood. She slid her hand, following its form. A long plank, standing tall, other planks ran across and soon she had a mental picture. Shelves. She continued running her hand through gauzy cobwebs and encountered something cold, hard, and smooth. The picture came faster this time. Wood shelves. Glass jars. She let out a breath.

She walked forward, feeling her way along the shelves, counting as she went. Every three steps, a standing plank supported the shelves. The shelves were sometimes empty except for cobwebs. Sometimes they held glass jars or wooden boxes. On her eighth step, her hand found something new. Something wet and slick with what felt like snot.

She yelped and jumped back.

Don't overreact.

Once again, she forced her hand forward. It was probably something normal. The feel of it had surprised her, that's all. Her fingers brushed up against the rough, slimy fabric. There was something hard underneath it, but she forced herself to feel around. Tiny threads poked up from the fabric, and then her finger plunged into a hole. An eye hole.

She yanked her hand back and had no problem imagining the thing. The image of it lunged at her in the dark.

Scarecrow!

Faith staggered back away from the shelves, not realizing how far she'd gone until she felt it behind her and panicked.

The nothing.

She drifted in the darkness, the ground beneath her feet her only connection to the world. Without the shelf to hold on to, she would float away.

Faith flailed her arms in front of her, desperate to touch anything. Her breath came out in shaky gasps, catching with each step that landed on solid ground and didn't continue forward, pitching her into an endless pit.

Her finger brushed against the cold, rough surface, and she shrieked before she realized what she touched. She rushed forward, arms out in front of her. Her fingers met resistance, and she pressed herself against the stone wall, hugging its surface like an old friend.

Then she felt the draft, a slight breeze from her left.

A way out.

The smell of the breeze made her gag, but it was the sweetest air she could imagine, because it meant leaving this place, and the bad man, behind her.

Edging along the wall, Faith found an opening in the stone. The breeze streamed through, faint, but steady. She mapped the edges of the hole with her hands and found it big enough to fit through. She reached inside. Her hand landed on the smooth, cool surface of a boulder.

The voice broke its silence.

Its harsh rasp boomed around her like wavering thunder, vibrating in her bones. "Don't you try to run, little rabbit! Don't you dare. I'll make you scream and scream."

Not if I don't give you the chance to.

Faith crawled through the hole before she lost her nerve.

42

The Visitor

Ray stood in the hall, watching the steps, waiting. There hadn't been another sound upstairs since he heard the footsteps for almost ten minutes now. And he couldn't help but wonder if Faith had been up there the whole time, hiding in a place they never checked. Unlike under the washer. Whatever the hell was up with that?

He was specifically told not to leave Grandpa under any circumstances, no matter what he heard or saw. Ray didn't need to be told twice that Jeremiah could mess with his head. His nose still burned from the mud that never existed, forcing its way up his up his nostrils.

But when the next sound came, nothing he had gone through earlier mattered, not the woods, not even the mud. The sob was gut wrenching. He'd never heard her cry like that before.

Ray didn't have a light. His phone was still charging, but he didn't care. Once he passed the midway point on the stairs and his head breached the second floor, the night-light sensed him and turned on. He swallowed his nerves and rushed up the rest of the way, suddenly worried the night-light would shut off before he got there, leaving him in the dark despite his motion.

When he reached the landing, the open door to his grandfather's bedroom caught his eye. The dim light from the night-light barely reached the room. Its dull glow formed a small puddle inside the door, a small dent in the darkness.

As long as he was moving nearby, the night-light would stay lit, but once Ray crossed into the bedroom, he'd be on a timer. He'd been trapped in the dark once already today and wasn't sure he'd make it through a second time. Not without losing it. He needed the light from the bathroom.

A sob came from the bedroom, from deep in the shadows. Ray turned, forgetting the bathroom light, and made his way down the hall. The twisting ball of anxiety in his gut spurred him on, reminding him the light wouldn't last much longer. But the darkness of the room in front of him slowed his feet. There would be a light switch just inside the door. There had to be.

It was dark in Grandpa's room, but not like the pitch black of the woods. He could make out the twinkling of stars in the night sky past the bedroom windows. Murky shadows formed obscure shapes that didn't resemble bedroom furniture at all, and he didn't let his eyes linger on them, afraid they would start to resemble something else. He reached his left hand through the doorway, let it slide up along the wall, feeling for the switch. His finger brushed the toggle, and he flicked it. A hollow click was all he got in return.

He still had the night-light. It didn't do much, but it was better than nothing. Taking a deep breath, he crossed the threshold. "Faith?"

Across the room, a shadow lashed out in front of the window, blotting out the stars, and he jumped. It drifted back, then lashed out again. And he realized he watched a curtain billow in and out. But there was no breeze, at least none that he could feel. None that could move the curtain like that.

Faith wasn't here. Jeremiah herded him into Grandpa's room. That much was clear. He wanted Ray to look out the window and see whatever new lie he cooked up.

Fine, I'll play.

Even in his own head, the bravado sounded forced.

He crossed the room, stepping deeper into darkness, expecting to lose what little light he had at any moment. Ray swept the curtain aside and looked out the window. It was a moonless night, and only the stars were visible. Everything else, the driveway, the fields, the forest beyond the farm, was a featureless landscape of night. But he had no problem getting Jeremiah's message.

The dry thrashing carving its way through the corn towards the house came from the field to his left. Then another from the right. Others joined in until they came from every direction. And Ray knew what they were. Or at least, what Jeremiah wanted him to believe they were. But he was done letting Jeremiah scramble his brain.

Faith giggled behind him. He turned to the door and found her silhouetted against the light in the hall. But that wasn't his sister. He knew that even before the shape began to morph and the figure launched itself towards him, its long, gangly arms stretching out as it ran.

Just before the night-light turned off, snuffing out the shadows, he made out the points of sharpened fingernails reaching for him.

In the chaotic rush of it all, Ray screamed and, with no instincts for the layout of the room or which way to run, backed up against the window. The thing hit him like a freight train. The screen ripped behind him, and stars swung into view. He hit the porch roof. Momentum took him. His legs kept going, sending him rolling, blotting out the stars, as Ray tumbled backwards towards the edge. He landed face down, but still in motion. His cheek caught traction on the asphalt tiles, slid the last few inches, leaving a layer of skin behind. He got a hold of the gutter on the way over, just long enough to slow his descent down, and did a half-assed hang jump into the wildflowers bordering the porch.

Outside, the thrashing was so much louder. Louder, and more threatening. That none of it was real meant nothing when the sound of them rushing through the corn filled his ears. Expecting to feel their fingers to dig into his flesh at any moment, he scrambled to his feet and made a run for the house.

He yanked open the screen door and threw himself at the wood one, twisting the knob as he went. The door slammed open and Ray staggered into the hall, not bothering to close it behind him. He caught sight of the shotgun, still laying on the floor near where they found Grandpa. He lunged for it, swept it up, then turned back and moved towards the open door.

The shotgun felt heavy in his arms, the weight both comforting and terrifying. He leveled it, aiming out towards the steps, waiting for the first scarecrow to reach the house. The scarecrows weren't real, but real didn't matter when the pain came. And Grandpa's heart couldn't take any more pain.

"Ray." His grandfather's exhausted voice called to him from the living room.

"It's okay Grandpa, I won't let anything happen to you."

Rustling thundered at the edge of the field. By the sound of it, there were dozens. He waited for them to breach the light of the porch.

"Ray."

So close now.

He hoped they rushed the house in groups. He didn't know how many he could take out with one shot, but years of playing video games taught him his best bet was to wait for close proximity and try to catch as many in each blast as possible. Assuming his grandfather had fully loaded the gun, and they came at him in clusters, he might have enough shots to keep them out.

"RAY!"

The voice roared so close behind him, he felt a rush of breath against his ear. He swung around, nearly pulling the trigger by accident, but managed to stay his finger. There was no one in the hall. He glimpsed Grandpa on the recliner through the living room arch.

Feet stomped up the porch steps behind him.

He turned back in time to see it before it crossed the threshold. It was no scarecrow. It was so much worse. The whites of its crazed eyes stood in stark contrast to the red mask of blood flowing down from its scalp-less skull. It rushed at Ray, its mouth wide open in a soundless scream.

Reflexes squeezed the trigger before Ray even thought to twitch his finger. The blast knocked the thing from the corn clean off the porch and Ray staggered back from the kick of the recoil.

The corn lay silent.

Even the crickets had gone quiet. The only sounds came from the thing. Wet, sputtering coughs. The dull thud of limbs twitching on the ground.

Ray slammed the door shut.

The flash of the gun had seared the thing's face onto his eyes. He tried to blink it away, but it wouldn't fade. The thought of that image, forever branded on his corneas, a tattoo of light and blood, and pain, threatened to make him scream.

It had walked straight out of a nightmare. It wasn't real, couldn't be. Ray remembered how the mud felt. The sensation of the fingers wrapped around his head, pressing him down. How sure he had been that he was drowning.

The thing was just another one of Jeremiah's tricks. Had to be.

But then Ray remembered its eyes and his stomach lurched.

What did I do?

43

There's Nothing

The woods were a kaleidoscope of morphing shadows in the headlamp's beam. Laney tried to steady herself, to minimize the unsettling motion around her, but the ground was uneven. Each unbalanced step over a tree root, or down into a depression, jerked the light around, leaving her flinching at lurching shadows. Any real threat would be on top of her before she could distinguish it.

To make things worse, the gas continuously sloshed around in the cans over her shoulder. Waves, set in motion with each step she took, rang against the metal sides, making it impossible for Laney to hear anything else around her.

She was going in blind, deaf and about as stealthy as a one-man band.

But her pace never wavered. It couldn't. Faith needed her. She plowed forward, determined the tree would burn, no matter what Jeremiah threw at her.

Even when she felt his breath on her ear.

There's nothing.

Laney kept moving, and the scent of his aftershave followed. His exhalations moistened the back of her neck.

There's nothing. There's nothing. There's no-

Her head snapped back.

The fist entangled in her hair yanked hard. She spun with it, swinging the sack like a flail, hitting nothing. The momentum of the swaying cans threw her off balance, staggering her onto the empty trail behind her.

"Fuck you!"

She fought back the tears from the shock of it, forced herself to turn back towards the tree, and walked faster still. The light jostled chaotically. Shadows lunged. His breath was with her every step of the way. Its cadence matched her footfalls, panting like a pacing tiger. So loud, it drowned out the sloshing liquid.

"You're going to die here." Troy said.

Laney spun on her heel, not swinging the bag this time, anticipating the momentum of the cans. The path behind her remained empty.

He was never there.

And she needed it to stay that way. At best, he was a distraction, at worst a threat.

She backed up against a tree and tried to calm her breathing, slow her pounding heart. Even with her head steadied against the trunk, shadows seemed to move beyond the trees. So, she closed her eyes and kept them closed. Gas lapped from one side of the cans to the other and continued with diminishing force until the liquid settled.

It took some time—time she didn't have—but the normal sounds of the forest returned, crickets and katydids, mating calls of frogs. The air carried the scent of pine trees and the sweet decay of decomposing leaves. All hints of cheap aftershave were gone.

Laney opened her eyes, calmer now and ready to go. She readjusted the rope holding the cans on her shoulder and stepped away from the tree.

She didn't get far.

Her head slammed back against the trunk, yanked by fists twisted through her hair on both sides. Her ears rang. Sparks of light danced in front of her eyes.

Trapped behind her shoulders, the gas can forced her neck to arch back at a sharp angle. Laney tried to pull away, but couldn't. Not without leverage. And the fists held tight.

Her scalp stretched taut away from her skull as strands of hair ripped out one by one. She put her hands on the sides of her head and grabbed the clenched fists, trying to pull them forward, or at least stop them from pulling her back. But they were too strong.

Releasing one hand, she hammered her fist back behind her, where Troy's arm should be, but only scraped her knuckles raw on the tree bark.

The heat of his breath washed the side of her face. The pain was bad, but his proximity was worse. It was suffocating. In a moment of panic, she let out a scream, not of fear or rage, but of animalistic intent.

A trapped animal would gnaw off its own paw to escape.

Laney tucked her elbows against the bark and pulled her feet up underneath her. Bracing against the tree, she pushed away with all her strength. Hair ripped out in bloody chunks, leaving patches of scalp raw and bleeding. She broke free, staggered forward, and got her feet under her. Then she spun around to face him, breathing hard. Her lips drew into a snarl and her eyes darted as she turned a circle, searching for him, forgetting he was never there.

She found only careening shadows. But as she turned, with warm blood running down her neck from her ravaged scalp, she recognized a new scent in the air.

Fear knows fear.

44

Skeletal Fingers

The floor of the cave kept changing, sometimes leading up, sometimes down. Smooth stone would give way to gravel and back again. There were places Faith could crouch, but the cave had never been tall enough for her to stand.

Roots, twisted and ropey, poked through the stone walls in places. There weren't a lot at first. Every now and again, one would catch her skin or clothes and poke at her like a skeletal finger. But soon they were everywhere, grabbing at her, and sometimes forming tangles she had to push her way through.

She crawled, ignoring the ache that throbbed between her shoulder blades. The skin of her battered knees, pressed between bone and boulder over and over again, had become tenderized flesh, burning each time a knee took on weight. But she kept crawling. It was all she could do, and she couldn't do nothing.

When the stone ended out of nowhere, her right arm dropped to a boulder a foot below with a hit that sent pain shooting from her hand to her shoulder. She groaned but kept moving. The whole "surprise, the floor is gone" thing was getting old fast. After the first time it happened, she tried to be careful, feeling ahead before she crawled. But that took too long, and she was so tired. She had to plow ahead just to keep moving. If she stopped, she might not have the energy to start again. If she stopped, she might be in the dark forever.

This new part of the tunnel was flat. But she had been crawling so long, her arms felt as heavy as the boulders around her. Every time she moved ahead, she promised her body it could stop soon. Just one more. One more. Numb arms lifted and dropped. Legs slid forward on raw knees. Then she promised again.

Sweat dripping down her face, jaw locked so tight her teeth hurt, she brought her shaking arm up, moved it ahead, then let it drop.

This time her hand didn't hit stone.

She broke through something smooth and brittle and it crumbled under her weight like a stale cracker.

Faith stopped. Her tired brain didn't have the energy to care about something new, unless that something was a way out. But what if it was important? So far, all the crawling through the cave got her was more crawling. What if this crumbly thing was a clue, like in The Goonies? She couldn't just ignore it, no matter how tired she was. She just needed to take a minute and get her brain back in gear so she could figure it out. Locking her elbows, she let her arms rest. Her head drooped as she knelt there, catching her breath, fighting the desperate urge to lie down.

The stone wouldn't be the worst place for a nap. It would be like going to bed, and slipping between cool sheets after a day of playing in the sun, letting tired muscles go limp, drifting off-

Her head jerked up, snapping her awake.

Have to keep moving.

She couldn't let that happen again. Her mom would never find her here. This part of the cave was too small, and Mom wouldn't fit.

Faith felt around ahead of her, trying to figure out the—fingers crossed—clue. Her hand found more smooth things, some long, some small, wrapped together with cloth, lots of cloth. Tree roots wrapped around the smooth things, and in some places, went right through them. She found a big chunk that was left of the thing she had crushed and picked it up, ran her fingers along the row of teeth-

She dropped the skull and shivered.

The broken skull hit the rock below with a hollow thump, and the stone rumbled, vibrating all around her. Dirt rained down from above her, sifting through the gaps between shifting rocks. Faith let out a shriek, but her raw throat only managed a harsh rattle. She had to move before the tunnel caved in and she got pancaked.

She crawled as fast as she could, and kept crawling, even when

the rumbling passed. Faith crawled until the space between ceiling and floor closed in, and she had no room left to crawl. Fighting the urge to panic, she laid on her belly and slid herself forward, hoping she would find the way out before the tunnel got too tight. Tears tried to form in her eyes at the thought of being stuck down there, but she sweat so much crawling through the cave, she had no water left in her body for tears.

Faith had been terrified earlier when there was nothing around her. When she thought she might float away in the dark, but now, with the rock so close, she craved the nothing. She'd give anything for the open space to stretch and breathe, even if it meant floating away. Her whole body shook with the need to pound her way out of the cave until she could move again. Her lungs tried to suck in air as fast as they could, but they could only fill up so much before her back hit the stone above her. A humming filled her ears, and she knew if there had been any light to see by, she would see the darkness creeping in before she passed out.

But then she felt it. The breeze was stronger here.

The way out!

Suddenly, her muscles weren't so tired anymore. She just had to get through this tight part of the tunnel. The way out was on the other side. It had to be.

Faith flattened her body as much as she could, head turned to the side, arms and legs stretched out. She pressed her toes against the stone and pushed. Her fingers clung to any crack or bump they could find, and she pulled. Every inch felt like a lap around the gym at school, and soon her muscles remembered how tired they really were.

And then it happened.

She reached the point she was afraid of. Ahead, the tunnel shrunk until it was too flat for her head to fit. She had nowhere to go but back, and she was too tired for that. She let herself go limp against the stone, and the breeze, cool and strong, washed over her.

Faith cried dry, hitching sobs. Her mouth formed the silent words her voice couldn't. "Mommy, where are you?"

45

The Murmuration

Ahead, trees on either side led to darkness, and the space beyond the path stole the light. The dank smell from earlier now mingled with cheap aftershave and rot. As she entered the clearing, Laney sensed the oak looming over her. An ominous hum resonated from it. Its gnarled branches, a vast network of limbs blotting out the stars, spread out above, waiting for her to get closer.

Her headlamp found the trunk of the tree. She stared at the moving curtain of shadows surrounding it. Her mind, at first, couldn't interpret what her eyes were seeing. A tiny insect breached the headlamp's beam, buzzing near her face. Laney slapped at the sharp bite of pain that flared from her cheek and she understood.

Fuck.

Thousands of midges surrounded the trunk, maybe hundreds of thousands. The tiny insects, swarming in the beam of her light, formed a defensive force at least ten feet deep.

She stood clear of the swarm and sloped her shoulder to release the rope. The cans slid to the ground beside her, revealing an indented rope burn on the skin of her neck. Fighting the sense of urgency, she took a moment to rotate her arm at the joint in circles to loosen the muscle, and to think. Without the constant sloshing of the gas cans drowning it out, the hum of the swarm was unnervingly loud and made concentration difficult. Once she started what she came here to do, she'd have to move fast and keep going until it was done. And to do that, she needed a plan.

Laney would have to go through the barrier of insects to get in close enough to douse the tree with gasoline, but she wasn't sure how long she could stay in the swarm. Already stragglers were venturing out of the cloud for a taste test, and the painful bites were like electric shocks to her already frayed nerves. She slapped at them, crushing their tiny bodies against her skin, wishing she had some bug spray.

Maybe I do.

She unscrewed the metal lid on one can and tilted it, pouring some gas into her palm. Laney rubbed the liquid onto her arms, neck and cheeks like a lotion. The fumes burned in her nostrils, and made her eyes water, but at least the gas smelled better than the tree. She grabbed a handful of dirt to wash her hands, then rubbed them on her jeans, trying to get as much of the gasoline off of them as possible.

With a can in each hand, she took a deep breath, squinted her eyes, closed her mouth tight, then breached the swarm.

The tiny insects mobbed her as soon as she stepped into the cloud. They avoided her skin where she applied the gas, but that didn't stop them from crawling elsewhere. Attracted to the bloody patches on her scalp, the bites there were sharp needles of burning pain.

They crawled into every open orifice they could find. She thought the noise was bad before, but the invasive, chaotic droning inside her ears was maddening. The only thing worse were the bites on the tight flesh of her ear canal. She clenched her jaw to keep from screaming and tried shrugging and rubbing her shoulders against the side of her head to knock them away.

Laney snorted air out her nose to dislodge the midges crawling up her nostrils. She parted her lips to suck breath in through a narrow opening, but not narrow enough to keep them from crawling into her mouth. They crawled over her eyelashes, constantly assaulting her vision. She had to blink to keep them off her eyes.

Keep moving. Don't scream. Don't scream.

When she got close enough, she put down the closed can. Taking the open can in both hands, she started splashing gas on the bark with big swinging motions, trying to cover as much vertical distance with each splash as she could. Laney worked her way around the circumference of the trunk until she reached the point she started at.

She tossed the empty can and tried to open the lid on the second, but it wouldn't budge. Why didn't she loosen it before stepping into the swarm? She wrapped the bottom of her shirt around the lid for more grip, exposing the pale skin of her belly to the insects. Gritting her teeth at the pain of the fresh assault, she gripped the lid tight, trying to turn it. But it didn't move.

Laney dropped the can and franticly searched the ground around her until she found a rock with a point. She knelt down, trying to ignore the insects swarming at her head, and pounded the rock into the metal side of the can until it punched through. Tossing the rock aside with relief, she got to her feet. She picked up the can and tilted it, pouring out a generous line of gas as she backed out of the swarm, emptying that can too.

Once free of the cloud, she allowed herself a moment of frenzied retribution against the insects still assaulting her. She dug them out of her ears with her fingers, crushed the ones in her hair and under her shirt and scrubbed her face with her palms. Their crushed bodies became bloody smears, trailing tiny, disembodied legs and wings down her cheeks.

The tickle of phantom insects still crawled on her skin, as she rubbed her hands in the dirt again to cover any vestiges of gas left behind and fought to ignore the random muscle twitches and the urge to slap at her head and face.

She got the torch out of the bag, and removed the flint igniter from where it hung around the neck of the tank, then turned the knob to release the gas. Hoping she got enough of the fuel off of her hands, she gave the igniter a few quick squeezes until she got a good spark from the flint. Blue flame erupted from the nozzle with a whoosh and she managed to not set herself on fire.

The moment of truth.

Please work.

Laney touched the torch to the trail of gasoline. A line of flames raced towards the massive oak.

At once, the swarm defied their nature. Moving together like a murmuration of sparrows, like a single organism, they swirled up, then dove, crashing down on the burning line. Tiny bodies exploded with pops and hisses, and in an instant, the density of the swarm smothered the flames.

It all happened so fast. She stood, mouth agape, trying to comprehend what she just saw. As smoke rose from the line of tiny crisped and blackened husks, the remaining insects reverted to their previous behavior and became a living shield around the tree once again.

Laney closed her eyes, took a deep breath, shuddered, then once more breached the swarm.

46

Grandpa

The acrid gun smoke hung over Ray like a storm cloud, stinging his eyes.

"Grandpa?" Ray placed the shotgun on the floor with care. "I think I did something bad. I think...." His breath hitched in his throat. All at once, the enormity of what just happened drained the heat from his body, replacing it with an arctic blast that spread numbing tendrils of ice throughout him.

Staccato flashes of the thing's face, a private film shown only in his head, flickered every time he closed his eyes. With each flash, its eyes got wider, more terror filled. It wasn't running at him. It, no he, it was he. He, Johnny with the green eyes, was running away from something. Something terrible.

And I shot him.

Tears welled up in his eyes.

"Grandpa?" He didn't recognize his own voice. It was the high-pitched whine of a little kid.

He turned towards the living room, and through his tear blurred vision saw his grandpa was awake, an arm reached out, waiting to comfort him. Ray shuffled over to him on lead filled legs, then dropped to his knees beside him. He took his grandfather's rough, calloused hand in his, held it tight to his chest, and sobbed.

"I killed him. I didn't mean to. I swear. Please tell me what to do? I'm sorry. I know you're sick right now, but I need you. I don't know what to do." His grandfather's hand hung limp in his grasp. "Grandpa?"

Ray rubbed his tears away with the palm of his hand and met the old man's eyes before the relentless flow blurred his vision again. He knew. He knew the moment he looked into the slackened, staring eyes. No smile creased their corners. No warmth shone from within. But he refused to believe it.

He swiped his hands across his eyes, wiped the tears away again and again. Each time, he met the same lifeless stare.

"Grandpa?" He placed a tentative hand on his grandfather's chest and gave a small shake. When nothing happened, Ray shook again, harder, with both hands, throwing his weight into it. Pete's body limply rocked with the motion. His hand shifted, slid off the recliner's arm, and fingers rapped the floor, with a dull clattering of fingernails against the wood.

The reality Ray had been denying came rushing in all at once. Grandpa wasn't just out of it. No amount of shaking would wake him up. And with the realization came a panicked need to do something before it was too late. Before, his grandfather had gone too far.

Ray ran to the kitchen, to the phone on the wall, and picked up the handset. Grandpa didn't want an ambulance. But Ray didn't know what else to do. He put the phone to his ear, and immediately yanked it away, held it far from him, eying it like it was a rabid snake.

The screaming on the other end didn't belong to Faith. That much he knew.

The raw wail of pure, terrified agony that crawled under his skin and slid along his nerves like a razor blade came from a boy. A boy his age, by the sound of it.

Ray slammed the handset home and ran to his cell phone, charging next to the coffeemaker. He hit the power button, and waited ages for the loading bar to fill, pacing as far as the charging cord would allow. Finally, the home screen cycled up, and he punched in his pass code, dialed 911.

This time he held the phone at arm's length, waiting for the scream. It rang instead. Once. Twice. He put the phone to his ear, expecting another ring, but got a barely perceptible click. Someone had answered.

The words shot out of him at high speed. "Hello! I'm at...at...

Killian Farm. I don't know the address. My grandpa had a heart attack. He need's an ambulance. He's not breathing. What do I do? I don't know what to do."

No response. Just the soft hum of an open line.

"Hello? Is someone there? Can you hear me? What do I do?"

There was an inhalation of breath, and Ray flinched, expecting the scream again.

"Mind the road." The voice was weak and far away, but he recognized it immediately.

"Grandpa?" Ray spun to look at his grandfather lying limp on the recliner in the living room. Dull, vacant eyes stared back at him as the line disconnected.

He was too late. Grandpa had already gone. He put down the phone, closed his eyes, and took deep breaths until the shakes hit. Then he paced, trying to keep it together, to keep the voice, the scream, all of it out of his head. He banged clenched fists against his skull. A keening moan clawed its way out of his throat.

Then, all at once, he stopped. His eyes shot to the living room, to Grandpa.

"Fuck this." He rushed to his grandfather.

It took all his strength, but he grabbed Pete's feet and pulled, sliding him down the recliner until the chair shifted forward from the weight. Resting Pete's legs on the floor, Ray rushed up and got his arms under his grandfather's shoulders before they could tilt to the side. He crouch walked to the left, straightening out his grandpa's body. Then he knelt down slow, muscles straining from the effort to be careful, and laid his grandfather's head gently on the floor.

Though he had never learned how—he'd seen it done enough on TV—Ray started chest compressions.

"You're okay. Come back. Please, grandpa. You're okay. You're okay."

He threw the weight of his body down into each push. His grandfather's chest flexed beneath him. His arms pistoned again and again, until he couldn't feel them anymore. The tears stopped flowing, replaced with dripping sweat burning his eyes.

"You're okay. You're okay." The words became a mantra, breathlessly repeated, blending together with each compression in his exhaustion. He lost count. Lost track of time. Only the pain in his arms and shoulders gave him any sense of how long he'd been going at it.

It was only a muffled pop.

But to Ray, the sound of Pete's rib cracking shot through the air like a cannon blast, and he yanked his hands back in horror.

"I'm sorry. I'm sorry. I didn't mean to hurt you," he said in a quiet voice, as if soothing a child. He reached out with shaking hands and gently smoothed the wrinkles out of his grandfather's shirt. "I didn't know what else to do. Please don't go."

His arms fell away from Pete's chest and lay limp in front of him. He sat, a slack and unmoving hull, mouth hung open, panting for breath.

A small spot of grease from his mother's car stained Pete's t-shirt near the pocket. It drew Ray's eyes like a magnet and he couldn't pull them away from it. Not that he tried. If he looked away, he might see his grandpa's face, and he couldn't look at him like that again. He let the spot fill his vision until his breath evened out and he felt empty.

In his emptiness, Ray's senses absorbed every minute detail of the surrounding space. A bead of sweat on the tip of an eyelash throwing fractals in the corner of his eye. The hollow tick, tick, tick of the clock on the mantle. The droning hum of the refrigerator. Wind gently rattling the corn outside. The tingle of sweat dissipating from his skin in the cool evening breeze coming in through the open windows.

The click of the pantry door opening. A long, drawn out creak of invitation.

Jeremiah beckoned him.

Ray closed his eyes as he kissed his grandfather's cheek. Stubble rubbed against his lips. The scent of sweat and motor oil filled his nostrils. The thought that he'd never smell that specific scent again, Grandpa's scent, that there would be so many *nevers* now, threatened to trigger a tsunami inside him. Until a few days ago, he barely knew the man existed. Now, he couldn't imagine not having him in his life. He got to his feet before the loss could wash over and drown him.

Jeremiah took enough from him. Ray wouldn't let him have Faith.

47

The Whoosh

Faith came out of her daze, still wedged between the boulder above and below her. The humming wasn't just in her head anymore. The stone around her vibrated with the thrashing movement of something above, making her teeth rattle.

Earthquake.

She ignored that thought, threw a blanket over it and pretended it wasn't there, knowing that if she acknowledged it, it would tear her mind apart with fear.

There was something new in the tunnel, other than the earth-

Don't even think it.

A gas station smell. Was she near Grandpa's barn?

And something else. The breeze had changed. It was stronger near her right arm. Fresh clods of dirt spattered her skin there. She reached for the rock face above her and found a new crack between boulders where the dirt had dislodged. A small ember of hope ignited in her. Her hand reached up through the crack, fingertips tantalizingly close to something she thought she'd never feel again.

Outside.

A sharp pain pricked her finger, and she realized the source of the humming. There were bugs. Flying bugs.

It's so close.

Working her hand through the crack, she tried to dislodge more dirt and widen it.

Please be big enough. Please.

It wasn't.

Freeing all the dirt she could reach gave Faith a better sense of the gap between boulders. It was small, only big enough to poke her hand through. She let her hand fall limp back to the rock, wishing she had the tears to cry.

"Faith!" It was her mother's voice.

The ember roared back to life. She shoved her hand up through the hole, exhaustion gone in an instant. "Mommy!" It hurt her lungs and tore at her raw throat, but she yelled as loud as she could.

She came for me. It's finally over.

A loud whoosh roared above, and a wave of heat washed over her.

Faith screamed.

48

The Torch

Vibrations emanated from just below the ground beneath her feet. Laney took a step towards the trunk. Ropey tendrils of tree roots ruptured from the soil and writhed on the broken ground, threatening to entangle her. She staggered forward, struggling to stay on top of the undulating mass.

Waving the torch around, she caught hundreds of tiny flies with the flame. Their bodies tumbled to the ground as burning embers. But the insects weren't smart enough to see the creature that was thousands of times their own body size, and armed with fire, as a threat. Once again, Laney became their pin cushion.

She thought she might scream when the first midge entered her already ravaged ear and assaulted her with the amplified sound of buzzing wings foretelling the pain to come. The shrill humming drilled into her head like a root canal. Two steps closer to the tree, she lost count of how many insects had joined the first. By the droning cacophony inside her head, it seemed like a thousand.

Burn the fuckers out.

The thought of a cleansing flame brought a grim smile to her face. Every microscopic bit of the insects completely annihilated, leaving only a purifying warmth and her ear free of the unendurable buzzing and pain. Intense heat neared her cheek, and she realized her hand intended to comply. She caught herself and swung the torch at the swarm in retaliation. A fresh pinprick of pain erupted in her ear and, once again, she had to stop her hand from reflexively turning the torch on herself.

Get your shit together.

She'd never save Faith if she couldn't get control of herself.

Another bite came, this time on her left eyelid, and her resolution for self control was gone in an instant. She roared a guttural, incomprehensible scream, and spun, swinging the torch wildly, trying to kill every last one of them.

Not one more fucking bite! Not one more!

Stomping, she lurched over the moving tree roots, trying to crush the insects underfoot. She felt a bite on her back and spun to get the fucker who bit her. Then she stomped some more, grinding them under her heels. It wasn't enough just to kill them. They had to cease to exist entirely. If even the tiniest shred of their bodies existed, she would never stop feeling them crawl on her skin.

She went on her path of destruction, stomping and waving the torch in the air, until she stumbled on the roots and the flame of the torch brushed her leg. It took a second for the pain to reach her brain, but once there, the searing didn't just clear her head. It blasted her with a burning sanity.

She had one goal here.

One.

"Faith!" Her daughter's name was her rallying cry.

Laney threw the torch at the tree.

As soon as it left her hand, something in the roots near the trunk caught her eye. Small dirty fingers wiggled up through an opening in the ground.

"Mommmmmeee—"

The blue flame kissed the gas soaked bark, and flames engulfed the tree with a deafening roar, lighting up the night. A blast of intense heat staggered Laney back, and she fell. The roots writhed beneath her with a panicked fervor as she struggled to get to her hands and knees, desperate to find her daughter's hand amongst the roots again.

The flames spread fast, catching the midges and turning them into a swarm of embers. Tiny sparks of flaming insects danced in the turbulent currents of heat.

Laney stood and stumbled forward, the roots constantly threating to take her feet out from under her. If Faith was below the tree, there had to be a way for her to get in, too. She had to find it before it was too late.

But fire owned the tree and the waves of heat radiating off of it burned her skin. The air baked her throat and lungs with every breath. She knew she'd die if she went much further.

Shrieks and groans came from the burning oak as the bark and wood split. The roar of the blaze filled her ears as the flames climbed high towards the branches. But she could only hear her daughter's voice calling for her. The voice had been raw like sandpaper, but Laney knew it was Faith.

I have to find my baby.

She closed her eyes and staggered into the overwhelming heat.

49

Following

Shadows surrounded the wide-open door, shielding it from the light. The pantry beyond the door itself was even darker. Even though they had left the light on in there when they pulled the washer out. It was as if the threshold didn't lead to a simple room, but the deep dark of space, a black hole with gravity so strong that light couldn't escape its pull. Nothing could.

Ray stood at the other end of the hall across from it. He held a fireplace poker in one hand, and his cell phone charged to thirty-two percent in the other. A modern warrior prepared to enter battle with a creature from a campfire tale. He glared at the dark entrance, his jaw clenched tight.

Despite the hatred boiling inside of him, it took all his will to take the first step into the shadows. With each step deeper, the air grew cooler. Until his breath fogged before him and goosebumps crawled up his arms and the back of his neck.

The closer he got to the door, the more the light slunk away behind him. He fumbled, one handed, with the flashlight button on his phone. His stomach lurched when the phone nearly slipped from his fingers. Though it would only hit the wooden floor beneath him, he was sure, once it left his hand, he would never find it again.

Flashlight on, Ray pointed the phone in front of him. It barely penetrated the murk beyond the opening. Vague shapes of boxes and canned goods lurked in shifting shadows just beyond the light.

Did something just move in there?

One step away from the door, his will faltered and his feet rooted to the floor. An icy knot grew in the pit of his stomach.

This is fucking suicidal. If I go in there, I don't come out.

Don't give a shit.

That was grandpa's trick to deal with fear. But Ray gave a shit. Above his need for vengeance, for all that Jeremiah put him through, put his family through. Even above, he admitted to himself with shame, finding his sister. He wanted to live.

For all he knew, Faith was already gone. The thought of it was a gut punch, but it was the most likely reality. Grandpa was gone. Faith was gone. Probably his mother, too. And he was about to check into the same roach motel that took out the rest of his family.

Above all, he wanted to live. The mud taught him that.

He couldn't take the next step forward. But he also couldn't turn around, couldn't step back, couldn't leave his sister to her fate, gone or not.

Standing at the threshold of the door, staring into the gloom, a realization came over him. An understanding beyond his years. There was living. And then there was living in fear, or worse, guilt. Which wasn't really living at all.

Grandpa taught him that.

Ray stepped a trembling foot over the threshold.

The damp, sickly smell hit him as soon as he crossed into the room. It was just like the tree, but so much stronger. It cloyed to his skin like an oily sheen. The stench forced its way into his nostrils. He could taste it in the back of his mouth. The revulsion was instantaneous and he wretched, splattering the dinner he ate a lifetime ago all over the floor and his sneakers.

Bent over, leaning against a shelf, he waited for his stomach to decide it was empty, and dry heaved a few times more before it did. Something ran across his hand and he pushed away, straightening with disgust.

He let the light play around the room. The bi-fold doors were open, and the washing machine sat where he and his mother had left it in the middle of the room. But when he cast his light towards the laundry closet, something beyond the washer ate it.

Ray walked closer, revealing a jagged hole in the floor where the washer had been. Something had ripped away the wood planks in an uneven circle about three feet wide. Dust sifted from the broken planks into the darkness below. He leaned over the opening, the wood creaking beneath his front foot. The chilling stench that shot up at him nearly knocked him from his feet. His stomach convulsed once more, but there was nothing left to purge.

He shined the light down. Insects skittered out of sight. An old wooden ladder, spotted with dark rot and broken steps in places, leaned up against the lip of the hole. The missing flooring lay scattered on the dirt floor below him. Among the planks was a doll house figure wearing a pink dress. It sprawled, limbs askew, like a mangled body at the bottom of a cliff. A roach ran over the doll's face, fleeing the light.

Ray's empty stomach lurched at the thought of Faith being down there alone in the dark.

"Faith?" He said, his voice barely above a whisper. He tensed, waiting for something in the darkness below him to respond.

Standing at the edge of the hole felt like swimming in the deepest part of the ocean, kicking legs dangling like bait for whatever lay below him. Every instinct he had screamed, run. Get away from the hole, from the house, the whole damn farm and keep running.

There was more than cold and stench emanating from the pit below him. A malevolent power radiated from the dark. An icy hand wrapped his intestines through its gnarled, bony fingers and squeezed.

He knew this was the place where Jeremiah was his strongest.

Grandpa wasn't tough enough.

How am I supposed to be?

His lip quivered as he took a step away from the hole, head shaking a definitive "no".

I can't go down there. Mom wouldn't want me to. She'd want me to do the safe thing. I found Faith. I did that much. Now mom can go get her. She has to. It's her job. Not mine. It's her job.

"Ray." Faith's tearful voice echoed from the pit.

Impulse took him, and he let it. Ray was on the rickety ladder the moment he heard his sister's voice.

He made it two rungs down.

The next rung crumbled to dust without a sound when his foot bore weight on it. He let the poker go and flailed, grabbing a broken plank jutting out over the edge. It held him for less than a second before the splintered wood gave way and he fell.

He hit the ground hard, landing flat. His head bounced off the dirt floor and a cracking sound resonated from where his back landed on the poker. The impact knocked the wind out of him. For the moment, there was no pain, just the panic inducing need to breathe. He rolled onto his hands and knees, still somehow holding the phone, and sucked in wheezing gasps of dank air.

A far off scream echoed faintly in the darkness, but he was so focused on filling his lungs, he barely noticed it.

After a few minutes of catching his breath, he forced himself to his feet.

He took a deep breath, preparing to yell, and a sharp knife of pain flared in his back.

"Faaaith." His sister's name came out a breathless croak that trailed off to a whisper.

There was no answer.

Ray shone the light in front of him. The beam shook with his hand as he turned a circle. The ladder stood near a wall at one end of the rectangular room, a room about twelve feet long and half as wide. Wooden shelves covered in dusty boxes, and glass jars filled with dark liquid lined the gray stone walls. Thick logs, covered in cobwebs, loomed heavy two feet overhead. A large, cobweb covered wheel lay nestled among debris near where he landed.

I'm such a fucking idiot.

Faith wasn't here. There was no way out. He let Jeremiah sucker him again.

The ladder was rubbish. He might make a jump for the top of the hole. But even if he pulled off the jump with his broken ribs, he didn't think the planks would hold him.

A bead of sweat ran down his back, causing him to shiver. The tremor sent a fresh stab of pain through his ribs and confirmed it. He wasn't climbing out of there.

Worse, he got the sense he wasn't alone.

With nowhere else to go, he turned towards the wheel. Goosebumps prickled his flesh as he walked closer. A large, rusted metal wheel, bent at an angle, lay on top of what looked like a woven chair rotted in some places, chewed through in others. Wood armrests, any polish they might have held once, now long gone, lay near the wheel. Below the chair lay a second wheel, just as damaged as the first. In the scattered debris of wood and leather straps lay two more small wheels.

Jeremiah's wheelchair.

Angela told Ray Jeremiah had been in a wheelchair for years before he died. And from what she said, it really pissed him off.

But how the hell did it get down here?

Ray shone the light up at the hole. He could make out the partial frame of a what must have once been a hatch. Metal brackets screwed into the wood near where remnants of the ladder were attached.

Jeremiah must have fallen. Or, more likely, Grandpa was right. Someone pushed him.

Ray turned the light back to the chair.

If that's his chair, where's Jeremiah?

There was a pattern on the ground, just beyond the chair, undisturbed by time except for the occasional crossing of rodent footprints. A staggered groove carved the surface of the dirt, as if something had been dragged in fits and bursts a long time ago. Ray followed it to the other end of the room, where scuffled impressions had erased the drag marks a foot from the wall. The stone of the wall had collapsed at the base, and the gap it created opened to a cave.

He squatted to get a better look and played his phone light around the hole. Imprinted on the dirt, just in front of the opening, were five warped oval shapes. His breath caught in his throat when he recognized the pattern, and realized Jeremiah wasn't taunting him with the dollhouse figure. Faith had actually been here. Like right *here*, at this hole, and she left the toe prints to prove it.

The mouth was tight, but the tunnel dropped about a foot and opened up into what looked like a natural cave. Massive boulders leaned and stacked against each other, forming the chamber. The gap was just large enough for him to make it through if he crawled. It went on for at least ten feet on a downward angle. Tree roots poked through the boulders here and there before it curved up and out of sight.

Maybe a way out? Jeremiah must have thought so. Faith too.

He reached into the cave mouth with his phone, then shifted his weight to get another angle on the end of the tunnel, hoping to see where it continued.

Something heavy dragged across the dirt floor behind him.

Startled and off balance, Ray tried to straighten too fast. His phone caught on the edge of the broken wall, knocking it from his hand. Pain shot through his back and his balance tipped backwards. He only staggered a foot before the wall caught him. But even this was enough to trigger a muscle spasm, sending waves of excruciating pain through his back. Leaning against the cool, rough wall, he hugged his arms around his body, trying to stop the onslaught.

The phone must have landed face down, but not completely flat. There was just enough light spill to mark the cave entrance. Ray stood in the dark, taking shallow breaths, tears running down his face, as he waited for the pain to ebb.

Sound came again from the direction of the ladder, this time a soft impact, then something long and heavy dragging across the dirt floor. Ray pictured the trail in the dirt he followed to the cave and he knew what made the sound.

Jeremiah was coming for him.

He had no choice now. Wincing at the pain, Ray slid into the hole on his belly, then pulled his way through the cave entrance. It would have been an easy maneuver on a good day, but with the broken ribs, it was anything but. The pain in his back was agonizing. The rough edges of the stone wall scraped traces in the flesh of his stomach as he pulled himself into the hole. He reached for the next handhold, feeling around for anything that would give him leverage, then finally gripped a crack in the rock wall. Straining his back muscles, setting off a new flare of pain, he pulled himself in further.

He paused for a moment to reach for his phone, that lay slightly behind him to his right. But the sound came again. It was close and moving fast.

Panicked, ignoring the pain, and the grinding he felt as his ribs shifted, rubbing bone against bone, he flailed around for another handhold. An icy breath caressed his left calf, and he yanked his leg and tucked it up underneath him, then dug his toes into a crevice and pushed himself forward.

Knotted fingers, icy cold, and slick with rot and dangling flesh, wrapped around the ankle of his right leg still protruding into the root cellar. The hand gripped tight and pulled. A bony ribcage covered in coarse cloth slid up and over his calf.

Ray kicked out, bashing his leg against the edges of the hole until the thing let go, leaving bits of rotten flesh smeared onto his skin. His hand swept over a gap in the rock, and he jammed his fingers in. Planting the toes of his sneakers against the boulder beneath him, he pulled hard and gained another foot. Then another. And another before he stopped to listen for it. He sucked in slow, shaky breaths until his pounding heart slowed.

There was nothing but silence from the cellar beyond the hole.

He expelled a breath of relief and let his head drop to the cool stone below him. But the damp surface that met his face wasn't stone. Jeremiah's breath, cold and foul, dampened Ray's skin as his cheek laid against a thin layer of slick flesh, stretched taut over a bony skull. He immediately tried to pull away, but the decayed skin had fused with his and when he pulled, the rotted flesh stretched with him.

"Raaaay." It was a simple, drawn out whisper, but the word splintered into tiny pieces that pierced his skull and wormed their way into his brain. Jeremiah's gnarled hand slowly caressed Ray's face, starting at his forehead, sliding down until bony fingertips reached his eyes.

"You won't need these where you're going."

Sharpened points of long nails punctured the thin barrier of his eyelids before a sickening pop released a rush of warm fluid down Ray's cheeks, and the nails continued on, driving deep into his skull.

A new sound filled the cave, careening through every tiny crack, every narrow fissure, bouncing off the hard granite rock faces, gaining power.

Ray screamed and screamed.

50

A Real Mother

When Laney opened her eyes again, she found herself on the outskirts of the clearing, not knowing how she got there. She looked up at the tree. There was no sense of the trunk anymore, just a column of flames holding aloft fiery branches. She dropped to her knees and watched the tree burn through tearing eyes and shimmering air.

Coward. Fucking disgrace of a mother. You didn't deserve her. A real mother would have saved her or died trying.

She expected the voice inside her head to be Troy's. Only he would be that cruel. But it was her own voice.

And it was right.

She hoped against hope for a break in the flames, or to hear her daughter's voice again. But she knew the truth of it. When she tossed the torch, she killed her daughter.

Laney wanted, more than almost anything, to lie down beneath the canopy of burning limbs and wait for them to succumb to the fire and take her to Faith.

Only one thought kept her moving.

Ray.

51

The Light

The chill creeped into Ray's cheek and jaw bones with a dull ache as he slowly became aware of the cool stone beneath him. His screams wound down. His hand went to his face, where his eyes used to be, expecting gaping holes, but found the rounded flesh of eyelids. He opened them and took in the smooth rock beneath him in the dim light. Ignoring the pain, he contorted his body to search the small chamber, and found no sign of Jeremiah.

An hour ago, he believed that no pain could be worse than the burning pressure of mud filling his lungs. Jeremiah proved him wrong. Ray wouldn't underestimate him again. His hand brushed the skin of his face, confirming it was still there.

His phone lay back at the entrance, leaning against the rock. The gaping hole leading to the root cellar loomed over it. He knew he had to go back and get the phone, but there was nothing he wanted to do less. He turned to the absolute darkness that lay in front of him.

Scratch that. Something came to mind.

Climbing further into the cave without a light would not happen. Who know's what Jeremiah had waiting for him? He didn't have a choice. There was nowhere else to go, but he needed the light.

He pulled his pocketknife out of the side pocket on his cargo shorts and opened it. The blade that impressed him so much back in town now seemed woefully small.

With no room to turn around, he wormed his way backwards towards the entrance, a maneuver that had him grimacing in pain. When he reached it, he braced his legs on either side of the hole, and stretched the hand with the knife back for the phone, trying to ignore the grinding in his ribs from the twisting.

No good. He couldn't reach.

Taking a deep breath to force down the rising panic, he backed out through the hole, feeling the weight of darkness on his back. He snatched the phone and shined the light behind him, doing a quick pass around the cellar, thinking it would make him feel better. That it would ease the threatening presence at his back. Despite the lack of a decomposing Jeremiah waiting to pounce, it didn't. Finding the cellar empty just made him feel like he was missing something. He forced himself to turn his back to the dark space and crawled into the cave to find Faith.

52

The Axe

Vacant green eyes stared up at her in the beam of her headlamp. The body lay sprawled on the front steps of the porch, surrounded by a puddle of sticky, drying blood and buzzing flies. His scalp was gone. His face and chest were pocked with bloody holes. But Laney knew who he was. She'd expected to run across him after she found his brother in the barn. She didn't expect to find him like this, but that hardly mattered now.

Laney skirted the mess and walked up the other side of the steps. An axe, retrieved during a pit stop at the barn, hung heavy in her right hand. Without hesitation, she swung the front door wide open, expecting the worst, and wanting to get it over with. Her headlamp barely breached the darkness at the other end of the hall. Even without the light, she would have known the pantry door was open, but the sense of overwhelming dread that emanated from beyond the door was lost on her.

She was full up.

The lights were on in the living room, revealing her father's body. Laney had walked through the front door expecting nothing less. But the reality of it weakened her knees, and she leaned against the arch to steady herself.

When she saw no sign of Ray, a small spark of hope ignited in her. And that was all it took to crack the dam. It was a small crack, just a hairline fracture. Tears welled in her eyes, just once. She wiped them clear, and they were gone.

Her father didn't look peaceful in death. He looked old and weak. His hand, lying limp on the floor, reached out to her, as if to say "look what you did". He'd spent years defying Jeremiah, and was stronger for it. Just three days with his family left him small and vulnerable. She did this to him. She killed him. Just like she killed-

Laney shut that thought down, straightened off the arch, and walked through the pantry door.

The space where the washing machine used to be waited for her. She thought about that on the walk back from the tree. She thought about a lot of things on that walk. But mostly, she thought about finding Jeremiah and making him pay. And he had told her where to find him earlier that day in the pantry.

Laney swung the axe with all her strength. The hungry blade tore jagged holes in the floor where the washer had stood, revealing an empty darkness below. She swung again, and again widening the hole until her arms were numb.

She shone her headlamp into the void, illuminating the still settling cloud of dust from her demolition. Through the particulate fog, she could just make out the pink dress of the tiny doll sprawled on the dirt below, covered in a layer of sawdust, and her breath caught in her throat. If she had followed her instincts, had smashed through the floor earlier, Faith would still be alive. For the thousandth time since she left the burning tree, Laney pushed all thoughts of Faith to the outskirts of her grief ravaged mind. The guilt would have to wait. She needed to find Ray. She needed to end Jeremiah.

Laney grabbed the fold-up ladder from the corner of the pantry, then dropped it into the hole. It clattered dully on the dirt floor. She dropped the axe down next. Easing herself over the edge, she let her feet drop to the ground.

It was an old root cellar, maybe a foot taller than her. She shone the light around, her nose wrinkling at the smell. A pile of debris that looked like an old wheelchair lay near the crumbled wooden ladder, and she offhandedly attributed it to the noise she had heard in the hall, not caring why it was there.

Footprints, Ray's footprints, led across the cellar.

She swung the beam along the shelves on the wall, and a sob

caught in her throat. Another footprint, small, delicate, each toe clearly defined, imprinted the dirt a foot from the shelves. The smaller footprints continued along the wall.

Two sets of prints, leading in the same direction. She picked up the axe and followed them, alternating the light between the parallel paths walked by her children. Both sets converged near a dark hole at the base of the wall, where the foundation had collapsed. Faint clouds of smoke drifted out of the hole in a gentle breeze.

Smoke from the tree.

The implications staggered her. Her legs went weak, and she dropped to her knees in front of the hole. Faith must have crawled through this cave to get to the tree. There was no other way. And Ray followed his sister in.

She lost both her children tonight.

The crushing weight of grief threatened to collapse in on her. She dropped her head to the floor, clawing up handfuls of dirt as the first gut wrenching sob struggled to work its way up through an esophagus far too small to handle the enormity of guilt it carried.

A wet slap of flesh on stone echoed from the cave. Laney straightened, let the dirt grasped in her hands fall to the floor, and shined her headlamp into the hole. A tiny glimmer of hope carried on the beam of light. Motion disturbed the smoke where the cave turned up at the end. Someone was coming down. Laney held her breath, waiting, hoping. Despite the whispers creeping in from the outskirts of her mind, warning her that hope would be her downfall.

The sounds drew closer.

Finally, a hand came down at the turn of the cave. Laney froze, trying to process the sight of it. A low moan rose from somewhere deep inside her. The second hand came down into the light and she couldn't look any more. She grabbed the axe and slid away from the hole, got to her feet. Though she couldn't bear it, she forced her eyes back to the dark opening at the base of the wall.

Staggering back, dragging the axe along the floor, her mind tried to comprehend what she saw, ignoring the voice in her head screaming for her mind to bury it deep and never think of it again.

Dark smoke billowed from the hole.

A ghastly hand followed.

53

The Hand

Its crisp flesh burned and peeling, the hand grasped the wall on one side of the opening. A second hand reached through, and fingers melted to nubs, braced the other. Together they pulled, and a head burned clean of hair, save patches that were still aflame, emerged. Its small face was a featureless mass of burned and bloody, sloughing skin except for one untouched eye. The bright blue orb, perfection in a sea of destruction, smoldering with a hatred hotter than the burning oak, turned in its socket to look at Laney.

The child-thing bared its teeth through fused lips. Strands of flesh stretched and pulled like taffy to reveal the blackened teeth behind them. It squatted near the rubble of the wall, a wet growl rumbling in its throat. With a curious tilt of its head, it watched its mother back away in fear.

Without warning, it coiled and launched.

Laney brought up the axe in front of her, gripped tight in her hands, and let reflexes take over. She stepped to the side, and the thing flew past. It hit the ground behind her, then slid into a set of shelves. Glass jars rattled, then fell to the ground, unleashing a new stench of rot.

She turned to face it, but saw only a pile of broken glass mixed with the rotted contents of the smashed jars.

Frenetic movement came from behind, crashing into the side of her knee. She fell against the shelves next to her. More jars clinked and rattled before crashing to the floor. The cacophony of breaking glass masked the things next strike. This time it hit her in the small of her back, sending her flailing against the shelves again. She grabbed the top shelf to stop her fall. A muffled snap was all the warning she got before the rotted plank collapsed, sending her and dozens of jars to the floor.

Laney landed on her hands and knees amidst a sea of broken glass, driving a shard the size of a steak knife into the meat of her left palm. It crunched and broke off when it hit bone. Dozens of tiny slivers pierced the skin of her knees and she let out a scream of shock more than pain.

The thing rushed her again and again, taking frenetic shots at her ribs and head. Each blow left its mark on her skin and clothes in moist shreds of burned flesh.

Laney struggled to get to her feet, but fell twice, embedding new shards into her legs, before staggering to a leaning stand against the shelves. Her ears rang. The axe dangled from her right hand, hanging limply at her side. The cloth of her jeans hung damp and heavy with blood.

"Stop." It came out as a gasp, barely audible, surprising Laney when she heard it come from her mouth.

"Stop," she said again, this time louder and on purpose, a pathetic plea in her voice. She loathed herself at that moment. All thoughts of revenge were gone, and any strength of conviction she had coming down, abandoned her. Reduced by the mind ripping chaos of it all, to a distraught and grieving failure of a woman with nothing left to live for, she slid to the ground, numb to the fresh shards of glass greeting her skin.

Still, it came for her. Hitting her over and over. A relentless onslaught of attacks that made her want to crawl into a ball, lay on the ground, and wait for it to be over. In her mind's eye, Ray rolled his eyes in disgust. And at the thought of him, that spark of hope—rekindled when she first heard the noise in the cave—flared to life again. She clung to it. What if Ray was still alive?

Finding motivation in the dimmest, most masochistic of sparks, she struggled to her feet again.

A maniacally fast patter of footsteps came from her left. Laney turned just in time to see it running on all fours.

It leaped at her. She swung the axe out in front of her to block it. That did nothing against the momentum of the thing. Laney flew backward, hitting more shelves, shattering the jars. The back of her neck erupted in pain as glass covered in rotted, fermented fruit sliced her skin. The axe fell from her hands. She dropped to her knees, glass shards crunching as they ground against bone.

She didn't have time to recover before the flutter of footfalls came from the darkness again.

It hit her from behind. Clung to her back, and held fast. Its arms, wrapped tight around her neck, legs braced against her sides. Its face, slimy with blood and loose scraps of skin, pressed firm against her cheek.

In Faith's sweet voice, it whispered in her ear. "You said you'd never hurt me, mommy."

"Oh, baby, mommy didn't m–" The nubbed hand came loose from around her neck, and shoved its way into her mouth.

"Liar!" it screamed.

Laney gagged against the taste of burnt flesh. She got hold of the thing's arm and tried to pull it out. With each grip, flesh shed away through her fingers, until she was gripping nothing but bone and sinew. The hand shoved deeper as if it intended to rip out her guts from the inside.

With her airway cut off, everything went mercifully dark. She listened from a great distance, as the thing skittered away, the echoing sound of tinkling glass following it.

When her vision returned in flashes and sparks, it revealed a dirt floor covered in glass, scuffed and smeared with blood. She was on her hands and knees, gasping for air. A high pitch whine filled her ears, masking the sound of its footfalls. It clubbed her head as it flew by, sending her sprawling on her side.

The light from her headlamp flickered. In the stuttering light, it came for her, creeping forward, drawing the moment out. The large piece of broken glass in its good hand glinted savagely in the light.

Laney saw the axe on the ground in front of her before her headlamp sputtered out for good. But she didn't reach for it.

She had never, in her life, been more done.

54

The Nightmare

Crawling through the root infested tunnel with broken ribs was exactly as bad as Ray thought it would be. Navigating the changes in direction and pitch of the cave had been tricky, but he figured out some ways to move without triggering too much pain in his back. They mostly involved keeping his posture stiff. That wouldn't be possible here.

Shining his flashlight through the light smoke—his mother's work, he guessed—and beyond the tangle of roots currently blocking him, the tunnel headed down for a few feet before pitching sharply upwards again. That angle change at the bottom would require him to contort his body in ways he was already dreading. But first he had to get through the roots.

Ray pulled out his pocket knife, hand cramping as he gripped it. He'd already stopped three times to saw his way through root tangles he couldn't squeeze through. The blade had dulled by the time he finished with the first tangle. By his third, it was like trying to cut through rope with the edge of a ruler.

It felt like it took forever to clear the way. Sweating and out of breath, he checked his phone. The charge was down to nineteen percent. He had dimmed the power of the phone's flashlight. In total darkness, a dim light was sufficient, and it saved on battery. He hoped it would be enough to take him wherever this tunnel ended.

Ray slid down the smooth rock until he reached the bottom. The angle of the pitch change was more severe than it looked from the top. This was going to suck. It was going to suck real bad. He took a deep breath to prepare for the coming pain and pushed himself down the easy part. Then, he arched his back for the up pitch and the familiar stab of pain pierced his ribs. Reaching for hand holds only made it worse, but there was no going back from this point. He let out a grunt with each bone grinding pull and finally rounded the angle.

By the time he made it through, his whole body shook with pain. And the shaking only made the pain worse. A vicious cycle. Crying, he laid up against the cool stone to wait it out.

The smoke got worse as the shakes were winding down. The dull roar of the blaze, muffled down to a white noise by barriers and distance, washed over the walls of stone.

If the smoke came from the tree, that meant the tunnel exited near the clearing. Ray wasn't sure if it still made sense to keep going. Would he even be able to get out with the fire? If the smoke got any thicker, he might have to turn back, anyway. He still didn't know if there even was a way out at all, or if Faith even entered the cave. But what choice did he have? He'd gotten this far, and he had to know for sure. Dread filled him at just considering the possibility of having to crawl back the way he came.

A dry hiss came from above him. He swung the light of the phone up to where the tunnel widened and slanted out of view. The sound came again, two distinct sounds really, dull smacks followed by the whisper of something dragging on the stone. Something big.

Ray's hand instinctively went to his cheek, and it surprised him yet again to find intact skin where Jeremiah's rotting flesh had touched him. His face crawled, remembering the sensation of melding skin, like thousands of maggots burrowing violently in and out, stitching his flesh to Jeremiah's. A shiver ran through him, threatening to trigger the cycle of pain all over again.

Pebbles rained down on him. Jeremiah had reached the slant of the tunnel.

Maybe he should retreat, try to go back the way he came. There was room enough to turn around in here. But the idea of Jeremiah reaching him while he contorted himself through that angle in the tunnel was more than he could handle.

Not wanting to see it, not even for a second, Ray pocketed his phone, pulled his t-shirt up over his head and wrapped his arms around it, shielding his face. His heart pounded in the darkness. He gripped his knife hard, ready to swing when Jeremiah got closer. Though he didn't think it would do any good.

Heavy breathing filled the tunnel. The slap and drag of flesh on stone inched towards him. The clumsy cadence of meaty smacks echoed through the cave. Drags, like sandpaper, left the image in his head of a trail of grated flesh marking the granite in the thing's wake. The phantom stench of sweet, nauseating rot assaulted his nose.

Ray couldn't take it anymore. The only thing worse than seeing what was coming for him was being in the dark with it. He untangled his arms from around his head, grabbed the phone from his pocket, and poked his face through the neck of his t-shirt up to his nose.

His hand shaking, he pointed the beam of light at the approaching nightmare and screamed when he saw it.

55

Gone

As Laney lay there and waited for the thing—for her daughter—to take her vengeance, she tried to picture Faith as she was before. She searched for that ever smiling, perfect little face, for the warm light that filled every room she was in. But its face, that monstrous, ravaged face, wormed its way into her head, corrupting every memory. She could no longer form a picture of her daughter in her mind's eye, without seeing the horrifying visage the fire left behind.

Faith was gone. Laney had lost her daughter in every conceivable way. There would be no last moment of solace before the end.

The rage came suddenly.

It erupted, filling Laney's core with heat so blindingly hot that she felt nothing at all. Her fatigue was gone. Guilt gone. Fear gone. The drone of blood pumping through her veins hummed in her ears like electricity. It flowed with such power, a coppery taste filled her mouth.

A lucidity, pure in its emptiness, the kind that can only be achieved when all the distractions, all the sum parts of a life, have been destroyed, washed over her. In the calm center of her fury, she realized that the rage had been building the whole time. It didn't start today when she lit the tree and heard her daughter scream. It didn't start when she had to abandon the life she worked so hard for. It started years ago, on the first day her family had set foot on Killian Farm.

Laney found the axe in the darkness in front of her, then got to her feet, numb to the pain of her cuts, but not the warm rivulets of blood flowing down her back.

She didn't mask her sounds as she moved. The crunch of broken glass beneath her feet was a beacon for the thing to find her.

And it did.

Swift footfalls came at her in the dark. Laney swung the axe hard, getting nothing but the whistle of empty air and a hard clap to the side of her head for her effort.

She turned in the direction it had gone, and stood her ground, axe drawn back, ready to swing. Waiting for what seemed like minutes, she held her breath, and wished her heart wasn't pounding so loud in her ears.

There it was.

The slightest tinkling of glass. It must have circled behind her. She turned, swung with everything she had. The blade of the axe connected with a wet crunching sound, and the thing fell to the ground before her.

Laney raised the axe high above her head and brought it down as hard as she could. Feeling the blade sink into yielding flesh and bone triggered a churning revulsion in the pit of her stomach, and a disturbing sense of satisfaction.

The only sounds in the cellar were the whoosh of the axe, the wet, meaty thud when it hit, and the pounding of her heart. The world spun around her, and she stood in the eye of its cyclone, disconnected from everything. Each time she brought the axe above her head, raining warm drops of blood down on herself, she thought, "That's enough". But she swung the axe again.

And with each hit, the thing's flesh–Faith's flesh–resisted less, until Laney felt the impact of solid ground reverberate through the handle. There was nothing left of the thing—her daughter—but a decimated pile of gore. She let the axe drop to the ground with a soft thud, and stood in the quiet, glad for the darkness.

56

Back Again

As soon as the light from his phone hit her, she grunted and closed her eyes. Ray didn't recognize her at first. She was filthy, scratched up, wild hair sticking out in all directions. She kept moving, coming at him fast, like he was a brick wall that she intended to punch a hole right through. Jaw clenched, teeth gritted, she snorted air out through her nose like a charging bull. But when he realized it was really her, he let out a scream of joy that echoed through the cave.

"Faith?"

Hands slapping hard on the stone, she tilted her head down, picked up speed and plowed forward.

"Faith!" Ray yelled.

Her head swung up for a second at the sound of her name, but she kept moving.

Ray covered his head with his arms, bracing for the impact. She slammed against his forearms like a battering ram, then stopped, backed away. A few seconds later, her hand tentatively felt along his arms, then pulled back.

Ray brought his phone light up, shining it against the cave wall to soften the beam. Faith covered her eyes with her hand and squinted through her fingers.

"Ray?" she croaked, her raspy voice echoing off the stone. "Are you real?"

The pain in his ribs barely registered as Ray scrambled to hug his sister. She flinched at his touch, as if she still didn't believe it was him. Then all at once, she hugged him back.

Aches and pains forgotten, Ray smiled when they took the last turn of the tunnel that led to the entrance of the root cellar. If someone had told him a week ago that he would be relieved to see a dark hole that led into an even darker cellar where he last encountered his long dead great-great-grandfather, he would have called bullshit.

"We're here," He said. Faith responded with a sniffle, and he could only imagine she was crying in relief.

But the nagging worry that they had it all wrong clouded his eagerness to escape the tunnel. What if killing the tree did nothing? What if Jeremiah waited for them on the other side of the hole? His stomach tightened as they got closer.

They reached the end of the tunnel, and he stopped. Faith bumped into him from behind. His worry that burning the tree didn't work, and the two of them being trapped between an undead psychopath and a raging fire with no way out, became more than a worry.

"What-," she rasped, but he shushed her.

Quiet, ragged breathing whispered in the cellar's dark. With a shaking hand, he pointed his phone light through the hole and the sight took his breath away.

His mother stood there swaying, splattered in blood, shards of broken glass poking from her skin. The glass caught the beam and sparkled, washing his gore covered mother in a surreal fairy tale light.

It took her a few moments to notice that she was no longer in total darkness. She turned and squinted at him until her dull, empty eyes adjusted to the light. Then she calmly bent down, grabbed the handle of an axe, and walked towards him, dragging the axe head along the dirt floor.

The thought of what she might do sent a chill rushing through his bowels. He struggled to find his voice, and when he did, it was high pitched and squeaky.

"Mom! It's Ray."

If she heard him, she didn't show it. She kept coming. His mother might be just another one of Jeremiah's mind games, but that did nothing to curb the rising panic. Knowing what it felt like to get an axe between the eyes was not something he would regret missing out on.

"Mom, stop! It's me. It's Ray and Faith."

He turned to his sister. "Back up! Back up!"

Ray started back before Faith could move, pushing his sister in his panic.

Laney neared the hole, and swung the axe up into a two hand grip, held high, and at the ready.

"Mom! It's Ray!" He turned the phone light on himself.

She stopped.

Her eyes changed, like he found the switch, and the light inside her turned back on.

"Ray?" she asked.

"Yeah mom. Ray and Faith, mom. Ray and Faith."

His mom dropped to her knees, and he cringed at the crunch of glass that she showed no sign of feeling. The axe dropped to the ground beside her with a dull thump.

He scrambled out of the hole, Faith right behind him.

Laney held her arms wide for a hug, then caught sight of the blood covering her, and let them drop to her sides. Ray hugged her anyway.

"My babies. You're okay." Tears streaked down Laney's cheeks.

Faith's face softened. Her lip quivered. She squeezed in next to Ray, threw her arms around their mother's neck and hugged tight.

"My babies are okay." Laney said again, as if trying to reassure herself it was really true.

Ray pulled away. "I'm, most definitely, not okay," he said in a winded, pain cracked voice, but managed the ghost of a smile. Then the smile faded as he remembered. "Grandpa's–"

"I know," Laney said. "I know."

"What?" Faith asked.

But Ray could tell she knew from the look on her face. It seemed she didn't have any tears left. She laid her head against their mother's blood stained shoulder and closed her eyes.

They climbed the fold-up ladder out of the root cellar and into the warm glow of the rising sun. Putting herself between her kids and the darkness at their backs, Laney went last. She had pulled out what shards she could from her hands before attempting the climb, and left a bloody handprint on every rung. When she reached the top, Laney grabbed a couple of towels from a shelf in the pantry and wound them around her palms.

Ray led the way, shuffling out of the pantry and down the hall towards the front door. He kept his eyes on the floor, averted from his grandfather's body. Laney hugged Faith tight beside her and guided her towards the kitchen as they neared the arch. A quick hobble, and she caught up to Ray, gently grabbed the back of his shirt. He turned, giving her a confused look.

"Let's go out the kitchen," she said, nodding towards the arch.

He went pale beneath the scrapes and bruises, remembering what lay beyond the front door. And Laney knew, in that moment, that he had pulled the trigger. He'd been through so much, and she couldn't protect him.

"It wasn't your fault." She said.

He nodded in reflex, but his eyes didn't agree.

"Mommy," Faith said, her voice a painful rasp, "I want to say goodbye to Grandpa."

"Okay baby." Laney walked Faith into the living room and watched her exhausted seven-year-old daughter kneel with all the grace of an octogenarian, to hug goodbye the grandfather she had only just met. She viewed the scene filled with a hollow ache that she knew time would eventually fill with grief, or anger, or both. But for now, she clung to the reality of just being in the same room with Faith, knowing it was everything.

After a while, her little girl sat up, then put her hand on Pete's cheek. "I didn't know you long, but I love you and am going to miss you very much. You were the best grandpa ever." Faith kissed him gently on his cheek, then slowly got to her feet and went to the kitchen to hug Ray.

Laney took the blanket from the recliner and draped it over her father.

"Best dad ever too," her voice cracked as she pulled the blanket up over his face.

57

The Road

"Sit down. I'm going to need a minute," Laney said, doing a stiff-legged walk across the kitchen floor to the cupboard where her father kept the first aid kit. With the adrenaline wearing off, the pained ebbed in giving her awareness of every piece of glass puncturing her skin. Each shard throbbed, sending out pings of pain, pinpointing their location on the map of her body.

The kids slumped into chairs around the table. Faith crossed her arms on the Formica, laid her head down, and closed her eyes.

A new first-aid kit in a white plastic case had replaced the well-worn canvas bag containing the grab bag assortment of cartoon themed band-aids and half-used tubes of ointments from her childhood. She took the kit, pulled the roll of paper towels off the holder near the sink, then dragged the trashcan over to the kitchen table. Laney slowly lowered herself into the nearest chair, letting out a hiss as she went down, like bleeding air from a pneumatic piston. Despite the pangs from muscles tensing around the broken glass as she sat, sitting was heaven.

After she bandaged her hands, Laney started with a large shard, sunk deep into her thigh, carefully avoiding the sharp edges. The last thing she needed to do was to shred her fingers any more than they already were. She wasn't sure what her quota was, but death from a thousand cuts didn't feel like hyperbole at the moment. A quick tug released a piece of glass, the shape of a shark's tooth—a great white by the size of it—from the glue of dried blood mostly sealing the wound. She dropped the glass in the trash and stuffed a wadded up piece of paper towel through the hole in her jeans to staunch the fresh flow of blood. Then moved on to the next piece.

The tinkling of glass joining the growing pile of broken shards in the garbage, and the hiss of breath Laney let out as she mined each piece were the only sounds in the kitchen until Ray's stomach rumbled. The clenched look on his face made it clear there was an internal debate going on, but finally, he stood, groaning as he rose. He shuffled to the fridge, pulled out plastic containers—the remains of last night's dinner—and plunked them down on the table. Reaching to get the mugs from the cabinet proved to be another groan worthy effort. But he delivered them and a pitcher of filtered water from the fridge before easing himself back into his seat.

Faith perked up at the swish of water when the pitcher hit the table. She poured herself a full mug, chugged it down, and refilled twice before trading the pitcher to Ray for the container of mashed potatoes.

Laney tossed the last manageable shard of glass into the trash. Then she took the roll of gauze from the first aid kit and wrapped her legs over the jeans to keep the wads of paper towel in place. The rest of the shards were above her pay grade. She only needed to patch herself up enough to drive to the hospital.

Half-assed, self surgery complete, she propped her elbow on the table. Resting her chin on her palm, she watched her kids devour cold leftovers with their fingers, like a couple of raccoons on a trash raid. A troubled warmth filled her. Not for the first time, her whole world fit tucked around the same old, green Formica table. A small, precious, terrifyingly fragile world.

When the kids finished eating, Laney forced herself to stand. Getting up was the last thing she wanted to do, but the thought of them dozing at the table, of passing the day there in their exhaustion only to wake in the dark, sparked a fire under her. She made her way to the sink. Patches of red bloomed on the white gauze, wrapped around her legs, as she lumbered.

The cabinet next to the sink held the coffee can. The one she should have accepted that first day.

Eyes closed, Laney stood on the porch and tilted her head back, taking a moment to let the morning sun warm her face. She needed the time to rationalize away the sudden blooming guilt at leaving her father behind. The idea of him being all alone in that house, of abandoning him just when he had a family again, was unbearable, but he wasn't there anymore. The shape that looked like him, lying under a blanket in the living room, was just a remnant. But that knowledge didn't keep stepping out into the warmth of the beautiful day feel any less a betrayal.

The sun cast the cornfields in a golden light, and a strong, warm breeze kept the smell of burning oak downwind. Birds chirped away in easy conversation, the nightmare of the night before lost on them.

The world had gone on like nothing had happened.

They climbed into the truck, Ray up front and Faith on the bench seat in the back. Laney turned the key, and the finely tuned engine growled to life like a final gift from her father. She put the truck in gear and drove.

"Don't look." She said, as they passed the front of the house. She didn't have to tell Ray twice. He squeezed his eyes shut, as if simply closing them would not be enough. The Hess boy's body lay there, a stark red blight against the white porch, and a meal for a half-dozen crows.

Laney looked away when she spotted the empty rocking chair.

She turned down the long driveway, just as a car turned off the road. It came at them fast, kicking up a cloud of dust. Laney stopped the truck and sighed. The gray sedan kept up its speed until the last second. Then, its brake lights flared, and it skidded to a stop feet from the truck.

"Oh Fuck." Ray watched his father get out of the car, sporting a pair of shiners, and a crooked nose. The side of his face where the pan hit him was a blistered mess. Troy slammed the car door, slid over the hood, landing on the driver's side of the truck, and kept moving. Ray turned in alarm as his mother opened the truck door.

"Mom, what are you-"

"Stay here." She got out and closed the door behind her.

Troy stopped inches from her. "Woman, I have been looking-"

Laney stepped up into his face. "You found me."

Troy's eyes flared. He cocked his arm, readying a balled fist. She looked him in the eye.

Unflinching.

Unblinking.

He clenched his jaw, coiled the muscles in his arm to swing. His fist shook with the urge to fly.

Laney stared him down, not caring if he threw the punch, not sure she'd even feel it. The scope of the last three days rendered his fist trivial. Her son had gone missing. She'd thought she lost her daughter twice, and her father, who had finally come back into her life, lay dead in the house behind her. Compared to all that, the pain Troy promised was nothing.

Troy was nothing.

And he must have realized it, too. He must have seen how pathetic and small he was in the depth of her eyes, and couldn't bear the sight of it. His eyes flicked away. His arm fell limp at his side. He took a shaky step back, and looked at her again, finally *saw* her. His face twisted, a mixture of shock and disgust, as he took in her state. The blood, the cuts, the torn out hair. He staggered back, wide eyed, and looked at the kids watching him from the truck. The both of them, bleeding and filthy, looked back at him. Faith yawned and leaned out of sight in the back seat of the truck. Ray gave him a glassy-eyed stare.

"What the hell happened here?" Troy looked Laney in the eyes and flinched. She stared back at him, calm, clear-eyed and without a shit to give. He took another step back, his eyes darting, landing anywhere but her.

The breeze carried the sound of sirens in the distance.

Betrayed by the half smile that twitched across his lips, Troy forced his face into a scowl and finally let his eyes settle on Laney. "You're so lucky." He back stepped to the car, nodding all the way. "You're so fucking lucky."

Laney cocked her head to listen to the sirens. "They sound pretty far." She shrugged. "We've got time."

"Are you fucking kidding me?" A high-pitched snort of incredulous laughter shot out of Troy. "What the fuck is going on here?"

He didn't wait for an answer. Troy turned and walked around the car to the driver's side. His fingers fidgeted with the door handle for a moment, pulling at it a few times, never hard enough to open it, as if he couldn't just let himself walk away. "Nope." He finally shook his head. "You're just not worth it." He opened the door, slid into the driver's seat, and started the engine.

Still shaking his head, he put the car in reverse, hit the gas. The car tore back ten feet, then Troy slammed on the brakes. The driver's side window rolled down with a motorized hum, and he leaned his head out, finding his nerve in the safety of the car. "You're not worth going back to prison for, but this ain't over, bitch. I'm going to find you again, and when I do-"

Laney turned away and started back towards the truck, waving a hand over her shoulder as she went. Troy threw a fit on the horn at her dismissal. He punched out a barrage of short bursts to punctuate the stream of fucks spewing from his mouth and ended the tantrum by hitting the gas.

She turned back to watch him accelerate down the driveway until there was nothing left of him but a trail of dust. When she got back into the truck, Ray looked up at her with a smile on his face. A smile just for her.

A last look in the rear-view showed black smoke blighting the sky behind the house as the tree still burned. The house itself looked deathly still. Too still. She watched it, waiting to see the front door burst open, spilling out a plume of darkness. But the door didn't open and after a few minutes, she started down the driveway, kicking up the dust that had just settled from Troy's exit.

She stopped where the driveway met the road and put on her blinker. A tractor trailer approached from her left, thick tires rumbling on the asphalt. Waiting for the truck to pass, Laney glanced at Ray, who was already nodding off, his head leaning against the window. Half asleep, he mumbled, "mind the road."

"I see it, honey," she said as the truck got closer.

Laney glanced in the rear-view mirror to check on her daughter and motion caught her eye. A gust of wind rushed at them. The corn bent in a rippling wave as it passed over. Her hands clenched the steering wheel. Jeremiah came for them, one last attempt to stop them during the death throes of the tree.

But the wind passed, and the corn settled. She let her hands relax on the wheel, and glanced at Faith.

Her daughter looked back at her, a burning hatred in her one perfect blue eye.

Panic took over and Laney tried to wrench her way around to face the child thing, to get it in front of her, not behind her. Her foot, digging for traction, came off one pedal, hit the other.

Hard.

She didn't realize the truck was moving until the corn rushed past in a blur. Scrambling for the brake, the wheel, anything to regain control, Laney couldn't tell where her screaming stopped, and the tractor trailer's horn began. But it only lasted a split second before the thunderous crunch of metal turned everything black.

Ten Years Later

The jeep, its windshield aglow with the pinks and purples of the setting sun, turned onto the driveway at Killian Farm. The wooden sign marking the drive had long ago succumbed to a swerving tractor trailer driven by a man far past the need for sleep. Unkempt fields overgrown with weeds lined the drive. Though, where the corn still grew in sparse patches, the stalks were tall and healthy in the late summer heat.

The jeep stopped just inside the driveway. A handsome young man with dark hair and a strong, wiry build got out, leaving the engine running. Lines marked the outer corners of his gray eyes, the result of a kind and frequent smile.

He crossed the empty road to the split tree carrying two bouquets of flowers. The tree still thrived. Its scars, both old and older, had grown over with moss. He knelt, cleared the withered bouquets, and laid the fresh flowers at the base of the trunk.

"Hey mom. I'm back in the states. You don't have to worry about me anymore. Though I know you will." He smiled and rolled his eyes. "Got my honorable discharge two weeks ago."

"Tell grandpa I still give a shit, and-"

His voice caught in his throat, and he waited for a moment, taking slow, controlled breaths in through his nose, hissing out through gritted teeth, until his jaw unclenched. Finally, he wiped tears from his eyes, kissed his fingertips, and gently touched the moss.

"Love you."

He stood, crossed the road, and got back into the Jeep. All he had to do was put the car into gear, and the slope took him the rest of the way down the drive until the Jeep drifted to a stop in front of the farmhouse. Ray shifted into park, turned the key, letting the engine go silent, and looked up at the house through the bug smeared windshield.

Backed by the setting sun, the farmhouse wore a veil of shadows. Darkness stared back at him from behind broken windows framed by crooked shutters dangling from their hinges. The once pristine siding, now wore a guise of weathered skin as a dingy shroud of dust and mildew, carved through by slug trails, covered the boards. Pale, lifeless wood, as stark as bone, poked through in places where the paint peeled back and the elements had washed the dust away. Vines strangled the flowerbeds wrapping the porch out of existence.

Without his grandfather's vigilance, the house showed its true face. It finally looked haunted.

The house was Jeremiah's last refuge. Since the burning of the oak, his influence around the farm had died with the tree's roots. The thick protrusions that had spread like pervasive veins pumping Jeremiah's vitriol throughout the farm, the first time Ray was here, had disappeared, like they never existed. And, though the sense of dread no longer hung over the property, it still lingered with the house. The large door of the front entry loomed above him past the dirt stained steps, daring him to enter.

Ray didn't know what made his uncle decide to gift him the farm. Maybe it was worthless, or maybe Uncle Philip couldn't bear to sell the only family legacy. But Ray saw the gift for what it was—a burden.

A burden his grandfather had carried alone for all those years.

A burden that Ray was finally ready to accept and put an end to.

His phone chimed, and he answered it without looking, just knowing who it had to be because of where he sat. The hum of a crowd sounded on the other end, a hesitation. But he recognized the airport noises in the background, and knew he was right, waited for her to talk.

"Tell me you didn't go there." She finally spoke, the strain in her voice saying more than her words.

"Had to."

"Why?"

He looked around him, took it all in, the dead corn, dead flowers, the decrepit house, and shrugged. "If I don't finish it, it was all a waste."

"They wouldn't want you to throw your life away, too."

"I'm not. I'm ending Jeremiah's."

There was an impatient sigh on her end. "And exactly how do you plan on doing that?"

"I've got some ideas. I'll figure it out."

She hesitated again, like maybe she didn't want to know. "How bad is it?"

"Honestly, I might be wasting my time here. So far, there's nothing. Not even sure he's still here," Ray lied.

A flight announcement broke through the background buzz, high pitched and tinny over a loudspeaker.

"That's me," she said. "Please... just keep your eye holes open."

"Always do."

"And be strong. Like Mom."

"Always am." His voice cracked, hoping he wasn't lying, that he could face this shit head on, no matter what he was up against. Like Mom always did. He always thought the running was weak, but protecting your family, starting fresh, was the braver thing to do, the harder thing. Something he didn't understand until she was gone, and he, and Faith, were shipped off to Aunt Ellen and what was left of Uncle Philip. They went from one nightmare to another. He enlisted the day he turned eighteen, petitioned for guardianship of his sister, and got her out, too. Uncle Philip didn't fight him on it, and Aunt Ellen was all too happy to see them go.

"You have a good time. And don't worry about me. I won't do anything stupid," he said.

"Love you, jerk-face."

"Love you too, dog breath. Have a safe flight."

He ended the call. A picture of a smiling young woman standing in front of the Eiffel Tower with a scar barely visible along her hairline —blond, like her mother—faded from the screen.

Reaching in the back of the jeep, he pulled his duffle bag up through the space between the seats, took a deep breath, then stepped out into the twilight.

Killian Farm belonged to him now.

Acknowledgements

This novel wouldn't exist without the help of Bruce Costa, Carla Hill Meehan, Matt Schick, Ami Shah, Rhonda Viscusi-Babb and especially Lauren Lepkowski. Without their encouragement and invaluable feedback, Killian Farm would still be collecting digital dust bunnies on a hard drive somewhere.

Thank you.

About The Author

L.M. Meehan enjoys reading and writing horror while nestled in the dark woods of the Pocono Mountains.

Thank you for reading Killian Farm. I hope you had as much fun reading it as I did writing it. If you are inclined to leave a review, I'd appreciate it. If you'd like news about future projects, please join my mailing list.

https://www.lmmeehan.com

I hope you enjoy whatever reading adventure awaits you next.

Psion
Eridanus [3h6m33.5s, -6°,5'18"]